SOCIAL CREATURE

SOCIAL CREATURE

TARA ISABELLA BURTON

R A V E N 🐦 B O O K S

LONDON • OXFORD • NEW YORK • NEW DELHI • SYDNEY

RAVEN BOOKS
Bloomsbury Publishing Plc
50 Bedford Square, London, WC1B 3DP, UK

BLOOMSBURY, RAVEN BOOKS and the Raven Books logo are trademarks
of Bloomsbury Publishing Plc

First published in Great Britain 2018

A catalogue record for this book is available from the British Library

ISBN: HB: 978-1-4088-9611-2; TPB: 978-1-4088-9610-5;
eBook: 978-1-4088-9609-9

2 4 6 8 10 9 7 5 3 1

Printed and bound in Great Britain by CPI Group (UK) Ltd, Croydon CR0 4YY

MIX
Paper from
responsible sources
FSC® C020056

To find out more about our authors and books visit www.bloomsbury.com
and sign up for our newsletters

For Brian—

who has been on this adventure from the beginning

1

THE FIRST PARTY LAVINIA TAKES LOUISE TO, she makes Louise wear one of her dresses.

"I found it on the street," Lavinia says. "It's from the twenties."

Maybe it is.

"Someone just left it there. Can you believe it?"

Louise can't.

"They probably just thought it was trash." She puckers her lips. She puts on lipstick. "And *that* is the problem with people. Nobody understands what things *mean*."

Lavinia fiddles with Louise's collar. Lavinia ties the sash around Louise's waist.

"Anyway, the second I saw it—Christ! I wanted to—oh, I just wanted to *genuflect*, you know? Kiss the ground—do Catholics kiss the ground, or is that just sailors? Anyway, I wanted to put my mouth right there on the sidewalk on somebody's chewed gum and say, like, *thank you, God, for making the world make sense today.*"

Lavinia puts powder on Louise's cheeks. Lavinia adds rouge. Lavinia keeps talking.

"Like—it's all so fucking *perfect*, right? Like—somebody's grandmother or whoever, dies in some random brownstone in the East Village nobody's even visited in twenty years and they dump all her shit out into the street and then at sunset—here I am walking across East Ninth Street and I find it. This old woman and I who have never met have these two beautiful, poetic, nights ninety years apart, wearing the exact same dress—oh, Louise, can't you just *smell* it?"

Lavinia shoves the lace in Louise's face.

"You could fall in love," says Lavinia, "wearing a dress like that."

Louise inhales.

"So you know what I did?"

Lavinia gives Louise a beauty mark with her eyebrow pencil.

"I stripped down to my underwear—no, that's a lie; I took my bra off, too. I took off everything and I put on the dress and I left my other one in the street and I walked all night, wearing it, all the way back to the Upper East Side."

Lavinia does Louise's buttons.

Now Lavinia is laughing. "Stick with me long enough," she says, "and I promise—things will just *happen* to you. Like they happen to me."

Lavinia does Louise's hair. At first she tries to do it, like she's done her own: savagely and exuberantly tendriled. But Louise's hair is too flat, and too straight, and so instead Lavinia braids it into a tight, neat bun.

Lavinia puts her hands on Louise's cheeks. She kisses her on the forehead. She roars.

"God," says Lavinia. "You look so beautiful. I can't stand it. I want to kill you. Let's take a picture."

She takes out her phone. She makes it a mirror.

"Let's stand against the peacock feathers," Lavinia says. Louise does.

"Pose."

Louise doesn't know how.

"Oh, please." Lavinia waves the phone. "Everybody knows how to pose. Just, you know: Arch your back a little. Tilt your head. Pretend you're a silent-film star. There. There—no, no, chin down. There."

Lavinia moves Louise's chin. She takes their photo.

"The last one's good," Lavinia says. "We look good. I'm posting it." She turns the phone to Louise. "Which filter do you like?"

Louise doesn't recognize herself.

Her hair is sleek. Her lips are dark. Her cheekbones are high. She's wearing a flapper dress and she has cat's eyes and fake lashes and she looks like she's not even from this century. She looks like she's not even real.

"Let's go with Mayfair. It makes your cheekbones look shiny. Christ—look at you! Look. At. You. You're beautiful."

Lavinia has captioned the photo: alike in indignity.

Louise thinks this is very witty.

Louise thinks: *I am not myself.*

Thank God, Louise thinks. *Thank God.*

They cab it to Chelsea. Lavinia pays.

It's New Year's Eve. Louise has known Lavinia for ten days. They have been the best ten days of her life.

Days don't go like this for Louise.

Louise's days go like this:

She wakes up. She wishes she hasn't.

Chances are: Louise hasn't slept much. She works as a barista at this coffee shop that turns into a wine bar at night, and also writes for this e-commerce site called GlaZam that sells knockoff handbags, and is also an SAT tutor. She sets an alarm for at least three hours before she has to be anywhere, because she lives deep in Sunset Park, a twenty-minute walk from the R, in the same illegal and roach-infested sublet she's been in for almost eight years, and half the time the train breaks down. When they call her, once every couple of months, Louise's parents invariably ask her why she's so stubborn about moving back to New Hampshire, say, where *that nice Virgil Bryce* is a manager at the local bookstore now, and he won't stop asking for her new number. Louise invariably hangs up.

She weighs herself. Louise weighs one hundred fourteen and a half pounds on a period day. She puts on her makeup very carefully. She draws on her brows. She checks her roots. She checks her bank balance (sixty-four dollars, thirty-three cents). She covers up the flaws in her skin.

She looks in the mirror.

Today, she says—out loud (a therapist she had once told her that it's always better to say these things out loud)—*is the first day of the rest of your life.*

She makes herself smile. Her therapist told her to do that, too.

Louise walks the twenty minutes to the subway. She ignores the catcaller who asks her, every morning, how her pussy smells, even though he's probably the only person in the world she interacts with regularly. She spends the ride into Manhattan staring at her reflection in the darkened subway windows. Back when Louise was sure she was going to be a go-down-in-history Great Writer she used to take a notebook and use the commute to write stories, but now she is too tired and also she probably will never be a writer; so she reads trashy *Misandry!* articles on her phone and sometimes watches people (Louise enjoys watching people; she finds it calming; when you spend a lot of time focusing on the things wrong with other people you worry less about everything wrong with you).

Louise goes to work as a barista, or at GlaZam, or to give an SAT lesson.

She likes lessons best. When she speaks with her very carefully cultivated mid-Atlantic accent and puts her very carefully dyed blonde hair into a bun and alludes to the fact that she went to school in Devonshire, New Hampshire, she gets $80 an hour, plus the satisfaction of having fooled somebody. Now if Louise had actually gone to Devonshire Academy, the boarding prep school, and not just the public Devonshire High, she'd get $250, but the kind of parents who can pay $250 are more assiduous in checking these things.

Not that most people ever check these things. When Louise was sixteen, she took to leaving her house early and eating breakfast and dinner at the Academy's dining hall. She made it a whole three months, watching people, before anybody noticed, and even then it was just her mother who found out, and grounded her, and by the time she was allowed out of the house again she'd started AIM-chatting Virgil Bryce, who didn't like it when she went anywhere without him.

Louise finishes work.

She looks in her phone-mirror, a few times, to make sure she's still there. She checks Tinder, even though she hardly responds to anybody she matches with. There was one guy who seemed really feminist online but turned out to practice relationship anarchy; and another who was really into kink in ways that she was never entirely sure were not abusive; and one guy who was really great, actually, but he ghosted her after two months. Sometimes Louise considers going out with somebody new, but this seems like just another thing to potentially fuck up.

Sometimes, if Louise has been paid cash that week, she goes to a really nice bar: on Clinton or Rivington, or on the Upper East Side.

She orders the nicest drink she can afford (Louise can't really afford to be drinking at all, but even Louise deserves nice things, sometimes). She sips her drink very, very slowly. If she doesn't eat dinner (Louise never eats dinner) the alcohol will hit her harder, which is a relief, because when Louise gets drunk she forgets the invariable fact that she is going to fuck everything up one day, if she hasn't already, whether it's because she loses all her jobs at once and gets evicted or because she gains twenty pounds because she is too tired to exercise and then not even the catcaller will want to fuck her or because she'll get throat cancer from all the times she has made herself throw up all her food or because she will get another kind of even rarer and more obscure cancer from all the times she obsessively dyes her hair in a bathroom without ventilation or she will fuck up by unblocking Virgil Bryce on social media or else because she will get into another relationship in which a man who seems nice on Tinder wants to save her, or else to choke her, and she will do whatever he says because the other way to fuck it all up is to die alone.

Louise waits until she sobers up (another very certain way to fuck up is to be a drunk woman alone in New York at night), and then she takes the subway home, and although Louise no longer writes in her notebook, if she is still tipsy enough to feel that the apocalypse is no longer imminent she tells herself that tomorrow, when she is that little bit less tired, she will write a story.

They say if you haven't made it in New York by thirty, you never will.

Louise is twenty-nine.

Lavinia is twenty-three.

This is how they meet:

Lavinia's sister, Cordelia, is sixteen. She's at boarding school in New Hampshire—not Devonshire Academy but one of its rivals. She's home for Christmas break. Their parents live in Paris. Lavinia found one of Louise's SAT TUTOR? AVAILABLE NOW! flyers at The Corner Bookstore on Ninety-third and Madison, which has a free Christmas champagne reception Louise has been crashing for three years, even though she lives so far away, just to drink for free and watch rich, happy families be happy and rich.

"I'm afraid I don't know a damn thing," Lavinia says over the phone. "But Cordy's brilliant. And I know I'll corrupt her—unless somebody else is there to stop me. You know what I mean. A good influence. And anyway she's here for a whole week before she goes to Paris for Christmas and we've watched every single Ingmar Bergman DVD in the house and now I'm all out of ideas to keep her off the streets. I can pay. How much does a person pay for these things? You tell me."

"One fifty an hour," says Louise.

"Done."

"I'll start tonight," Louise says.

Lavinia lives in a floor-through brownstone apartment on Seventy-eighth Street between Park and Lex. When Louise arrives on the stoop, there is opera blaring from an open window, and Lavinia is singing along, off-key, and this is how Louise figures out that Lavinia lives on the second floor without even having to check the buzzer.

Lavinia has flowers in all of her window boxes. All of them are dead.

Lavinia answers the door in a sleeveless black dress made entirely of feathers. Her hair comes down to her waist. It is wild, and coarse, and she has not brushed it in days, but it is the hue of blonde Louise has spent many hours experimenting with drugstore dyes to achieve, only it is natural. She is not tall but she is thin (Louise tries to calculate exactly how thin, but the feathers get in the way), and she fixes her eyes on Louise with such intensity that Louise instinctively takes a step back: half-knocking into a vase filled with dead lilies.

Lavinia doesn't notice.

"Thank God you're here," she says.

Cordelia is sitting at the dining-room table. She is wearing her hair in one long thick braid, coiled and pinned. She doesn't look up from her book.

There are antique hand fans all over the walls. There is a gold-embroidered caftan hanging on a wall, and a powdered wig on the head of a mannequin whose features are drawn in lipstick, and there are several illustrated tarot cards—the High Priestess, the Tower, the Fool—in rusty art nouveau frames on all the surfaces in the room. The walls are all a regal, blinding blue, except for the moldings, which Lavinia has made gold.

Lavinia kisses Louise on both cheeks.

"Make sure she goes to bed by ten," she says, and leaves.

———

"She does that."

Cordelia finally looks up.

"She isn't really that oblivious," she says. "That's just her sense of humor. She thinks it's funny to tease me. And you."

Louise doesn't say anything.

"I'm sorry," says Cordelia. "I started studying already." Her smile twists at the edges.

She makes Louise a pot of tea.

"You can have chocolate-vanilla or you can have hazelnut-cinnamon-pear-cardamom," she says. "Vinny doesn't have any normal tea."

She serves it in an intricately patterned teapot ("It's from Uzbekistan," Cordelia says. Louise doesn't know if this is a joke). She sets it down on a tray.

Cordelia forgets a teaspoon, although there is one in the sugar pot, but after the second cup Louise realizes if she stirs the tea it will wet the spoon and then ruin the sugar. If she keeps the spoon dry the sugar will settle in the cup.

Louise sips her tea without any sugar in it. She briefly considers asking for another spoon, but the thought of doing this makes her nervous, and so Louise doesn't say anything at all.

They do SAT words: *What is the difference between* lackluster, laconic, *and* lachrymose? They do math: all the 3-4-5 triangles, surface areas of different shapes. Cordelia gets all the questions right.

"I'm going to Yale," Cordelia says, like that's a thing people just decide. "Then I'm going to a pontifical university in Rome for my master's. I'm going to be a nun."

Then: "I'm sorry."

"For what."

"I'm trolling you. I shouldn't. I mean—I do want to be a nun. But even so."

"That's okay," says Louise.

She drinks another cup of sugarless hazelnut-cinnamon-pear-cardamom tea.

"I feel guilty," says Cordelia. "Keeping you here. I don't really need a tutor. Don't feel bad—I mean, you're doing a very good job. Sorry. It's just—I know all this already." She shrugs. "Maybe Vinny really does want you to be my babysitter. Only—she won't be back by ten."

"That's okay," Louise says. "I trust you to make your own bed-time."

"That's not an issue." Cordelia smiles her strange half-smile again. "Vinny's the one with the cash."

Cordelia and Louise sit in silence on the sofa until six in the morning. Cordelia puts on a dressing gown covered in cat hair (there is no cat to be seen) and reads a paperback copy of John Henry Newman's *Apologia Pro Vita Sua*. Louise reads clickbait articles from *Misandry!* on her phone.

She is very tired, but she also needs four hundred fifty dollars more than she needs sleep.

Lavinia comes home at dawn, covered in feathers.

"I'm so terribly, *terribly* sorry," she exclaims. She trips over the threshold. "Of course, I'll pay you for the hours. Every hour. Every one."

She catches her skirt in the door. It rips.

"Christ."

Feathers slice the air as they fall.

"*All my pretty chickens,*" Lavinia cries. She gets on her hands and knees. "*All? What, all my pretty chickens and their dam.*"

"I'll get some water," Cordelia says.

"It's a bad omen." Lavinia has fallen over, now, laughing, with a black feather in her hand. "It means death!"

Louise grabs the trailing feathers from underneath the door.

"No, don't! Let them be!"

Lavinia grabs Louise's wrists; she pulls her in.

"It died a noble death." She hiccups. "This dress—it has been *felled in battle.*" Her hair fans out on the floor all the way to the steamer trunk she has made into a coffee table. "And what a battle! Oh—what's your name again?"

"Louise."

"Louise!" Lavinia yanks her wrist again, but joyfully. "Like Lou Salomé. [Louise doesn't know who that is.] Louise! I've had the most wonderful, wonderful night in the world. One of *those* nights. You know?"

Louise smiles politely.

"Don't you?"

Louise hesitates.

"I *believe* in things again, Louise!" Lavinia closes her eyes. "God. And glory. And love and fairy dust—God, I *love* this city."

Cordelia leaves a glass of water on the steamer trunk.

But Lavinia is scrambling to the sofa. She's beatific and dark with glitter, and light with different glitter, and Louise doesn't know what to do or say to make Lavinia like her but she is good at watching people and she knows what they need and so, like she always does, she finds an opening.

"I can fix that, you know."

Lavinia sits up. "Fix what?"

"It's just the hem. I can sew it back on. If you have a needle and thread."

"A needle and thread?" Lavinia looks at Cordelia.

"My room," says Cordelia.

"You can fix it?"

"I mean—unless you don't want me to."

"Don't want you to?" Lavinia gathers up her skirts. "*Lazarus, back from the dead.*" She piles them in her lap. "*I have come to tell thee!*" She flings back her arms. "Oh, I'm so—so!—sorry."

"Don't be," Louise says.

"I know—I know—you must think I'm ridiculous."

"I don't think you're ridiculous."

"Are you sure?"

Louise doesn't know what Lavinia wants her to say.

"I mean—"

Lavinia doesn't even wait.

"You're not judging me?"

"I'm not judging you."

"You're *sure?*"

Louise speaks very slowly. "Yes," she says. "I'm sure."

"It was just—it was only just a few of us. Me and Father Romylos and Gavin—Gavin's a narcissistic sociopath. He told me so, once. One of the nicest people in the world, but technically, a narcissistic sociopath. Anyway, we decided to see if you can break into the Botanic Garden. Apparently you can! Look!"

She shows Louise a photograph. Lavinia and an Orthodox priest and a bald man in a turtleneck are collapsing in a hedgerow.

"Father Romylos is the one in the cassock," she says.

"Are there even any flowers this time of year?" Cordelia has returned with a sewing kit. She hands it to Louise.

"It's my favorite thing in the world, breaking into places! It makes you feel so alive—to be somewhere you're not supposed to be. We got caught, once, had to pay an awful fine at the Central Park Zoo, but other than that! Oh—don't look at me like that."

"Like what?"

Louise is sewing the hem. She hasn't even looked up.

"Like you think I'm horrible!"

"I don't," says Louise.

What she is thinking is this:

Lavinia isn't afraid of anything.

"I'm not drunk, you know," says Lavinia. She sways her hair—her long, coarse, wonderful hair—across Louise's shoulder. "I swear. Do you know what Baudelaire said?"

Louise puts another stitch in the hem.

"Baudelaire said that you should get drunk. On wine. On poetry. On virtue—as you choose. But get drunk."

"Vinny's drunk on virtue," says Cordelia.

Lavinia snorts. "It's only prosecco," she says. "Even Cordy drinks prosecco. Mother makes us."

"I abhor alcohol." Cordelia winks at Louise as she picks stray feathers out of the couch cushions. "It's a vice."

"God, don't you just *hate* her?" Lavinia puts her feet on the steamer trunk. "I bet you don't even believe in God, do you, Cordy? She's kept it up a whole year—can you believe it? Before that she was vegan. And—oh, God, you're *brilliant!*"

She has seen the hem Louise has fixed for her.

"Are you a costumier? I have a friend who's a costumier. She makes eighteenth-century outfits every year for Carnevale in Venice."

"I'm not a costumier."

"But you can sew."

Louise shrugs. "Lots of people can sew."

"Nobody can sew. What else can you do?"

Louise is caught off guard by the question.

"Not a lot."

"Don't lie to me."

"What?"

"You're special. You have the mark of genius on your brow. I could tell—soon as I saw you. And you—you kept vigil with Cordy, didn't you? All night long. *That's* special."

Louise isn't special. She knows this. We know this. She just needs four hundred fifty dollars.

"Are you an actress? You're pretty enough to be an actress."

"I'm not an actress." (Louise is not pretty enough to be an actress.)

"An artist?"

"No."

"Then you're a writer!"

Louise hesitates.

She hesitates because you can't really call yourself a writer when you haven't written anything anyone else likes enough to publish; not when you haven't even written anything you like enough to even

ask somebody to publish; not when there are so many failed writers
to laugh at in this city. But she hesitates long enough before saying
"no" that Lavinia seizes.

"I knew it!" She claps her hands. "I knew it! Of *course* you're a
writer. You are a woman of *words*." She scoops up the flash cards:
assuage, assert, assent. "I shouldn't have doubted you."

"I mean—"

"What have you written?"

"Oh, you know—not a lot. Just a couple of stories and things."

"What are they about?"

Now Louise is fully afraid. "Oh, you know. New York. Girls in
New York. The usual stuff. It's dumb."

"Don't be ridiculous!" Lavinia is staring up at her with those
bright and blazing eyes. "New York is the greatest city in the world!
Of *course* you want to write about it!"

Lavinia's hand is so tight on her wrists and Lavinia is staring at
her so intently and blinking so innocently that Louise can't bring
herself to let her down.

"You're right," Louise says. "I am a writer."

"I'm *never* wrong!" Lavinia crows. "Cordy says I have a sense about
people—I always can sense if a person is going to be interesting.
It's like telepathy, but for poetic qualities—it makes things *happen.*"
She stretches like a cat along the sofa. "I'm a writer, too, you know.
I mean—I'm working on a novel, right now. I'm on a sabbatical,
actually."

"A sabbatical?"

"From school! That's why I'm here." She shrugs. "Living in squa-
lor, you see. I've taken the year off to finish it. But my problem is
I don't have any discipline. I'm not like Cordy. She's so smart."
(Cordelia is back at her Newman and doesn't look up.) "Me, I just go
to parties." She yawns, long and luxuriant. "Poor Louise," she says,
so softly. "I've ruined your night."

The light streams in through the window.

"It's fine," Louise says. "You haven't."

"Your beautiful Friday night. Your beautiful winter Friday—right in the middle of the holiday season, too. You probably had plans. A Christmas party, right? Or a date."

"I didn't have a date."

"What did you plan, then? Before I smashed it all to pieces?"

Louise shrugs.

"I dunno. I was going to go home. Maybe watch some TV."

Truth is, Louise was planning to sleep. Sleep is the most seductive thing she can think of.

"But it's almost *New Year's Eve!*"

"I don't really go out, much."

"But this is *New York!*" Lavinia's eyes are so wide. "And we're in our *twenties!*"

It is expensive to go out. It takes so long to get home. You have to tip for everything. It's too cold. There are puddles in the subway stations. She can't afford a cab.

"Come with me," Lavinia says. "I'll take you to a party!"

"Now?"

"Of course not *now,* silly—what am I, crazy? There's a New Year's Eve party happening at the MacIntyre—it's going to be *wonderful.* It's going to be their best party yet. And I owe you! All those extra hours you stayed—I owe you interest."

"You owe her one-fifty an hour," says Cordelia, from the armchair. "Seven until"—she checks her wristwatch—"seven."

"*Jesus fuck,*" says Lavinia, so violently Louise starts. "I gave all my cash to the busker. He was playing "New York, New York" outside the Bandshell. *We were very tired—we were very merry.*"

She straightens up.

"Now you *have* to come," she says. "If I don't see you again, I won't be able to pay you for tonight."

She smiles so ecstatically.

"I owe you more than money," she says. "I owe you the most beautiful night of your life."

———

This is the first party Lavinia takes Louise to, and the best, and the one Louise will never stop trying to get back to. She goes in Lavinia's dress from the 1920s (it is actually a reproduction from the 1980s, store-bought, but Louise doesn't know this), which she found on the street, because that is the kind of thing that happens to people like Lavinia Williams, all the time.

Now, the MacIntyre Hotel is not a hotel. It's kind of a warehouse and kind of a nightclub, and kind of a performance space, in Chelsea; there are a hundred or so rooms over six floors. Half of them are decorated like a haunted hotel from the Great Depression, but also there's a forest and a whole insane asylum on the top floor where Ophelia goes mad (they also perform *Hamlet,* but they do it without any words), and Louise hears that sometimes actors take you into secret bedrooms or chapels and kiss you on the cheek or on the forehead or on the mouth, but tickets are a hundred dollars each (and that's before you add the coat check, or the ten-dollar ticketing charge), and so Louise has never been herself to verify this.

Some nights, *those nights, one of those nights,* they do special themed costume parties in the space: all-night open-bar kiss-a-stranger-and-see parties where everybody dresses up and lurches through all the labyrinthine interconnected rooms, where every floor has its own sound system and even the bathtubs in the insane asylum are full of people making love.

Louise has never had one of those nights before.

Don't worry. She will.

Here is what's inside the MacIntyre, in the order Louise makes sense of it: red velvet, candles, ostrich feathers, champagne flutes, people with *Happy 2015* glasses, people taking selfies, a woman in a red backless sequined dress singing Peggy Lee's "Is That All There Is?," people taking selfies. Lavinia. A girl in a tuxedo. Marie Antoinette. Someone in a lion tamer uniform. Lavinia.

People in black tie. People who actually own black tie in black tie. People in corsets. People in lingerie. Lavinia.

A man in a cassock ("Don't tell him I told you, but he's actually defrocked"). A woman six feet tall wearing nothing but pasties and feathers with the most grating and New York accent Louise has ever heard ("Her burlesque name is Athena Maidenhead. I don't know her real name"). A bald man in black skinny jeans and a turtleneck who is the only person there not in costume and who doesn't seem to notice ("That's Gavin. He keeps Excel spreadsheets of all the women he dates"). Lavinia.

Lavinia dancing. Lavinia drinking. Lavinia taking so many photographs, pulling Louise in with her, pulling her so close Louise can smell her perfume. It's made for Lavinia, Louise will learn one day soon, at a Chinese hole-in-the-wall over on East Fourth Street, and it smells like lavender and tobacco and fig and pear and everything beautiful in this world.

Peggy Lee sings the line *is that all there is to a fire?* and Louise downs a flute of champagne like it's a pickleback and then she starts to get nervous because when she drinks she stops concentrating as much on not fucking up, and when Louise stops concentrating is when she fucks up most; but Lavinia puts one hand on Louise's waist and uses the other to tilt a bottle of Bombay Sapphire straight into Louise's overflowing mouth, and even though Louise is not stupid and she is so good at watching people and she is so very careful—all the time she is so careful!—the intense pressure of Lavinia's hand on the small of her back makes her think that if the world is going to end, anyway, it might as well end tonight.

"Friends! Romans! Countrymen! Bring me more gin!"

Lavinia. Lavinia. Lavinia.

When Louise lived in New Hampshire, she often imagined that once in New York, she'd go to parties like this.

When she and Virgil Bryce would stand on the railroad bridge, and she would beg him to touch her breasts and he would finally, magnanimously agree, and they would talk about running away together (he wanted to live in Colorado and illustrate manga), and he would remind her how cruel the world was, she would try to explain to him that New York wasn't like anywhere else.

It didn't matter if you weren't that special, she'd say, or even if you weren't pretty, not even by the standards of Devonshire, New Hampshire, as long as you wanted it badly enough. The city would scoop you up and carry you skyward to all your vaulted aspirations; every single party on every single night in that whole, glistening, glaring city would make you feel like you were the only person in the world, and also the most special, and also the most loved.

You and I, of course, we know the truth.

We know how easy it is to fake it. All you need is to keep the lighting low; all you need are a couple of showgirls with cheap feathers superglued to the end of their corsets; all you need is to keep people drinking.

But girls like Louise don't know this. Not yet.

This is the happiest Louise has ever been.

Nine o'clock. Lavinia and Louise and Gavin Mullaney and Father Romylos and Athena Maidenhead and so many other people without names are dancing the Charleston on top of a stage, underneath a chandelier the size of a giraffe. "Are we even allowed to be onstage?" Louise asks, but Lavinia can't hear her over the music. Two aerialists are knotting their bodies together, kicking the crystals in the chandelier, and Athena has abandoned her feathers and there is nothing between her skin and everybody else's sweat except for two pasties and a merkin in the shape of the moon.

"New Year's resolution," Lavinia roars. "Be it resolved: we shall drink life to the lees."

Lavinia's dress has fallen off her shoulder, exposing her breast. She doesn't even care.

Then two hands close over Louise's eyes. Someone kisses her on the neck.

"Guess who," she whispers, into Louise's collarbone.

Louise jerks around so quickly.

The girl is so confused. "But . . ."

"*Mimi?*" Lavinia has stopped dancing. She isn't smiling.

"*Butyourdress.*" The girl's voice is loud and monotonous and artificial, like she's speaking lines from a high school play. "I thought . . ." She laughs. It is no less artificial, and no less loud. "*Yousee?*" Her smile hangs desperately off her mouth. "*Shetookyourdress!*"

Nobody says anything.

"*SorryImlate,*" she says. "*Therapytookforever. AndthenIcouldntfindmyniceunderwear.*"

Nobody reacts to this, either.

"*HesaysIhaveneuroticdespair.*"

The music is so loud. The girl gets closer. She blinks very intently. "*ISAID: HESAYSIHAVENEUROTICDESPAIR.*"

Nothing. Not even a nod.

"*IT'SNOTEVENINTHEDSMYOUKNOW.*"

Father Romylos lamely nods at her and this is worse, Louise thinks, than if nobody acknowledged her at all.

The worst part is that she's still smiling.

Even when she goes over to Lavinia. Even when Lavinia recoils.

"I've missed you," she says.

The girl gyrates up to Louise.

"I'm me," she says. "Me."

"What?"

"Mimi," she says, like Louise is supposed to know her.

"Oh," says Louise.

Mimi hands her her phone. She knots her arms around Lavinia's neck.

"Take a picture!"

Lavinia isn't smiling.

Mimi snatches the phone back. She scrolls through the photos.

"We look great," she says. "I'm gonna post them all."

Now it's ten. Now the moon is full.

"Promise me something," Lavinia says. They're smoking on the rooftop; they're in a hedgerow or a maze or something full of rose-bushes that are still in bloom despite the frost; Louise has no idea how they got here. "I want to usher 2015 in right. I want things to be as they should be. I want it to be a better year than the last one." She breathes out smoke. "It's got to be." (Nobody else is here, not Mimi nor Gavin nor Father Romylos nor Athena Maidenhead, but Louise doesn't remember saying goodbye to them, either.)

"Of course," Louise says.

"I want to recite poetry with you tonight."

At first Louise thinks Lavinia is joking. But Lavinia is tight-lipped and unsmiling and more serious than Louise has yet seen her.

"Don't let me forget, okay?"

"Okay," Louise says.

"Promise?"

"Yes," Louise says. "I promise."

Louise can't remember any poems.

Lavinia takes a pen out of her purse. She writes it on her arms. MORE POETRY!!! The letters are misshapen. She writes it on Louise's, too.

"There," Lavinia says. "Now we'll remember."

Together they gaze out over the city. There are so many stars, although Louise knows some of them must only be city lights.

"Hey, Louise?" Lavinia's smoke spirals from her lips.

"Yes?"

"What's your New Year's resolution?"

Louise has so many: *eat less lose weight make more money get a better job write a story write that story finally write that fucking story and send it somewhere if you only had the nerve stop reading* Misandry! *at four in the morning when you can't sleep read an actual fucking book sometime maybe maybe write a fucking story.*

"I don't know." (*Be less boring, that's another one.*)

"Come on—you can tell me!"

She says it like she means it. She says it like Louise is safe.

Louise wants to believe her.

"It's stupid," Louise says.

"I bet it isn't! I'll bet you a hundred dollars it isn't." Technically Lavinia owes Louise between four hundred fifty and eighteen hundred dollars, depending on whether or not Louise counts the hours spent with Cordelia waiting for Lavinia to come home, but Louise is no longer counting.

"I want to send one of my stories out. Maybe. If it's good enough."

Louise is so afraid that, having said it, she will have to do it.

"To a magazine?"

"Yes."

"You've never done it before?"

"No. I mean—I have. But not in years."

"I bet they're brilliant," says Lavinia. "I bet they're *genius.* I bet everybody's going to love you."

"Come on, that's not—"

"Don't contradict me. I have a feeling. I *know.*" Lavinia throws back that never-ending hair.

"What's yours?"

Lavinia shakes the last ember out of her cigarette. "Same one I make every year. Same one I'll make every year until I die." She takes a deep and delicious breath. "I want to *live,*" she says. "I mean really, *really,* live. Do you know what Oscar Wilde says?"

Louise doesn't but she knows it was probably witty.

"He says—*I put my talent into my work, but my genius into my life.* That's what I want to do, too. Or maybe you think that's *trite?*" She spits the last word.

"No—no!"

"Probably it is. Fuck it. I don't care. That's what I want."

———

Now it's eleven. Now they're on the dance floor, again; now everybody on the dance floor is kissing everybody else; everybody except Lavinia, who is standing in a spotlight in the center, inviolate, dancing alone.

"*Whatawildoutrageousnight.*"

Mimi's lipstick is smeared. So is her eyeliner.

"Come *on!*" She's tugging at Lavinia's sleeves. She's still speaking in that clipped and amateurish way. "We'll have some champagne!" Mimi cries. "We'll take a selfie!"

Then Louise gets it: what's so uncanny about that strange, pantomime way Mimi is talking.

She's trying to talk like Lavinia.

Lavinia isn't smiling. "We've already taken a selfie."

Mimi is smiling so desperately. "Then we'll take another!"

She pulls herself against Lavinia and holds out the camera. She leaves a sloppy lipstick kiss on her cheek.

"Jesus, Mimi!"

"Shit—my eyes were closed in that one! *Let'stakeanotherokay?*"

She can't keep her hand steady. The photos all come out blurry.

"Okay, we're done here."

"Just one more! One more!"

Mimi keeps pawing at Lavinia, pushing her breasts against her, leaning in to kiss her.

"Just one more, come on!"

She reaches out for Lavinia's sleeve. She tears it.

Louise cannot believe how loud a sound the rip makes.

"For fuck's *sake,* Mimi, don't you know when to fucking leave?"

Lavinia's eyes are terrible.

Mimi's eyes fill with tears. She's still smiling.

"Come on," Mimi keeps whimpering, like a dog. "It's one of those nights. Isn't it? Isn't it?"

"You're drunk, Mimi. Go home."

Mimi does.

———

An hour later Mimi posts every photo she's taken that night. She tags Lavinia in all of them.

Me and bae, she writes, with a dancing fox emoji and a wiggling Hula-Hoop girl emoji and a cat that rolls over and over doing somersaults, like anybody even says *bae* anymore.

Now the music is so loud you can't hear anybody else unless you're close enough to kiss them; now we are dancing; now we're all standing four abreast on one of the raised columns, seven feet above the crowds, and here Lavinia stands, chin up, shoulders back, like a god.

Now they've lowered the big clock; now everybody's screaming *yes, yes;* now Lavinia's standing and scanning the crowd with those eyes so bright they burn.

"What is it?"

Lavinia doesn't answer her.

"Are you looking for Mimi?"

Lavinia keeps looking, looking, and Louise tries to follow her gaze but she doesn't see anything, just a couple of boys in black tie doing shots she doesn't recognize, and then it is like an electric shock, the way Lavinia digs her nails into Louise's wrist, and Louise asks *what is it* but by now she's so drunk that by the time Lavinia turns back to her Louise forgets what she was asking about in the first place.

Lavinia grabs Louise's shoulders.

"We should jump," Lavinia says.

"What?"

"You. Me. We should do it."

"You want to *crowd-surf*?"

Nobody crowd-surfs. Not in real life.

But this isn't real life.

"What's the worst that can happen?"

It's one minute to midnight.

"Trust me," says Lavinia. "Please."

———

Ten—nine—

Now Louise remembers everything she is afraid of.

She remembers that she doesn't have health insurance and if she breaks a bone she will not be able to afford to fix it and that she has work tomorrow and she can't afford to take off even if she could (*eight*) and she doesn't even know Lavinia that well and shouldn't even trust her because new people generally let you down if they don't do worse and (*seven*) even though Lavinia is looking at her so raptly Lavinia is a stranger and the most surefire way of fucking it up is to open up to another person and (*six*) she cannot afford to be stupid—stupidity, like happiness, is a luxury, but her heart is beating so fast, like it is a hummingbird that will beat out all its breaths (*five*) and die before midnight but for the first time in as long as she can remember Louise is happy, and she will spend all her heartbeats if she has to, if it means feeling like this (*four*) because in the end she only really wants one thing in the world and that is to be loved and (*three, two, one*).

The crowd catches them.

So many people—they bear up her waist and thighs and back and Louise isn't afraid; she knows, *she knows* they will not let her fall; she knows she can trust them, because they are all in this together and they are all so riotously, gloriously drunk and they all want her to stay up as much as she does, because it is a beautiful thing to be up so high, and they all want to be *a part of it.*

Lavinia reaches across the crowd; she is smiling; she is so far away and then she is closer, just a little bit closer, and then she is close enough to grab Louise's hand, and she squeezes it tightly.

Now it's almost dawn.

Everybody has spilled out into the street. They've taken off their heels. Girls walk barefoot on the ice. Taxis are charging a hundred dollars a person just to go to the Upper East Side.

———

Louise is a little bit sober by now; she can feel the blisters in her shoes, but she is too happy to care. She wraps herself in her coat, which is not elegant enough to justify how flimsy it is, and huddles against the wind, and Lavinia orders an Uber without thinking about it, even though the surge pricing must be insane at this hour.

"Where are we going?"

Lavinia puts a finger to her lips.

"I have a surprise for you."

The cab takes them through the West Village, the Lower East Side, across the Brooklyn Bridge.

"Was it what you wanted?" Lavinia is huddled in an enormous fur coat. She is blinking very intently.

"What?"

"The party. Was it what you wanted?"

"Yes," Louise says. "It was wonderful!"

"Good. I'm glad. I wanted to make you happy."

The cab rolls on past the water.

"Just think," Lavinia says. "You could be home in bed right now."

Louise should be home in bed right now.

"But instead . . ." Lavinia opens the window. The wind whips their faces. "You're going to watch the sun rise. Isn't that wonderful?"

The cab comes to a stop underneath the Ferris wheel: by the bright-painted gates, the freak-show signs, the Cyclone.

The park is closed for the season. But the streetlights illuminate the carousel, the haunted houses, the boardwalk beyond it: beyond that, the waves.

"I wanted to be near water," Lavinia says.

The boardwalk is frozen slick, and so Lavinia uses Louise to steady herself; both of them slip and both of them fall and they skin their knees a little bit, doing it, but there they are.

"At last," Lavinia says.

It is too cold to sit, but they squat, anyway, and huddle together under Lavinia's enormous fur.

Lavinia hands Louise a flask.

"Drink this," she says. "It'll warm you up."

There's whiskey in it—*good* whiskey, that's much too nice to be tippled out of a flask just to keep you warm when you can't feel your hands, but that's Lavinia for you.

"On the *Titanic,* they drank whiskey," Lavinia says. "They were going down with the ship and they saw the end before them and they said *fuck it, we might as well* so they got completely plastered on the finest whiskey, and then once the ship sank it saved them. They were so warm on the inside they didn't feel the cold. They swam all the way to the lifeboats. I think about—all the time—when—oh, your *dress!*"

Lavinia's dress—the one she has been so kind and good and generous enough to entrust to Louise, the one she found on the street in the East Village and which represents beauty and truth and everything good in the world and maybe, even, the existence of God, is in shreds. There are wine stains. There are cigarette holes.

And Louise thinks, *you fucked it up.*

She wasn't careful. She was selfish and thoughtless and she drank too much and she let her guard down—even animals know never to let their guard down—and now Lavinia will turn on her the way she turned on poor, pathetic Mimi, who ripped Lavinia's sleeve. It will be so much worse than before, now that the night has been so good, now that she knows what she's been missing.

Louise tries not to cry, but she is drunk and weak and so of course she can't, and so she starts to sputter tears, and then Lavinia looks at her with astonishment.

"What is it?"

"I'm sorry. God, I'm so sorry—your dress."

"What about it?"

"I ruined it!"

"So?"

Lavinia tosses that long hair of hers. It whips in the wind.

"You had a good night, didn't you?"

"Yes, of course, I—"

"So what's the problem? We can always get another dress."

She says it like it's so easy.

"I told you," Lavinia says. "Things happen around me. The gods will bring us another one."

Louise's tears freeze-dry on her face.

"It's a sacrifice," Lavinia says. "We'll sacrifice to the old gods—we'll put the dress in the water and let the water take it and, oh!"

"What?"

Lavinia shoves her forearm in Louise's face.

MORE POETRY!!! is mostly smudged by now, and really more like MRE PERY!1, but Louise can make it out.

"You almost let me forget! How could you?"

"I—"

"That clinches it."

Lavinia leaps to her feet. She lets the fur fall. She lets her beautiful white dress that makes her look like an angel fall, too. Against the snow she is cold, bitten, naked. Her breasts are blue. Her nipples are purple.

"Fuck, fuck, fuck!"

She's hysterical, laughing.

"Fuckfuckfuckit'ssocold!"

Louise gapes.

"Come on! Your turn!"

"You want me to—"

Louise is already shaking from the cold, now, under the furs.

"Come on! You have to do it!"

Lavinia's eyes are so wild, so wide. Louise is so cold.

"You *promised*!"

Lavinia extends her trembling, blue-veined hand.

"You *promised*!"

Louise did. So she does.

———

At first she thinks the cold will kill her. It is in the back of her eyes and at the back of her throat and up her nose and all the way down her esophagus, and not even the whiskey can help. If she were on the *Titanic* she would drown. Lavinia takes the dress from the crumpled heap of frost and sand and boardwalk splinterwood at her feet and gathers it up to her breasts and says "Come."

'Tis not too late to seek a newer world.

The thing about Tennyson's "Ulysses" is that everybody knows it. You're not special for knowing it. If you know one poem by Tennyson it's probably that, and if you know one poem, period, there's still a greater-than-fifty-percent chance that it's this one. Lavinia is not special for knowing it (some of it), and Louise is not special either, for having memorized it (all of it) back in Devonshire, nor for whispering it to herself on the railroad bridge, nor for trying so desperately to make Virgil Bryce see that *sail beyond the sunset* were the four most beautiful words in the English language, and if she could not sail then she would, at least, swim. There is no such thing as fate, probably, and it is probably just coincidence. It's probably trite: like Klimt posters, like Mucha, like "The Love Song of J. Alfred Prufrock," like Paris (Louise has never been to Paris).

But Louise has that poem written on her heart, and she is so relieved that Lavinia does, too.

Push off, and sitting well in order smite
The sounding furrows; for my purpose holds
To sail beyond the sunset, and the baths
Of all the western stars, until I die.

Lavinia hurls the dress in the water. It recedes; it comes back: borne up—like a drowned woman—on the waves.

Lavinia and Louise look at each other.

And they're so goddamn cold Louise thinks they will turn into statues, they will turn to ice like Lot's wife (or was that salt? she cannot think) and they will stay there forever, the two of them, hand to hand and breast to breast and foreheads touching and snow on their collarbones, and Louise thinks *thank God, thank God,* because, if they could petrify themselves for all time so that all time was nights like these and never any morning afters, then Louise would gladly give up every other dream she ever had.

They take a selfie of their naked bodies, from the lips down. They use their arms to cover their nipples, because otherwise Instagram will censor it, and so they have two remnants of MORE POETRY!!! across the center of the photo.

"We'll get that tattooed on our arms," Lavinia says.

They are huddled, now, under the fur. Lavinia has put her dress back on. Louise has nothing but a shift, and a useless coat.

"I want to remember this forever," Lavinia says. She can't stop laughing. "Until the day I die."

When somebody says *I will remember this until the day I die,* they usually mean *I had a pretty good time,* or else, just *I want to fuck you.* That poly male feminist Louise dated that time used to say that he'd never forget her; so did the guy who was really into kink (*I'll never forget what you let me do to you, you are so not like other women that way*); so did Virgil Bryce. Even the guy who ghosted her once said, the night he took her for a walk in Prospect Park in summertime, *I'm probably going to leave New York, eventually, but when I do I want to remember nights like this* (that was the night she fucked him).

But Lavinia isn't like other people.

And when, six months from now, Lavinia dies, she will be thinking exactly of this night, and of the stars, and of the sea.

Louise will know this. She will be there.

They walk toward the elevated train.

Lavinia hails a cab.

"Take it," she says. She is smiling. Louise marvels at Lavinia's lipstick, still so dark even after all that champagne. "My coat is warmer than yours."

Louise can't afford a cab.

"It's fine," Louise says. "I'll take the subway."

Lavinia laughs, like this is a joke. "God, you're beautiful," she says. She kisses Louise on both cheeks. "I miss you already."

She throws herself into the cab.

Two minutes later, Louise gets a notification on her phone. Lavinia has posted the photograph of the two of them on Facebook.

She walks ten minutes to the Coney Island Q, because none of the other trains are running, for reasons that passeth all understanding. She doesn't step on the cracks in the sidewalk.

She sits on the subway, shaking in her slip underneath her flimsy coat, with holes in the pockets, that she bought at H&M like four years ago when GlaZam gave her a hundred dollars for a Christmas bonus, tries to avoid eye contact with the man who wanders up and down the subway car in a hospital gown with a medical bracelet on his arm, but everybody else is doing this, too, and you have to watch out for yourself, especially when you're five-foot-five and weigh one hundred fourteen and a half pounds on a period day. She is drunk enough to be sick, and tries not to throw up when two young men get on at Kings Highway with Burger King bags and proceed to noisily chomp on their fries all the way to Atlantic Avenue.

Here Louise has to switch to the R, even though it means doubling back, and some girls who maybe were part of a bachelorette party are screaming and waving their sparklers, and on the R-train platform there's a man standing on a plastic crate prophesying the end of the world.

I hate, I despise your festivals, he is shouting, although nobody is looking at him. He is looking straight at Louise. (*Though ye offer me burnt offerings and your meat offerings, I will not accept them: neither will I regard the peace offerings of your fat beasts.*) At least, Louise thinks he is looking straight at her. (*Take thou away from me the noise of thy songs; for I will not hear the melody of thy viols.*)

Louise gets off the R at Fifty-third Street.

Her heels bleed. There is sand between her toes and it blisters. She keeps her keys between her fingers.

On the corner before her house she sees the man who catcalls her, every day, to and from the subway. He is smoking weed. He is looking at her.

"Hey," he says.

She keeps her head down. She does not look at him.

"Hey, little girl," he says.

Louise does not answer this, either.

"You know it's cold outside?"

She thinks *just keep walking; just keep walking.*

"You know I'd warm you up!"

He is smiling—like this is friendly, like she should be flattered, like this is the nicest thing anybody has ever done for her.

"I'd warm you up, little girl."

He is following her—sauntering, not running, like this is a pleasant stroll, like this is not something that makes her want to scream.

"Don't you want me to warm you up?"

Louise tries so hard not to hear him.

She is so fast, with the key in the door, even though her hands shake. She's had practice.

"Don't flatter yourself," he calls after her, when she has at last made it inside. "I wouldn't fuck a dog like you with a ten-foot dick."

By the time Louise gets to bed it's nine.

She sets her alarm for twelve.

When Louise wakes up she can barely move but she moves anyway, because her shift at the coffee shop starts at two, and the knee-fondling cokehead who runs it will dock her pay if she is even a half-minute late to work.

2

LOUISE DOESN'T HEAR FROM LAVINIA.

She'd think she'd dreamed it, were it not for the MORE POETRY!!! on her arm, that she cannot bring herself to scrub off underneath her sleeves, were it not for the bad cold she gets that week that makes her have to cancel one of her tutoring sessions with Paul, whose parents are so much more annoyed by this than he is. Nights like that, with people who know "Ulysses" and stroke your hair—are not real. People take what they want from you, and tell you what you want to hear, and forget if they meant it.

Louise wonders, from time to time, if it was because she tore the dress.

Louise works. She takes the subway. She fixes her roots, strand by strand by strand.

Lavinia does so many interesting things that week. Louise sees them all on Facebook and Instagram. Lavinia goes to a Russian Orthodox Christmas party and she goes to the season premiere of *Rusalka* at the Met and gets photographed for the opera fashion blog in a floor-length silver-sequined gown and she goes for a snow-capped tea-party picnic with Athena Maidenhead and Father Romylos at the Alice in Wonderland statue in Central Park, and she spends a whole night going back and forth, back and forth, on the Staten

Island Ferry (*we were very very tired,* she captions the Instagram photo, *and we were very very merry*). The official photographs from the MacIntyre hit *Urban Foxes* and also the gossip section of the *Fiddler* blog, which used to only cover literary gossip but now makes an exception every now and then for literary-adjacent party photos, and Lavinia is in every single photo in the gallery.

Louise finds herself in one of them.

It's not actually of her, exactly—she's reflected in a mirror on the hotel lobby floor where the gin bar was, her face half-turned, while Lavinia poses, but it's so beautiful she doesn't even recognize it at first.

She right-clicks it. She saves it. She even goes to the Staples near Union Square before her bar shift, and spends $4.99 to print it out glossy, just in case the whole Internet collapses one day because of nuclear holocaust or war or something and she is never able to look at it again.

After a week, Lavinia texts her:

Just a name—Bemelmans—and a time.

Louise is supposed to work a shift for GlaZam. She does a Google search for Bemelmans and finds out that it's in the Carlyle Hotel and that glasses of wine start at twenty dollars, before tax, before tip.

Lavinia is there first.

She has spread out over two stools. Her skirt is voluminous and she's slung her ratty mink and her purse over one of them, even though the bar is so crowded with hotel guests, tourists, businessmen, all of whom are staring with unacknowledged fury at Lavinia's accessories.

"Sit. I've already ordered us champagne. I'm on my second drink, already—you're late!"

Louise is out of breath. "I'm sorry. The train."

"Have you ever been here before?"

"Not that I can remember."

Lavinia tosses her hair back—it looks like she might have tried to pin it up, this morning, but since then it has come undone and the pins have relented and she doesn't care enough to try to fix it.

"It's my local," she says. "I'm the only person under forty here who isn't a prostitute."

The wood is dark and although the place isn't candlelit this early in the evening, it looks like it might be and that is the beauty of it. There are murals on all the walls. There is a piano in the middle of the room and the piano man is playing "New York, New York." Lavinia hums along.

"They always play that here," Lavinia says. "Everyone always plays it. I don't mind. It's comforting. Like Christmas."

She slides Louise a champagne flute.

"Shall we have a toast?"

Louise's hands are still shaking from the cold. "To what?"

"To our New Year's resolutions, of course!"

"Of course."

"And to us!"

"And to us."

They clink glasses.

Sure, Louise has been in beautiful places before. Sometimes, when she has time between tutoring sessions, she goes to the Met and pays a dollar admission to wander the halls alone, like a ghost, just to be around beautiful things. But she has always been an alien there. For Lavinia this is home. "Have you done it yet?" Lavinia is beaming. "Your story. How many journals have you sent it to?"

"Oh."

Louise hasn't worked on her stories at all.

"None, yet—but I'm almost ready!"

"Will you let me read it? I want to read it. I can't *wait* to read it."

"What about your novel," Louise says. The best way to get some-body to forget they've asked you a question you don't want to answer is to encourage them to talk about themselves. "How's it coming?"

"Oh. It is as it always is. Ever was. Ever shall be. But I won't go back to school until it's finished—I promised myself that—I swore the solemnest of oaths. I will not step foot in New Haven until the final period is on the final sentence. Not that anyone wants to ever step foot in New Haven."

Lavinia knows the bartender, and so they get another round without asking for it.

Across the bar, Louise sees somebody she recognizes. High cheekbones and a plunging neckline, lips that are wine-dark, and she is leaning on the arm of a man who is older, and whose wristwatch blinds Louise.

"She's always here," Lavinia says. "With *someone*."

She raises her glass. The woman winks.

"Mother would be horrified. *What company you keep,* she'd say. *You'd have more luck getting a boyfriend, you know, if you went to dinner parties with your Chapin friends.* But I don't think it matters what a person does for a living, do you? Paris in the nineteenth century had a demimonde. And nobody judged Baudelaire. Anyway, she looks perfectly all right without the feathers."

Now Louise gets it. It's Athena Maidenhead.

"Anyway, she's not *really* a prostitute," Lavinia says. She applies more lipstick. "She's just—you know. A *demimondaine.* She's on Whats YourPrice and everything." She purses her lips. "How do I look?"

"Beautiful."

"Perfect," Lavinia says. "Selfie."

They do.

"I'm sending it to you. I want you to put it up. And tag me. And make it public, okay?"

"Okay."

They have another drink, and then another, and then another still.

An ambassador buys them one, and Timmy the bartender brings them yet another round Louise isn't sure whether or not they've ordered, and they send one over to the piano man, and then—and then, the bill comes.

Lavinia picks it up without even looking at it.

"Come on," she says. "Let's go to my party."

The second party Lavinia takes Louise to is in a bookstore that is not a bookstore. It is a rent-controlled apartment on East Eighty-fourth Street whose tenant, a gap-toothed belly laugh of a man called Matty Rosekranz, used to have a real bookstore, only he lost it after the recession because nobody buys books anymore. So he gutted his apartment and threw out the sink and got rid of the gas stove and now it holds nothing but books—good books but also pulp erotica and science fiction novels from the 1950s that have been out of print almost as long. The people who know the number buzz up and they bring a bottle or a joint. If they're pretty girls they just bring friends, and read their work out loud, and Matty entertains them, and nobody really buys a book but everybody leaves feeling like they've been part of something special.

Nobody has ever seen Matty Rosekranz outside the secret bookstore.

"Gavin says he saw him at the DMV in Harlem once," Lavinia says, as she leans against the buzzer. "But I don't believe him."

"What the fuck are you doing here?" asks Matty Rosekranz, when they come up. At first Louise is afraid he means her, but then he laughs, and lifts Lavinia up by her waist. "I thought we got rid of you."

"You can't get rid of me," Lavinia says. "I'm like a bad habit."

There are so many people here. The air is swamp-like and smells of beer. Everything that isn't full of beer has been turned into a bookshelf, except for a bookshelf that has been turned into a table, and over this Matty Rosekranz presides, with a bottle of Tito's and a six-pack and a bunch of red plastic Solo cups that everybody keeps knocking over and which Louise automatically picks up.

"Identity politics have been decimated," insists a man in a bright turquoise-and-dandelion bow tie, "by the left. The whole basis of truth relies on that fundamental statement—*x* equals *x*. But then you say *oh, I'm a man, but I'm a woman*—sorry, I know it's not politically correct."

He's talking at a very thin, very frail-looking woman with wide eyes and flaxen hair who looks impressed.

Lavinia gets right between them.

"Hello, stranger."

She kisses him on the cheek like she's not even interrupting him.

"Lavinia!" It takes him a second. "How have you been? I haven't seen you since—"

"I'm doing *splendidly!*" Lavinia flings out her arms. "It's been *wonderful*—I've been doing such things lately—Christ—it's a wonder I get anything done, these days, it's just been so busy—thank God I have Louise." She grabs Louise's hand and holds it up in the air. "She's keeping me on the straight and narrow. She's so disciplined—she writes all the time. She's an inspiration."

"You're a writer, too, then?"

"Oh, I'm so sorry! You haven't met. Louise, this is Beowulf Marmont. Beowulf, this is Louise—"

"Wilson."

"Louise Wilson. Oh, you have *so* much to talk about. Louise is the most interesting person you'll ever meet. Christ—there's Gavin!"

She sails away.

This is a test, Louise thinks.

Lavinia is testing her: to see how well Louise gets on with her other friends, now that they're not all piss-drunk, now that they can hear one another speak.

Louise doesn't blame Lavinia—it's a thing you do with an outsider.

"So." She is so chipper. "How did you and Lavinia—"

"Yale."

"Oh. Of course."

"You?"

"Oh." Louise shrugs. "You know. Parties." She keeps smiling.

Beowulf sniffs. "Sure," he says. "Where are you from?"

"I went to school in Devonshire," Louise says. She does that thing she does—almost without meaning to, now—where she sounds so clipped, it might as well be foreign.

"So you know Nick Gallagher."

"Oh. No. I mean—he probably graduated after me."

"When did you graduate?"

She hesitates. She works out his probable age, how young she can get away with being.

"2008."

She hopes she can pass for twenty-five.

"You should know him, then. He was class of 2010. He's a good kid. He's on staff at *The New Yorker* now."

"Sorry. I mean—it was a pretty big place."

"You should look him up. I just had lunch with him—last week. At the *New Yorker* offices. You've been?"

"Not yet!" She is doing such a good job of staying so desperately chipper.

"You should look him up. If you want to, you know, write for *The New Yorker*." He shrugs. "I mean—like, a lot of young women writers don't. Because, you know, the patriarchy. They're really into, like, new media or whatever. Like, *The New Misandrist* or whatever." He snorts. "So where have you written for, then?"

She could lie. But she knows he already knows what she is. Insufficiency is a thing people can smell.

"Sorry," Louise says. "I'm not a writer."

"Oh, great."

Louise knows this look. He's looking over her shoulder for somebody more important to talk to. "Great, great, great."

"Where do you—"

He's already halfway across the room. Lavinia's in a corner, talking to Gavin Mullaney, grabbing books off the shelves, so unafraid, talking to one stranger, and then another, and looking so happy the whole time.

She's not even looking over at Louise.

Louise does her best. She smiles prettily in a half-frozen way so nobody registers how petrified she is, and makes herself look busy, fingering all the books on the shelves, and feigning intense interest. She overhears somebody else talking about how he's the online editor at *The Fiddler* now, which makes him generally speaking the second or third most important person under thirty-five in any given room. She watches people but not too closely, and she both wants and does not want them to approach her, because if they do she does not have anything impressive to say, and Lavinia will see.

The reading begins.

Beowulf Marmont reads his story, publishing soon in *The New Weehawken Review*. It's about a man who drinks too much and loves women with pillowy lips. Beowulf is so confident, the way he strides up, the way he clears his throat and silences even Lavinia, who is whispering to Gavin about Edna St. Vincent Millay, and the logical part of Louise knows that he isn't looking at her—that he doesn't even care about her—and maybe it's just the secondhand pot smoke making her paranoid but the whole time that Beowulf is reading and Lavinia is looking away Louise remembers what happens if you can't pull your own weight at a party. People look over their shoulder; they forget you; they talk about you once you've gone and they do not reinvite you; Louise knows she isn't pulling her own weight—not standing like a lump against the wall, not stammering at strangers (she could say something brilliant and witty to strangers, she thinks, if Lavinia were at her side), but the more conscious she is of this the drier her throat gets, and the more impressive she needs to be the more insufficient she knows she is.

She bolts.

There's only one open window in this whole mold-eaten warren of an apartment and that's in the room that was once a kitchen; Louise runs and she grabs a book, any book, one on the top shelf, so that at least she'll look like she's cool enough to leave a reading to focus on a better book and not like she's just too afraid to stand in a room with people who think they're better than she is without Lavinia by her side to guide her through it.

"Are you hiding out, too?"

Louise starts.

He is sitting, half-curled, on a pile of books. He is smiling at her.

He has floppy brown hair and the kind of tortoiseshell glasses nobody wears anymore. He is in tweed, which also nobody wears anymore. He has wide, childlike brown eyes and very thin lips.

"Is it that obvious?"

"I mean—don't we *all* just want to hide out at these things?" He laughs a strange, croaking laugh. "I guess some of us just have weaker constitutions. Or, you know, don't need to network so much."

"Lucky them," Louise says.

"Lucky us," he says.

"Sure," Louise says. "Lucky us."

Then: "So, you're not a writer?"

He snorts. "Oh, no. I make much more sensible career decisions."

"Such as?"

"Grad school." His smile flowers. "Classics."

"I hear it's a lucrative field."

"Oh, yeah." He makes room for her on the bench, which is really just more books. "The margins are huge." He lights a joint, offers her a puff.

"I don't know if I should," she says. "Pot makes me paranoid."

"I mean, so does everything, right?"

"Except *networking.* Obviously."

Louise takes a puff. It makes her cough, and splutter, and so he takes out a handkerchief from his blazer pocket and offers it to her.

"*Really?*"

He starts to stammer, a little, and Louise realizes she's embarrassed him.

"I mean—thank you. I'm sorry. I'm sorry—that was rude. I was just—"

He laughs.

"Well, you know, *someone's* got to keep up standards."

"Of course." She does not understand why he is being so nice to her? "Naturally."

"So, you're not a writer, either?" He takes the joint back.

"Yes. No. Maybe?"

"There is *no such thing* as a writer anymore." The ugliest man Louise has ever seen stumbles into the room. "That's what Henry Upchurch says."

He has a square, simian face. His jaw is too big for his skull, and his skin is stretched too tight over it, and he is pale in an uncomfortably yellow way. He is short, and a bit fat.

"Hal, don't—"

"*America was great once. Not now. Then. Then we had men of letters. Then we had men of action.* Really? Nothing?"

"I'm sorry," Louise says.

"Christ. Where did you go to school? *Did* you go to school?"

"Hal!"

"I'm not being an asshole! Genuinely—I'm curious." He rummages through the books. "Here. Take it. An education."

He holds it out. *A Dying Fall.* Henry Upchurch.

"Only the best opening line in American literature. A literary lion. And a Great Man. Don't you think he's a Great Man, Rex?" He pronounces it *Reksh,* but then again, he is very drunk. "Christ, Rex— *cheer up.* This is pathetic."

"I'm just tired."

Hal claps him on the shoulder, hard.

"Is my friend boring you?"

"No."

"Are you boring him?"

"No!" Rex gets up. "No—we're fine, Hal."

"Come on." He turns to her. "What's your name?"

"Louise."

"I want to do you a favor, young Louise." He presses the book into her hands. "I want to expose you to the great and the good and more dead white men and yet-living white men you can shake a stick at. Where did you say you went to school?"

"In Devonshire."

"Devonshire. Of course. Look. It's Faber. 1998. The thirty-year-anniversary edition." He takes the book. He opens it up. "And would you look at that. *Signed*, too!"

In the other room, Louise can hear Beowulf Marmont's voice drone on.

Hal squints. "*Dear Marcus*—how nice, good old Marcus, probably a fag. *Dear Marcus. I am so delighted to read your very kind letter of March 3rd and to learn all about your fondness for* Folly's Train. *Please do ass-cheept this copy with my very pesh wishes and my hopes that your coursh of study at Harvard will be a prospph-prospsp-profitable one.*" He coughs. "What a generous, generous man. And look—we have a dedication, too! Will you look at that? *With deepest gratitude to my comrade-in-arms and agent, Niall Montgomery, to my longtime editor, Harold Lerner, and, with affection, to my wife, Elaine, and to my son.* Would you look at that?" He slams the book shut. "And to my son." He's grinning, gap-toothed, like Louise is supposed to be in on the joke.

"I'm sorry." Rex stares at the floor. "Hal's drunk."

"I'm not drunk. I just appreciate literature, that's all—not like that cuckold in the other room. Christ! It's true. No great writers. Nothing new under the sun."

"Are you a writer, too?"

"Not for all the tea in China, young Louise. I'm just a humble insurance executive."

He waves the book in Louise's face.

"I'm going to go buy this book for you." He catches sight of what's in Louise's hand. "He didn't give you a handkerchief, did he?"

Louise doesn't say anything.

"You're such a faggot, Rex. Love it. Lawl."

It takes Louise a second to figure out he means *LOL*, like the acronym, and not *loll*, like what he does with his tongue.

Hal grabs the red Solo cups. "I'm getting us all refills. And one more thing. Rex?" His grin gets wider. "She's here."

They stand in silence for a while, once Hal has gone. Then Rex sits. He exhales. He picks up a book. He puts it down. He lights another joint. He drops the lighter.

"Are you okay?"

"I'm sorry," Rex says. "Christ—Hal. I'm sorry."

"No worries."

"He's an asshole. He's—I mean, he's not normally that bad. He just likes to troll. But he's a good person, deep down."

"Is he?" She tries to smile, a little bit, to let him know it's not his fault.

"Very deep down."

They laugh together.

"He just gets weird, you know, when he drinks. About his dad."

"His *dad*?"

"The Great Man of American Letters."

"*No.*"

"I've known him my whole life," Rex says, "and I still can't tell whether he knows we've figured out he means it."

"Darling."

Lavinia is brilliant in the doorway. Her pearls glimmer. Her hair cascades.

"Darling," she says, and it takes Louise another second to figure out that Lavinia means her.

"I've been looking for you *everywhere!*"

She is looking straight and steadfastly at Louise with a steely smile.

"I'm sorry!" Louise isn't even sure why she springs to her feet so quickly. "I needed some air."

"Darling—we'll get you all the air you need. I'm so excited. Don't forget our picnic."

Her smile is plastered on. Her teeth are sharp. Suddenly, without understanding why, Louise is afraid.

"Our picnic?"

"Don't you remember? It's going to be wonderful. I'm getting us champagne. I've been thinking about it—ever since New Year's—I just know you'll love it."

"Right," Louise says—so slowly. "Of course."

Lavinia takes Louise's hand. She pulls her in. She kisses her cheek. She leaves a lipstick mark.

Rex is silent. His cheeks are red. He does not move.

"Oh, Lavinia, I'm sorry, this is—"

"We're late." Lavinia's lips haven't faltered once. "Let's go."

"Who was that?" Louise asks, when they're on the stairs. Lavinia just keeps smiling.

They cab it to the High Line. Lavinia pays. They go to a liquor store and buy two bottles of Moët. Lavinia pays for that, too. They find this place Lavinia and only Lavinia knows, where the gate to the High Line is slightly bent, and then Louise follows Lavinia as they crawl on their stomachs through it.

Now, Louise knows she has another shift at the bar tomorrow, and her rescheduled lesson with Paul, and she'll have to be up at six to make up the work for GlaZam she missed today, and because she knows that getting arrested and having to pay a fine and spend a night in jail is definitely one of the ways a person can *fuck it up,* but Louise is so relieved to be away from the secret bookstore, and the people who see right through her, and she is so relieved to be with Lavinia (who maybe sees through her or maybe doesn't but in any case only sees what she wants to see), that Louise follows Lavinia, anyway, joyfully, by the light of the moon.

"How do I look?" They are standing alone on the High Line, with the snowflakes studding their hair and making flowers that are not flowers on all the branches. Lavinia adjusts her lipstick, the velvet, the pearls.

"You look beautiful," says Louise. She does.

"Will you take a picture of me?"

Lavinia holds out her phone.

"Of course."

Louise takes one of Lavinia making snow angels. She takes one of Lavinia leaning against the bushes. She takes one of her seated with her skirt spread out on the bench.

Louise shows them to her.

"Yes. Yes. No—delete that one. Yes. Post it."

She lights a cigarette. Her hands are shaking.

"Isn't it wonderful?" she says. "To be outside—on a night like this, under the moon and the stars."

Louise wants to laugh with relief.

"You didn't like the party?"

"God no! Did you?"

"God, no!"

"Beowulf Marmont—"

"God, I'm so sorry I left you with him! I was trying to get away—I made you a human sacrifice—oh, Louise, will you *ever* forgive me?"

"I thought you liked him."

"He wears a yellow bow tie. Who could like a man in a yellow bow tie?" She hands Louise a cigarette, and Louise doesn't like to smoke, really, not when she's sober, but she loves the way the smoke looks against the snow. "Back at Yale, he once told me male circumcision was as bad as rape. He wasn't even trolling."

"He was pretty awful."

"Did he hit on you? He hits on *every* girl he sees."

"Oh. No." This stings a little bit.

"Thank God. I think he's dating this awful girl with these huge fucking eyes—she looks like an anime character or something. And his writing is *terrible*."

"It's so terrible!" says Louise, even though she hasn't actually heard much of it.

"God—if only we lived in—in—in nineteenth-century Paris, or somewhere! Somewhere with *real* artists. Real writers. People who were above all this horrible, pretentious—"

"That's what Hal said."

Lavinia's smile freezes.

"Christ—*Hal!*"

"You know him?"

"You talked to him?"

"I mean—a little."

"What did you think?"

"I mean . . . he's a little . . ."

"He's an inbred moron, you mean?"

"Yes. Yes!"

It feels so good to be able to relax at last.

"He's a fucking mental Habsburg, isn't he? Brings up his father every five seconds just to sound like he's done anything of substance with his life!"

"That's all he did!"

"Of course he did! That's all he ever does! That and cocaine—he's such a fucking cliché I'm embarrassed for him. And Rex!"

"What about him?"

Lavinia freezes.

"You liked him?"

"What?"

"I mean—you two were talking."

"Oh. I mean. No. I mean—not really."

"You shouldn't talk to him. He's the worst of all of them." Lavinia lights another cigarette, but this time her hands are shaking too violently and she drops the lighter, and Louise is the one to pick it up. "He's a coward."

"What happened?"

"What do you mean? Nothing happened!" Lavinia laughs.

"You seemed—"

"It was nothing," Lavinia says. "It was stupid. It's in the past. He's nothing to me. I don't care about him."

"Wait, did you two—"

Lavinia doesn't say anything. She tosses her hair, like she always does.

"It doesn't matter. Let's take a selfie. The light's good. Your skin looks great. I wish I had your skin. God, I hate you."

"I'm sorry," Louise said. "I didn't know. If I'd known, I wouldn't have talked to him."

"You can talk to him. I don't care. I don't care about *him*. He's—he's normal and he's boring and he wants an ordinary life with an *ordinary* girlfriend he can, you know, get brunch with or whatever. That's his right."

Lavinia stubs out the cigarette in the snow. It sizzles, and then the fire dies out.

"Do you want to know something funny, Louise?"

"What?"

"He's the only person I've ever really loved."

Lavinia is leaning on the railing, looking out toward the river, and so Louise can't see her face to tell if she means it.

"Isn't that stupid?" Lavinia says.

"I don't think that's stupid."

Lavinia rounds on her. "Because you think he's worth it?"

"No, of course not. I mean . . ." Louise casts about for the right thing to say. "People fall in love for all sorts of reasons."

"He wrote *letters*. That's why. You don't think that's a stupid reason?"

"Depends on the letters, I guess."

"I mean—we were kids. Like—sixteen. I was at Chapin and he was at Collegiate and, you know, we'd go to all the same parties. Whatever."

"Whatever."

"Anyway, we exchanged numbers or whatever it was and he asked if he could write me a letter, sometime. Like—with stamps and everything. I didn't expect him to do it. People never do the things they say they will." She looks up. Her face is white with the cold. "I mean—normal people. Not people like us." She beams, and in the moonlight she is radiant. "You and me, we keep our promises. We say—*we're going to recite poetry by the sea*. We say—*we're going to break into the High Line*. And we do. Anyway, he did. Back then, Rex was a real person."

She has gone through half the cigarette pack.

"He used to hand-deliver them, sometimes. Quill pen. Green ink. A *seal*. Leave them with my doorman. He didn't even have Facebook for the longest time—he had a whole complex about it, too. He wanted to wear a wristwatch. Christ—he still used a *flip phone*. I loved it."

She exhales, slowly. In the distance, the lights are going out, one by one by one, all over the city.

"We were partners in crime—*contra mundum*. We used to hold hands and walk through the Met and talk about running away together. We had the whole itinerary planned out. It was going to be this Grand Tour—you know—just going everywhere beautiful and seeing every beautiful thing and we were going to go to Vienna to see Klimt's *The Kiss* up close at the Belvedere, and to Venice for Carnevale. When we were finally free."

Louise thinks about Virgil Bryce, on the railroad bridge.

"Anyway," Lavinia says. "We never went."

"What happened?"

"Nothing *happened*. He just got boring. That's all."

"When?"

Lavinia snorts. "A couple years ago. Anyway, it doesn't matter. I told you. He's dull. He's even got Facebook now. At least, I think he still has. I wouldn't know. He blocked me."

The snow shines on her cheeks. Her lips are red.

"God, I hope he hates me," Lavinia says, suddenly.

"Why?"

"It means they still think about you." Lavinia exhales smoke.

Lavinia leans out over the railing: "Have you ever been in love?"

Louise has to think about it.

"I don't know. Maybe."

"Don't be ridiculous. When you know, you know."

"I moved to New York with someone," Louise says. "I was in love with him. I think."

Louise does not talk about Virgil Bryce, ever. But then again, nobody has ever asked.

"Was he in love with you?"

"Yes."

"Where is he now?"

"I don't know. I blocked him."

"Did he break your heart?"

"I don't know. I think I broke his."

Lavinia claps. "I knew it. I *knew it*! God—you're such a little femme fatale."

"I'm really not."

"All quiet and haughty and mysterious—God, I *knew it*. The second I saw you—"

"I'm really, *really* not."

"I thought—a man would slit his wrists for a woman like that."

"He didn't," Louise says. "But he did threaten to, once."

Lavinia grabs Louise's wrist.

For a second, Louise thinks she has said too much, that she has shocked Lavinia, that she has done that awful over-sharing thing people so often do that makes the room go quiet, and makes everybody say something sympathetic, and makes everybody feel sorry for you, and makes everybody hate you.

Then Lavinia bursts out laughing.

"Jesus *Christ,* I love you."

There are tears in her eyes. She is shaking. She squeezes Louise's hand so tight.

Louise can't help it. She starts laughing, too.

It has never been funny before.

But with Lavinia, on this bridge, which is so much higher and so much brighter than any bridge in Devonshire ever was, everyone else seems that little bit less real. Everything about that other Louise—the Louise with mousy brown hair and a crooked smile and who was a little fat and whom nobody but the charitable and the insane could ever really love—is fiction.

"Of course he didn't do it, did he?" Lavinia is still racked with laughter.

"No, of course not." Not as far as Louise knows.

"Men."

"Men!"

"They never keep their fucking promises."

Lavinia is laughing so hard that tears seep from her eyes.

Louise offers her a handkerchief.

Lavinia stops laughing.

"Where did you get that?"

"Oh. Oh—Rex."

"He *gave* it to you?"

"I sneezed. I forgot to give it back. I'm sorry."

"Let me see."

Lavinia takes it.

"He probably still has his *wristwatch,* too."

"I'm sorry. I didn't see."

Lavinia is silent.

Then: "Hand me the lighter."

Louise does.

A slow smile spreads across Lavinia's face. She lights the corner of the handkerchief. The fire is slow, at first. Then the whole thing bursts into flame.

"Jesus, *fuck*!" Lavinia drops it.

For a moment the two of them stand there, staring, at the small, persistent fire in the middle of the path.

Lavinia sucks her thumb where she has burned it.

"You see," she says softly. "They don't mean a thing to us, do they?"

She is so beautiful by the firelight.

She is so beautiful, Louise thinks, that you even believe her.

Lavinia takes another step closer to the fire.

"We should be maenads, instead," she says, so softly. "We should abjure all men and tear them apart with our teeth when they come near us. *Fuck you, Rex Eliot! Fuck you, Hal Upchurch! Fuck you, Beowulf Marmont.*" She spins on her heels. "Your one—what's he called?"

"Um—Virgil?"

"What a name!"

"His mom was a history teacher."

"Virgil what?"

"Bryce."

"Fuck you, Virgil Bryce!"

Lavinia turns to her.

"Well, come on! Your turn—what's the point if you don't say it, too?"

"Fuck you, Virgil Bryce," she says quietly.

"Pathetic!" Lavinia grabs her wrist. "Do it again!"

"Fuck you, Virgil Bryce!"

"For God's sake—FUCK YOU, VIRGIL BRYCE!"

"FUCK YOU, VIRGIL BRYCE."
"FUCK ALL MEN EVERYWHERE."
It feels so good to scream.
"FUCK ALL MEN EVERYWHERE!"
The fire goes out.
Lavinia says, "Let's get drunk."

They do.

They go through both bottles of champagne, right there on the High Line, with nothing but the stars over them and the rails extending to convergence in both directions. They drink and Lavinia tells Louise about all the places they will go together, when they finish their stories, when they are both great writers—both of them—to Paris and to Rome and to Trieste, where James Joyce used to live, to Vienna to see the paintings, to Carnevale.

Lavinia will never go.

She is going to die soon. You know this.

They take more photos. Louise in the snow. Lavinia on the railing. Lavinia and Louise: leaning, about to fall.

They post them.

"You should add him on Facebook," Lavinia says.

"Who?"

"Rex. He's on there now, isn't he?"

Louise looks.

"Yes."

"Add him. Hal, too."

Louise does.

They drink until the stars spin. They lean on each other's shoulders. They make more snow angels.

"Hey, Louise?"

"Yeah?"

"Will you read my novel?"

"Of course."

Lavinia sits straight up. "Fantastic. Let us *set off.*"

"Wait, *now?*"

Lavinia's already on her feet. "It's not that far!"

"It's two o'clock in the morning!"

"So there's no point in you going all the way to, like, Bumfuck, Brooklyn, is there? You might as well stay at mine."

She is so charming, pleading.

"Oh, *don't say no,* Louise. Please—*please*—*please* don't say no!"

Louise can't.

They cab it back to Lavinia's. Lavinia pays.

Lavinia gets her enormous skirt caught in the cab doors. Louise pulls it out. Lavinia is drunker than Louise realized and she has to help her into the apartment. She doesn't mind. It's nice, she thinks, to be so necessary.

"Home at last!"

Lavinia tumbles in.

"Christ, it's so *empty.* I hate it when Cordy leaves." She sails to the kettle. "We shall have tea. From the shores of Asia! From the Edgware Road. Do you want chocolate-caramel or lavender-mint? And we should have music, too! Mood music! Atmosphere!" She makes her way to the computer; she blasts Wagner's *Tristan und Isolde* so loud Louise worries that the neighbors will hear, and come down, and start a fight.

"So they'll hear!" Lavinia shrugs. "Fuck 'em! If there's one thing the Upper East Side needs it's more Wagner!"

She turns the volume higher still.

"I love this part." She lets herself fall on the sofa. She closes her eyes.

Louise makes the tea because nobody else will.

"Do you want me to put milk—"

"Shhh!"

Louise puts milk in the tea.

"It's the lovers' duet. They're the only two people in the world, right now. The two of them."

Louise brings the tea over.

"Listen!"

Louise does.

"It never lasts, though, does it? It all falls apart in the end. Doesn't it?"

"Yes," Louise says. She sets the tea down. "It does."

"God, you're so mysterious—I love it! *Fuck*—my dressing gown!" She extends a long white hand into the middle distance. "It's in my bedroom."

Louise gets the dressing gown. It is powder-blue and silk and stained and very impractical, with little flowers on it. She helps Lavinia put it on.

Louise sits next to Lavinia on the sofa. Lavinia strokes her hair. "It's three in the morning."

"I know. I know. But—just one chapter, okay? Please? Then—then you can take Cordy's bed and—and I'll get up early and I'll make us pancakes tomorrow before your shift, okay?"

"Just one chapter?"

"It's just that I care so much what you think! You should be *flattered*!" Lavinia whines, a bit, and puts her shoes up on the steamer trunk. "I'd stay up all night reading yours, you know. If you had it for me."

She takes out her phone.

"Here," she says. "It's all on here."

The light is blinding. The text is so small.

Louise starts to scroll. "How long is it?"

"Just start it. If you don't like it you can stop. I promise."

"I can barely read it."

"I want to see your reactions. That's the best way. If I can see your face. And you don't have to like it, you know. In fact, if you like it too much—I won't respect you. So you should probably hate it, just a little bit."

"Come on—I'm not going to hate it!"

But here's the thing: Louise does.

It's not just that it's bad. It is bad—the prose is too purple and the sentences are too long and the literary allusions are too forced and every other line is a quotation or a character monologuing about the nature of Life and Art; or a character does something intensely symbolic but that doesn't quite come off. But it's worse: it's self-indulgent. There's a character called Larissa who is very beautiful and very blonde and is kind of like a saint because her passions are so much greater and more important and more significant than anyone else's.

Even Louise knows the first rule of good writing is to never assume that your life is more significant than anyone else's just because you say it is. And Larissa wants to live Life as Art, except of course she can't, because nobody around her understands concepts like Beauty and True Love the way she does. So she tries to make a suicide pact with her lover, who of course is undeserving of her, and of course he doesn't go through with it and so she throws herself off a bridge all on her own for no obvious reason.

Also, she uses too many em dashes.

Louise feels so many things. She does not show any of them.

She is embarrassed, like she has walked in on somebody watching porn. She feels that she has looked at something raw and quivering, exposed and unholy.

She is angry, too, because in everything Lavinia has written there is such a perfect confidence: that Lavinia's thoughts and Lavinia's passions and Lavinia's philosophy and Lavinia's heartbreak are worth hours of somebody else's time, and Louise has never had that confidence.

Also, Louise is relieved.

There is something she has that Lavinia doesn't.

Louise's eyes glaze over. She is tired; she wants to sleep—she wants to sleep so badly—but Lavinia is looking at her and bouncing on her knees on the sofa, and nodding, and smiling, and if she gives away a hint—a single hint—of all that she is feeling she will never be able to take it back again.

"What do you think?" Lavinia is breathless.

Louise hesitates.

"You think it's bad."

"No! No—I don't think it's bad at all!"

Lavinia lets herself laugh. "I wasn't sure."

"It's good! It's—I mean, it's *good!*"

"But?"

Louise takes a deep breath.

Lavinia takes a deep breath.

"But nothing—"

"Oh come on!" Lavinia pats Louise's hand. "There's always *something.*"

"It's just—"

"Yes?"

"I mean—Larissa is you, of course."

"Why do you say of course?"

Lavinia is blinking so quickly.

"I mean the name."

"Well of course the *name.*"

"I mean—I wonder . . ." Louise has to be so careful, now. "I mean—I wonder if there's just *so much* overlap."

"Too much? You can tell me. I can take it. I can take it. Tell me."

"No. No—not too much. Just—there's not a lot of distance from the protagonist, is there?"

"What's that supposed to mean?"

Louise has seen that face on Lavinia before. She saw it on New Year's Eve, when Mimi tore her dress.

"Nothing."

"You think I let her off easy, or something?"

"I didn't say that!"

"I'm sorry." Lavinia inhales. "I'm sorry." She pulls the throw over her knees. "I'm sorry. You're right. I should—I'm just tired, that's all. I'm tired and I'm in a bad mood. I should let you go home."

She pulls the blanket up to her chin.

And Louise thinks *she cannot mean to do this.*

You are crazy to think this of her, Louise thinks. *You are a bad person to think this of her. She just forgot. That's all. Just ask to stay—just remind her—that's all you have to do. You cannot always think the worst of people.*

Lavinia's eyes are already closed.

And Louise, she knows that all she has to do is say *it's still cool if I stay, right.* But she is so afraid Lavinia will say yes and mean *no,* that Lavinia will make pancakes and then never call her again, because she has fucked it up because of course, *of course,* she's fucked it up. Nobody ever wants to know the truth about themselves, not really, and she—of course—she should know this more than anyone.

It would be so easy, she thinks, just to ask for what she wants.

"I love it," Louise says.

Lavinia's eyes pop open. "You do?"

"That's what I was trying to say. It's so—emotional. It's so—*raw.*"

"Really? You really think that?"

"You're going to be Great, Lavinia. I don't have any doubt. I don't have any doubt in the goddamn world."

That night, for the first time, Louise realizes just how young Lavinia is.

It's so easy to lie to her.

That's the other thing Louise realizes.

Lavinia flings her arms around Louise; she squeezes her so tight Louise can't breathe.

"God, I love you so much," she says. "You really don't know how much it means to me." She draws the blanket over Louise's feet. "I wouldn't trust anyone else to read it, not even Cordy. Nobody but you."

Louise leans her head on Lavinia's shoulder. Lavinia squeezes her hand.

Louise thinks: *we cannot be known and loved at the same time.*

It is very simple, Louise knows. There are two kinds of people in the world: the people you can fool into liking you, and the ones clever enough not to fall for it.

The day Louise dyed her hair, that first time, the month she first moved to Sunset Park, the month she bought a book of mantras and changed her number and blocked Virgil Bryce on social media, she looked into the mirror and found, for the first time in her life, that she was fuckable.

It was like she was getting away with something.

It took her a month or two to get the measure of it. First the cat-callers, and then the older men in bars, and then even the men a little closer to her own age in bars, and on Tinder, back when she used Tinder (the polyamorist, the kinky one, the ghost). Men thought she was special.

They did this, you understand, because they were stupid.

They didn't notice *Louise.*

It was just that Louise *looked* blonde and thin and pretty, and they were dumb enough to think that all these things were true of her, and not just qualities she wore. And so they were dumb enough to think that her other qualities (she was so chill, she was so clever, she was so open-minded in bed) were real, too.

It never lasts, of course. Louise knows this. You can't fool them forever, not even the very stupid ones. They realize every good thing about you is a trick.

Louise has fooled Lavinia, she thinks, and so Lavinia must be stupider than she is. She hates herself for thinking like that about Lavinia, who has been nothing but kind to her, but she thinks it all the same.

Unless Lavinia said *go home* because she knew Louise couldn't—not at this hour, not in this cold—

Louise would hate herself for thinking that, too.

"Hey, Louise?"

Lavinia is half-asleep.

"What is it?"

"You don't think I'm, like—*too much,* do you?"

"Too much?"

"I mean. You know. *Too much.* Too everything."

"No," says Louise. "Of course not. Am *I* too much?"

"Of course not," Lavinia murmurs. "You're—I mean—you're the *opposite* of too much."

Louise doesn't say anything.

"I love you."

Lavinia starts to snore on her shoulder.

Louise tries to sleep on the sofa, because if she moves she will wake Lavinia. She plays with her phone. She reads stupid articles on *Misandry!*

She wants to cry.

She hates herself for wanting to cry, because she has had such a good night—not the assholes at the bookstore, maybe, but after that. They have had such a wonderful night and they broke onto the High Line and they burned Rex's handkerchief in effigy for all men, everywhere, who had ever hurt them, and they took so many cabs Louise didn't even have to pay for, and now Louise is sleeping in such a beautiful apartment surrounded by such beautiful things and there is somebody who has squeezed her hand and said *I love you* and everything they have done tonight is everything that Louise, in Devonshire, would have been so happy—so happy and so proud and so *justified*—to see Louise, in New York, doing now.

You're being dumb, she tells herself. *That's all.*

She keeps looking at the photograph Lavinia has posted of the two of them.

They're on the High Line. They're surrounded by snow and branches and stars that, on this filter, you can't even distinguish from the city lights.

We look happy, Louise thinks. Maybe they were.

Everybody's Liking it. Father Romylos and Gavin Mullaney and even Beowulf, and so many other names that are by now at least a little bit familiar.

Mimi Kaye.

hey lady.

Mimi has added Louise on Facebook.

you look super cute in those pics

Winking smiley cat-eye emoji.

Thanks (Louise says)

(flirty heart-eyed fox, says Mimi)

isn't it fun out there?

(boggle-eyed dancing-footed toad)

yeah it was nice thanks

lavinia and I used to do it alllll the time hahaha

one time we even slept out there

the cops found us but lavinia got us out of it

isn't that so funny

(chicken with clown makeup on)

don't you think that's funny?

(owl wearing a cap and gown and glasses looking inquisitive)

Louise doesn't answer.

She doesn't sleep, either.

3

THE THIRD PARTY LAVINIA TAKES LOUISE TO is a loft party off the Jefferson L at this performance space this guy she knows owns where they've turned the entire mezzanine into a poetry library. The fourth party Lavinia takes Louise to is this cabaret benefit at the Laurie Beechman Theatre over in Hell's Kitchen, where everybody but Louise and Lavinia is ninety and is wearing tattooed eyeliner and sequined shawls. The fifth is the release party in Gramercy for this coffee-table book called *Sexual Secrets of Europe* by this degenerate Australian travel writer called Lydgate who must only be fifty-five but looks eighty, and it is there that Louise does coke for the first time and races Lavinia all the way up First Avenue.

They go to parties neither of them is invited to.

"It's easy," Lavinia says. "You just walk right in."

They get matching tattoos. This is Lavinia's idea.

"I don't ever want to forget our trip to the sea," she says. "I want to think about that night all the time. I want to commemorate it."

They are standing on Saint Mark's Place, which is the most expensive and least hygienic place to get a tattoo in New York City. They are drunk because they've just gone to that speakeasy you can only get to by entering through a telephone booth and putting your name down two hours in advance. Earlier they'd gone to the perfume shop on East Fourth Street, because Lavinia had to get her signature fragrance made, which is called Sehnsucht and which Louise can by now smell on all her clothes, and that night is the night Louise gets her own (because Lavinia pays for this, too), which is made of dandelion and fern and tobacco and heather, but when she smells it now she thinks it smells all wrong, because it smells nothing like Lavinia's.

"Come on!" Lavinia says. She has gone into a shitty shop that even Louise knows only NYU freshmen patronize. "God, Louise, don't you want to *live*?"

Two hours later Louise sobers up in Washington Square Park and realizes that both of them have MORE POETRY!!! tattooed in tiny letters on their forearms, and she isn't as horrified as she should be.

"Worst case scenario"—Lavinia shrugs—"you get it lasered off. It's not that expensive."

She leans her arm against Louise's arm.

They take a picture of the two of them, holding hands.

There are so many wonderful pictures of them on the Internet. There's the one of the two of them in Lincoln Center, between the opera and a costume party at the MacIntyre, taking off their evening gowns to reveal the corsets underneath. There's one of them in drag at something called the Tweed Picnic, which is a flash mob in Bryant Park.

Everybody, everybody Likes them.

"You certainly look like you're taking better care of yourself," Louise's mother tells her on the phone. "Your hair looks nice."

Louise has been dyeing it a slightly more strawberry shade of blonde. It looks so good on Lavinia, she thinks, and the two of them have the same skin tone.

People from Devonshire Like the photos—people who have barely spoken to her. So does Beowulf Marmont. So does the guy that ghosted.

More than once.

———

Louise starts finishing stories. She even sends them out.

She and Lavinia sit on the divan in Lavinia's apartment that smells like incense and sit together at their laptops and set the timer for an hour and write, and even though half the time Lavinia gets bored and gets up to make a pot of cinnamon-raisin-date tea and then forgets about that, too, Louise sits and types. Lavinia orders dinner for both of them on Seamless and it is so glorious to eat food that somebody else has cooked, and not to have to clean up, after.

"It's the least I can do," Lavinia says. "You're keeping me on the straight and narrow. You inspire me."

She sends an essay about Devonshire to Gavin Mullaney after a *Fiddler* Valentine's Day party. It's not the one she deep down wants to write, which is the one about pretending to go to the Academy for a week, because she doesn't like writing about herself, but she writes a *reportage* kind of thing about this crazy thing that happened to her sophomore year when a couple of Academy kids went nuts and ran away and they had the whole police after them. Gavin likes it.

I'm not a really big fan of narrative, Gavin says, *and I don't also personally really care about things like characterization since personally I don't have a lot of empathy for other people but it's super-readable and people apparently really like stories that are very driven by primal emotions.*

Could you Tweet it when you get a chance?

A few days later he suggests she pitch his second-favorite person of all the people he's dating (he has a spreadsheet), a woman called Michelle-Ann who left *Misandry!* to start a new, more intersectionally aware magazine called *The New Misandrist.* Louise does.

Louise lets herself get stupid.

She stops paying such close attention to money (somehow, even with Lavinia paying for everything, Louise is always broke, and she isn't sure why). She starts missing GlaZam shifts. She starts eating bread (Lavinia loves the croissants from Agata & Valentina, and insists on buying a dozen even though she only ever eats one). She starts trusting people, the way Lavinia trusts people, secure in the knowledge that the world is a well-ordered and reasonable place in which nothing ever goes unsalvageably wrong.

Louise stops waiting for the world to end.

Until the night it almost does.

Louise is so happy, that night. They have gone to this erotic illustrator's art Ballets Russes party at this gay culture museum on the Lower East Side, and they have stayed out so late at this Marie Antoinette–themed cocktail bar, and she is so happy that she has that final glass of champagne that she knows she shouldn't have. She takes the long, slow train ride, and when she gets off she is singing.

Louise never sings.

When she walks home she always hunches over. She puts her hands in her pockets. She always stares straight ahead. She always puts her keys between her fingers.

Always.

But tonight Louise is drunk, and Lavinia has invited her to the opera, in a couple of weeks, and promised to sew her a dress. Of course Louise will do the sewing but Lavinia will buy the raw materials and the vintage base; and they have so many grand plans, so Louise is humming "As Time Goes By," because that's what they played over and over at the Ballets Russes party and she leaves her keys in her purse.

"You've got a voice on you, little girl."

He is always there.

Louise isn't afraid of him tonight. She tosses her long strawberry-blonde hair, and shoots him the kind of world-destroying smile Lavinia shoots bartenders when she doesn't want to pay for something.

"You want to give me singing lessons."

"No, thank you!"

She's almost skipping.

"What's your name?"

"What's it to you?"

God's in his heaven, Louise is thinking, with the part of her brain that can still think, *and all is right with the world.*

"I said—what's your name?"

"Artemesia Gentilleschi!" She flings out her arms.

"You fucking with me?"

He is so close to her. She has not realized how close he is to her.

"Hey! I asked you a question!"

He grabs her arm.

Here's the thing: there's only so much you can lie to yourself. You can blunt instinct, if you want to—you can drink too much, you can laugh and smile and reapply your lipstick and say *let us get drunk, on poetry and virtue,* you can pretend to be a human being, a little while—but in the end, you are what you are.

Somebody comes too close, you run.

He follows you, you run faster.

His steps meld into yours, you stop.

You turn.

He hesitates.

You do what you have to do.

And if you're lazy enough and stupid enough and arrogant enough to forget to put your keys between your fingers—the one time, that *one time,* you're lazy and stupid and arrogant enough to not put your keys between your fingers—you use whatever you have to hand.

Your elbows. Your nails. Your teeth.

You punch a stranger straight in the eye before he can tell you whether he wants to rape you or just tell you he likes your smile.

You keep hitting him, and scratching him, and pulling out his hair, and even kicking him, straight between the legs, until you have made sure he is on the floor.

You kick him once more, in case he still wants to follow you.

You run.

Louise doesn't stop shaking until she's on the stairs.

She doesn't let herself cry until she's inside.

She doesn't let herself scream. Not now. Not ever. She just holds her wrist to her chest, her wrist with the bruise where he has grabbed it and MORE POETRY!!! still healing on her forearm, and she takes very slow, very measured, very deep breaths, that rack and strangle but do not make any sound.

You little fool, she thinks. *You deserve everything bad that ever happens to you.*

Maybe the moon is full. Maybe the stars are bright. Maybe cigarettes smell like incense.

But not for her, she thinks. Never for people like her, who don't live on the Upper East Side, who don't go to Yale, who aren't even naturally blonde.

Everybody who has ever told her this was right.

"That's bollocks," says Lavinia, when Louise tries to return the opera tickets the next day. "It's the season premiere."

Louise has made some vague and unconvincing excuse. Paul needs extra SAT lessons because he smokes too much weed. Something like that.

"The tickets are paid for," Lavinia says, like that's all there is to it.

She catches sight of Louise's bruise.

"Jesus Christ."

Louise explains that it's nothing, that there's just some guy who likes to chat her up, that he got a little handsy because she was too sassy, that this kind of thing happens all the time.

"All the time?"

Lavinia stretches out her legs along the steamer trunk. She fans herself with the peacock feathers. She turns up the music.

"Just move into Cordy's room," she says. "She's going to be in Paris the whole summer, anyway."

It is a stupid thing to do. Louise knows that.

But so is turning down a free room on Seventy-eighth and Lex.

Lavinia hires a moving van a week later. She shows up at Sunset Park in palazzo pants, with a scarf in her hair, like she's some 1930s explorer, like she's off on an adventure to the land of here-be-dragons, even though it's only South Brooklyn (it's not even real South Brooklyn, like Gravesend or Bensonhurst, just Sunset Park). She looks with such bewilderment at the bodegas, at the white plastic chairs, at the Greek man pissing in the lobby.

"I love it," Lavinia says. She taps a cigarette against the lobby walls. "You should write about him. A mad Greek—maybe he's a prophet. I bet *The Fiddler* would love it."

Louise never wants to think about the mad Greek again.

They get in the moving van, which Lavinia apparently can drive ("I learned in Newport one summer. I destroyed a mailbox"), with the single box of useless shit Louise doesn't plan to keep anyway.

There he is, on the corner.

He has a black eye. He has a bruise on his lip.

He sees her. He looks up.

"What's wrong?"

"Nothing," says Louise. "Keep driving."

"You look like you've seen—"

"Let's go!"

A strange, slow smile spreads across Lavinia's face. "That's not—"

"Please, Lavinia."

All she wants is to go. All she wants is to never see this street or this apartment or any of these bodegas with their loose cigarettes and their hanging rosaries and their uniform packs of knockoff microwave meals again.

Lavinia stops the van.

She is a terrible driver, and Louise lurches forward so violently bile rises in her throat.

"How dare he," Lavinia says. "How *fucking* dare he?"

"I just want—"

Lavinia's already out of the van.

"Hey!"

She gets in his face.

"Hey! You!"

"What do you . . ."

"You—you—catastrophic piece of shit!"

Louise can't breathe.

She sits there, strapped in the passenger seat, and she knows she should get up or do something or say something or stop it but her heart is beating so fast that she can't stop it, and Lavinia looks so ridiculous—in her cream-colored palazzo pants that are already gray (for God's sake, it is only April), and the scarf wound around her head, shouting at this man with a black eye and a bruise over his upper lip.

The funny thing is: he looks so confused.

Louise almost feels sorry for him.

"Lady, I don't know what you're . . ."

"You ought to be—drawn and quartered. You ought to be *hanged*!"

He looks up at her.

Of course, Lavinia doesn't mean it like that. Lavinia doesn't live in the real world, which is a world where when a white woman tells a black man he should be hanged it does not mean what it means in Lavinia's world, where men still fight duels with muskets or swords or bow to each other in the morning—Louise knows this. It doesn't even occur to Lavinia—not even now, not even when he's looking at her like she's hit him—what she has done, and all Louise can think is *fuck, fuck,* and then she's running out of the van; then she grabs Lavinia so hard by the arm Lavinia yelps and she screams *let's go* and almost throws her in the passenger seat; she grabs the keys and presses the pedal down because God knows Lavinia can't drive this thing, and the tires screech and they are all the way into Park Slope before anybody says anything.

"What the hell was that?"

Lavinia is rubbing her arm where Louise has grabbed it.

"You shouldn't have done that," Louise says.

She keeps her eyes on the road.

"Done what? Defend you?"

"Said what you said."

"What did I say? He—he *insulted* you!"

"You can't just—" Louise's heart is only just going back to normal. "You can't just—fucking—*say* things without thinking about them."

She doesn't know why she is protecting him. He has done nothing for years but follow her home. He has done nothing but call her names, and tell her he's going to fuck her, or else he wouldn't if his life depended on it. She has given him a black eye.

Maybe he was just trying to be friendly (how can she even think that, now?).

Maybe I should have just asked his name.

And Louise is so angry with herself and angry with Lavinia for being so stupid and angry with Lavinia for meaning so well and angry with Lavinia for not knowing why she is angry and she doesn't say anything.

They drive in silence all the way to the Upper East Side.

"You know," Lavinia says, when Louise stops the truck, "I thought you'd be grateful."

The bed is soft. The bedspread is jacquard, fur-lined. The walls have moldings on them. There's a midcentury modern chandelier. There are Persian carpets, and an art nouveau wardrobe Lavinia bought at the flea market in the Flatiron and there are antique postcards from all the childhood places Lavinia and Cordelia have been to. There is a framed photograph of the sisters on the bedside table.

There is no room for Louise's clothing in the closet. Lavinia has filled it up with formal dresses—ball gowns and vintage taffeta and silks and sequins and feathers and the long velvet trousers Lavinia wears those nights she wants to look like Marlene Dietrich.

"I'm sorry," Lavinia says. She is in her powder-blue gown with the stains on it. Her hair is halfway down her back. "I didn't think. But, I mean—it's not like you have a lot of clothes, anyway. You can always wear mine!" She says this very brightly. "It's so good that we're the same size, isn't it?" She brings Louise a glass of champagne. It's ten o'clock in the morning. "Speaking of which . . ." She sits on the bed, right on top of Louise's sweatshirts. "I was thinking. You should join ClassPass. I'm going to. That way we can work out together, in the mornings. God, I know, I know—but I'm turning over a new leaf. I'm going to get up early—we both are. Apparently your metabolism starts to slow down before your mid-twenties—I'm going to have to be so much more careful."

It takes Louise a second to register that Lavinia has no idea how old she is.

"Here, give me your phone. I'll sign up for you." Lavinia grabs Louise's purse. "Do you have a credit card in there?"

"How much is it?"

"Not a lot. Like—two hundred? One ninety? Something like that."

Lavinia grabs the card.

"That's kind of expensive."

"Oh, don't worry!" Lavinia beams. "It's unlimited. You can take as many classes as you want—we can go *twice* a day, even!"

"I don't think . . ."

"It'll be so much *fun*! You know me, Louise—I'll never do anything unless you make me. I'm positively useless. I wouldn't even write—and then this whole sabbatical—it'd be a waste, wouldn't it? If it weren't for you I'd just lie around the house all day and drink—you see, you have a *moral* obligation to me. My life is in your hands!" She lies back on the pillows. "Besides, aren't you saving a bunch of money in rent?"

"I mean, some."

Lavinia sits straight back up. "How much did you pay? You know—in *that place*?"

Louise hesitates.

"Eight hundred."

"Is that *all*?"

"It was rent-stabilized." There were months eight hundred seemed impossible.

"So, that's perfect. Save eight hundred, spend two hundred— you've still got six hundred a month more than you did before, right?" She dangles the card. "And we'll both get so skinny—oh my God! We're going to be like—*sylphs*."

She cocks her head at Louise, like a dog.

"Come on—say yes, *please*."

Louise is so, so grateful.

Isn't she?

She takes her card. She takes the phone.

"Do it now—come on."

Louise does. Two hundred dollars a month.

"Thank you! Thank you! Thank you!" She kisses Louise on the forehead.

Then: "Come on!"

She holds out the phone.

"Photo," she says. "Wait—no." She puts on lipstick. She grabs another dressing gown. "Put this on."

They take a selfie lying on the Karabakh carpet in the living room.

Lavinia titles it en famille. Everybody Likes it.

Even Mimi Kaye.

"What are you going to wear tonight?"

Louise is very tired. She has a lesson with Paul and another with a boy called Miles and a third with a girl called Flora, all the way in Park Slope. She has at least three hours of work to do for GlaZam. She has a barista shift in the morning.

"What's tonight?"

"What do you mean, *what's tonight*?" Lavinia laughs. "God—what's *wrong* with you today?"

"I don't . . ."

"The premiere. *Roméo et Juliette*."

"Fuck. The opera."

Louise has completely forgotten.

"Christ—Lavinia—I'm so tired!"

"But don't you see—it's perfect! Now you don't have to worry about getting all the way home. We can just take a cab, after. On me." She says it so innocently, like Louise hasn't just spent two hundred dollars on ClassPass just to make her happy. "Come on—we should *celebrate*! We're roomies now—wasn't that the whole point?"

Her smile is frozen on.

"Of course," says Louise. "I'll be back after my shift."

"Right," says Lavinia. "There's just one little thing. The co-op board here, you know. They're really strict about copies."

"Copies of . . ."

"So Cordy has a set and I have a set, but that's it. Not even the maid has a set. So—I mean, you'll have to buzz up for me to let you in." She shrugs. "That's not a problem, right?"

"Of course not," says Louise.

She teaches her lesson with Paul. She teaches her lesson with Miles. She goes to Park Slope to teach Flora, and then comes all the way back.

She buzzes in.

"What took you so long?" Lavinia is in a long red silk dress that shimmers as she walks. She has pinned and gelled her hair into fingerwaves.

She has probably been getting ready since Louise left.

"Subway."

"Well, hurry . . ."

It's only four. Louise wants to get at least a couple hours of work in at GlaZam.

"I've just got some stuff I need to finish."

"Can't you do it tomorrow?"

There will be more work tomorrow.

"But it's a *gala* night," Lavinia says. "Listen—listen, I have the *perfect* dress for you. I want to dress you in white, okay? I have this one I got from this seller on Etsy I know in Paris. It's from the fifties—cost me an absolute fortune but it's so beautiful and I've worn it so much I'm just—I'm just completely sick of it. I've already laid it out for you."

It is taffeta and silk and enormous and princessy. It is not something Louise would ever wear.

"Are you sure?"

"You'll look gorgeous! And I'll do your hair, too—it'll take a while, but I think we should curl it, a little bit. Give it some body! God, I'm so excited! And Rose will be there tonight, too—she'll be taking photos for *Last Night at the Met*."

She has Louise strip. She zips up the dress. It just about fits.

"I'd never wear it again," she says.

"Why not?"

"Tragic memories." Louise can see Lavinia smile in the mirror. "I lost my virginity in this dress."

"Jesus!"

"It's dry-cleaned. Plus I took it off first. Obviously."

Lavinia sits Louise down in front of the vanity. Lavinia plugs in the curler.

"Stay still."

Lavinia yanks Louise's head to the left. She twists her chin up.

"How did you lose your virginity?"

Lavinia takes a chunk of Louise's fine, finely dyed hair, and wraps it around the iron. She burns her ear.

"I mean—the normal way?"

"Was it nice?"

"It was fine."

It was not fine. Louise had to beg for it.

Of course, she wasn't pretty then.

"Was it—what's his name? Victor?"

"Virgil."

Louise is so tired. Louise doesn't want to talk about it. But Lavinia is being so soft with her, now. She is stroking her hair idly.

"What an idiot," Lavinia says. "I mean—I'm assuming. He didn't know what he had with you. I can't imagine a man in the world deserving you—look at you." She tilts Louise's chin up. "You're beautiful."

Even now this makes Louise smile.

"He should have taken you to—to—what's the most romantic place in New Hampshire? The—the nature! He should have taken you to, like, a cabin with a great big roaring fire and animal skins."

As it happens, Louise did lose her virginity in nature. It was in the woods behind the Devonshire Academy tennis courts.

"I lost my virginity after the opera," Lavinia says. She says it so idly. "I was seventeen." She is staring, vaguely, into the mirror, which is the only way Louise can look at her. "Did you know that?"

"No."

"We'd been together about a year—it's a long time, now that I think about it. But we were both, you know. We were very sweet. He was very gentlemanly—I told you. He's old-fashioned. We got student rush tickets to the Met. It was the first time I ever went. We held hands the whole time—it was pathetic, the two of us, both of us, these scared little virgins, holding hands, but—it was *Carmen* and I was seventeen and there's that bit, at the end, when he kills her—and there's a bullfight and there's this great skinned bull on one side of the stage and he's got his hands around her throat on the other and—God, our hands were so sweaty. And it was so perfect. And I remember thinking—I remember exactly what I was thinking. *I want him to remember me.* If he hadn't been a virgin, too—I mean, I was such a little prude. I wouldn't want to be one of a litany."

She exhales slowly.

"Of course we couldn't go to my place and we couldn't go to his place because of our parents—my parents lived here, then; this is back before they fucked off and bought this place—and nobody would give us a hotel room because we were both underage and we went to the Carlyle and the Algonquin and all these places and we swore we had money but they didn't believe us. We had to go all the way to—God, it was so awful—to this horrible place near the Flatiron I found that had bulletproof glass at the check-in desk. We were both so embarrassed. But we closed the curtains and turned the lights down and lit a candle and put on Liszt's *Liebestraum* No. 3 and—well, it was the most beautiful night of my life.

"You know, he's the only man I've ever had sex with? It's stupid—I know. I just—if things can't be *that* perfect, you know, then I don't want them. I don't want an ordinary life. And—*fuck*!"

The fire alarm is blaring.

There's smoke coming from Louise's hair.

The thing is: Louise hadn't noticed, either.

She has been thinking of what it must be like, to go to the Carlyle, or the Algonquin. Or it wouldn't even matter if it were a by-the-hour place with bulletproof glass. Not if somebody loved you that much.

They tuck the singed strand of hair underneath.

"I think you're beautiful however you do your hair," Lavinia says. "But this is precisely why I need you. I'd set my house on fire, telling stories, without you.

"I need you," Lavinia says, and squeezes her hand, and then it all feels perfect.

Except when Mimi texts, while Lavinia is finishing her makeup.

omg did u move in w/ Lavinia?

(shocked-looking lipstick-wearing pig)

(yes, says Louise, today)

omfg that apartment is soooo nice
i loved living there.
(gingerbread man in a gingerbread house that gets smashed)
what are you two up to tonighhht?

"Hey, Lavinia?" They are in the cab.

"What?"

"Did Mimi used to live with you?"

"Of course not. Why?"

"It's nothing. She just sent me this weird message—"

"I let her crash for a couple weeks between places." Lavinia is re-applying her lipstick with her cell phone camera. "That's all."

She gets out of the cab.

She lets Louise pay.

Tonight the full moon is smiling on Lincoln Center.

They take so many photos.

Lavinia takes some of Louise, pirouetting on the fountain's edge.

Louise takes so many of Lavinia under the archways.

Lavinia posts them with the caption ah, je veux vivre!

They do a line of coke in the bathroom before the curtain.

Lavinia leaves a twenty in the bathroom attendant's tip jar.

They buy a glass and a glass and another glass of champagne, at fifteen dollars a glass, and Lavinia buys most of them but Louise also buys some, and because she is drunk she is not keeping track of how much money she is spending but she knows she has six hundred dollars a month that she did not have before, and that champagne tastes so good, and that they both look so beautiful tonight.

They really, really, do.

Even people they don't know tell them so. Old women and tourists stop them, to tell them so, and Lavinia smiles so magnanimously and says thank you, thank you.

———

On the stairway, Louise sees Athena Maidenhead. Her hair is piled neatly on her head. She's wearing pearls. She is in a long rose-colored dress and is on the arm of a man with no hair.

Also, Anna Wintour is there.

Lavinia takes Louise to the press room, which is half-hidden off the bathroom and which nobody but press (and Lavinia, who is not press but knows things) knows about.

Beowulf Marmont is there already. He is trying very hard to muscle into a conversation between two older men, making booming and staccato pronouncements about the significance of Wagner calling his operas *dramas*.

"That's the problem with Gounod," Beowulf says. "Their emotions are just so straightforward—it's all very expected, isn't it? It's emotive, but at the risk of complexity."

Gavin Mullaney punches Louise on the shoulder.

"I have to say," he says, "I'm impressed by you. And that's off-brand for me. So be proud." He turns to Beowulf. "Of course you know Louise Wilson. She writes for us now."

Beowulf looks appalled.

"Of course," says Beowulf. "What a pleasure."

He's still looking over her shoulder, of course (the two older men, who are married, work for *The New Yorker* and *The New York Times*, respectively), but this time he stays perfectly still.

"Wellhellothere!"

Somebody pushes in.

"You'reBeowulfMarmont."

Mimi thrusts out her hand.

She's wearing a sequined dress with a neckline that goes all the way down to her navel, and a hem that goes all the way up to her ass.

"I am," says Beowulf, who doesn't know who the fuck she is.

"You're Lavinia's friend."

"Sure."

"You write for *The Fiddler* and *The Egret* and you're doing your PhD at Columbia."

"Okay."

"*IreadwhatyouwroteaboutJoanDidionfor*TheEgret*Ithinkyou'retotally rightandshe'sabsolutelyresponsibleforthepervasivefeminizationofnarrative nonfictionwillyoupleasetellmemoreaboutit?*"

Then, and only then, does Beowulf Marmont smile.

He puts his hand on her back.

"Let's get you a drink," he says.

"Let's go," says Lavinia, grabbing Louise's hand. She doesn't even look at Mimi.

"What's her deal?" Louise tries again, as they make their way up the stairs toward their box seats.

Lavinia doesn't answer. She leans against the statue at the top of the stairs and scans the crowd.

"Who are you looking for?"

"Nobody," Lavinia says. "The only person in the world I care about seeing is you, and you're right here." She keeps her eye on the stairway.

"Let's take a selfie," Lavinia says. They do.

"God, I love opera," Lavinia says, as they shrug off their furs and take their seats, as Lavinia scans the horizon, once again. "It's so nice to close your eyes for three hours and really *feel* things.

"And—look!"

She has brought her flask, even though they are already so drunk.

"Take. Drink."

She raises the flask to Louise's lips and tilts it so Louise's mouth overflows and she chokes a little.

Lavinia laughs. "Don't worry," she says, so suddenly.

"What?"

"You're nothing like Mimi."

Louise hates how happy this makes her.

"You're smart. And you're strong. And you're not fucking *desperate*. You're like me. You get shit done."

She squeezes Louise's hand.

"I'm sorry I made you come tonight—I shouldn't have—I know how tired you were."

"Don't worry about it," Louise says.

"But you're glad you're here, now, right?"

"Yes," Louise says.

"You're not mad at me?"

"No."

"I'm so glad you moved in," Lavinia says. "I hate being alone!" She takes another swig from the flask. "We're going to be—you and me. *Contra mundum!*" She takes Louise's hand. She raises it, so slowly, to her lips. She kisses her knuckles. She pulls Louise's arm in. She kisses where it says MORE POETRY!!!

"We're going to have the most wonderful night," she whispers, as the curtain parts.

The music is baleful and wonderful and the sopranos are beautiful and Vittorio Grigolo is so handsome and so passionate and you really believe how much Romeo loves her. And Juliette sings *ah, je veux vivre* and the waltz is a trill and Louise's heart is beating fast. She thinks *yes, yes, I want to live, too* and then she thinks maybe it is not so bad that she has spent two hundred dollars today (maybe three hundred if you count the champagne, the cab) and maybe sometimes you can be a little late with your work for GlaZam and sometimes (if you are with Lavinia at the opera) you don't have to worry, so much, about the men who follow you home in Sunset Park, and maybe it isn't so bad that she doesn't have the key to Lavinia's apartment; maybe it isn't so bad that she doesn't sleep sometimes because she is reading Lavinia's novel over and over again; maybe it isn't so bad that she has no space in the house for her clothes; none of it is so bad, when Lavinia is with her.

Especially when Lavinia is holding her so close.

Especially when they smell like whiskey, and champagne, and they've done a couple of lines in the bathroom, and Louise can smell Lavinia's perfume which is like fig and pear and lavender and which smells so much nicer than her own.

Especially when the music is swelling.

Especially when Lavinia kisses her neck.

Louise freezes.

This is one of Lavinia's affectations, she thinks—just like kissing her hand, or her knuckles, or her tattoo, like falling asleep on her shoulder, like curling up next to her in the same bed. Lavinia is exuberant and she shows love too boldly. Lavinia has never had sex with anyone but Rex (*was it—any man; was that a hint?*). This is just a thing Lavinia does to let you know you matter to her.

Just kiss your neck. With tongue.

Just bite, a little bit.

Just put a hand on your knee.

Louise looks over at her, but Lavinia is smiling like nothing is different, like nothing is wrong or weird or strange about it, like there's definitely nothing, nothing gay about it, not Lavinia sliding her hand up Louise's thigh, not her squeezing the skin between her fingertips, not her leaning in, again, and kissing the back of Louise's ear.

And Louise is so confused, because in all the times they've been together and looked at one another's breasts and compared cup sizes or changed in the same room or peed in the same stall, has Lavinia ever stopped to stare at her (she has stopped to stare at Lavinia, but mostly to think *she is so perfect-looking* and *she is so thin* and Louise does not think there was anything sexual in that, exactly, but now she isn't sure), but Lavinia is kissing her so delicately and so expertly—that's the other thing; like she knows exactly what she's doing.

Here's the thing: Louise doesn't know if she wants to.

She knew she wanted to the time she begged Virgil Bryce to take her virginity, because even though she was fat then and she was not pretty he was dating her all the same and that must mean he wanted her on some level. He had so often said he loved her despite all her unlovable qualities (silence, ugliness, anxiety, unceasing need) that made her unlovable. But even then, she thinks, she wasn't sure if she wanted to fuck him, or just wanted him to want to fuck her.

So then. So now.

There isn't, exactly, a single moment when Louise goes from *is she . . . ?* to *she is.* Or it was always: *she is.* Lavinia's hand on her knee. Lavinia's hand up her thigh. Lavinia's fingers moving her underwear. Lavinia's fingers inside her.

It feels good. That's the other thing. There's sexual orientation but there's also biology and when somebody is lightly biting your neck and also fingering you under this rose-colored taffeta dress with so many petticoats (thank God, thank God, she wore this ridiculous thing with all the petticoats; *was that why Lavinia asked her to wear this dress with all the petticoats?*) that feels objectively good no matter who is doing it as long as they know what they're doing, and also a little strange (and also cold?).

And Louise thinks *how can she want this?*

And Louise thinks *I cannot say no.*

She's just spent half of her rent money; she has a free apartment on East Seventy-eighth Street; Lavinia paid for the cab; Lavinia paid for the tickets; Lavinia paid for most of the champagne (*so what? So what? Does it matter? It matters*) and she wonders *is that what Mimi didn't do* except she can't imagine Mimi *not* letting Lavinia finger her (she *can* imagine Mimi begging Lavinia to finger her).

But also, this means Lavinia thinks Louise is hot enough to fuck.

But also *of course we're not fucking,* not that Louise is sure what counts as fucking with girls. Maybe Lavinia is just drunk or maybe Lavinia has been in love with her the whole time (*I love you; you're beautiful; I need you*—how many times has Lavinia said those things?

Has Louise really been so stupid?). Louise can't say no and this makes her angry but also, also, she doesn't really want to.

And the music, the music, the music. And the velvet. And the lights. And the champagne.

Lavinia pulls back. Her eyes are shining.

"I told you," she whispers. "I told you—what an *epic night*."

And her fingers are still inside Louise and she's kissing Louise right on the mouth and she's using tongue which of all the unreal elements of what is happening to Louise right now is the one thing, the *one thing*, that makes Louise think *oh God oh God* and maybe this, this, is what it feels like to be wanted, and maybe this is what it feels like to be loved.

And Louise thinks: *maybe it is not so important, to be able to say no*.

"I love you," Lavinia keeps whispering, into her mouth. "I love you; I love you; I love you so fucking much."

Here's the stupid thing: Louise believes it.

For a whole minute (a whole aria; Mercutio thinks Queen Mab has been with everybody; maybe she has), Louise thinks that this is where it has all been leading (the night but also this whole year; this year but also her life); that every stupid thing she has ever been or said or done and every time she has ever fucked up has been in the service of being known, like this, and also loved.

Until she sees Rex.

He is in a box across the way.

He is with Hal.

He is watching them.

Louise yanks herself away so quickly she almost falls over.

"I have to pee."

She bolts.

———

You can lose weight. You can dye your hair. You can learn to speak with a very charming mid-Atlantic accent. You can stay up until four in the morning, missing your own deadlines, just to read somebody's novel and tell them how great it is.

But nothing, nothing you do will ever be enough.

Even if somebody loves you (or they think they do, or they say they do), it'll just be because you remind them of someone else, or because you make them feel a little less bad about having lost somebody else, or because somebody else is watching, across the auditorium, in an opera box, and they just want to make them jealous, and you were just an accessory to this.

I am almost thirty, Louise thinks, *how did I not know this by now?*

She runs out onto the balcony. It's so cold—she's shivering, even though it's April—but she'd rather be here, shivering, looking out over Lincoln Center and that moon-infused fountain and that empty, geometric square than be inside for another second anywhere, anywhere Lavinia's perfume still hangs in the air.

She can't even get her cigarette to light.

"Need some help?"

She rounds on him.

"Here," Rex says. "Let me."

She still can't talk.

She gets her shit together long enough to offer him one, too.

"I'd offer you a handkerchief," he says. "But I think you stole mine last time."

"Oh," she says. "Sorry."

"It's fine," he says. "You can keep it."

"Lavinia burned it."

She puffs on her cigarette. She doesn't look at him.

"Oh." He puffs on his. "Really?"

"Yep."

"Okay." He exhales. "I probably deserve it," he says.

Then: "I'm sorry."

"Why? You didn't do anything."

"I didn't know. At the bookstore—when we met. I didn't know the two of you were . . ."

"We're not." Another, furious, puff. "She's straight."

"Oh." Again: "Really?"

She shrugs.

"We both are." She doesn't care, anymore. "But, you know. I hear men really like it when straight girls hook up."

"So I hear." He swallows. "How have you been, Louise?"

She is being so rude to him. He is being so kind to her. She can't stop.

"We've been having so much fun." She flicks out some ash onto the railing. "All these parties—haven't you seen the photos?"

"Can't miss them."

"Of course you can't. That's the idea."

"What?"

"Nothing. I'm sorry."

Finally, finally, Louise breathes. "I'm sorry. I'm—I'm in a mood."

"What's wrong?"

She turns to him. "Why does she hate you so much?"

He leans out on the railing. He sighs. "It's not my place," he says, at last. "Look—she deserves to be happy. God knows—I don't want to fuck it up."

"Did you cheat on her or something?"

"No—no!"

"Hurt her?"

"No—I mean—not like that."

"What, then?"

"It's not my story to tell."

"It's hers, you mean?"

"Isn't it always?" He is smiling, just a little bit.

"I won't tell her you told me," she says. "If that's what you're worried about. I don't have to do everything she says."

"It's stupid," he says. "Even now. I feel responsible for her."

"Well, you're not. She's not your problem. She's mine. And I want to know."

"Look," he says, finally. "I loved her—I really did. For a long time. And I still care about her—a lot." He sighs. "Look—she's a *lot.*"

Too much, Louise thinks.

"When we were, you know—when we were growing up, it was just kind of, like, the two of us, you know? I mean, there was Hal, sometimes, but he was at school, and, I don't know—we found each other. And when you're with her—God! It's like a drug—you know that."

"Yes," Louise says. "I know."

"And you're, I don't know, breaking into places and you're writing each other secret letters and—I mean—it's the most wonderful thing in the world, but we were in *college,* and I wanted to do—you know, normal, college-kid things."

"Beer pong?"

"I mean, sure."

"A *frat!*"

"I mean, frats aren't really a Yale thing, but . . ."

"Football?"

He lets himself laugh.

"Yes. Exactly."

The wind has gotten chillier.

"We shouldn't have gone to the same school. I mean—I told her it was a bad idea—or, I don't know, maybe she talked me into it, you know. And the first year, whatever, even the second, we did it her way. Then—look, it's not a bad thing to want to grow up."

"Careful," says Louise. "You might regret it."

"I waited until Christmas break. We talked about it. And she seemed, I mean—she took it well. She didn't freak out or anything. She was calm. Then two days later she calls me at two in the morning and tells me she's in Central Park, that she's taken a bunch of pills and stolen a paddleboat and that she wants me to come find her."

"A boat? Really?"

"I'm just reporting," he says. "Look—maybe it sounds funny, now—but it wasn't. I mean—she was off her face and she'd taken a fistful of her mother's Xanax and a bottle of gin and she kept trying to tell me that I should do it, too."

"Did she mean it?"

He hesitates.

"Yes," he says, finally. "She meant it. She told me that—that I'd promised to love her forever and she didn't want to live in a world where people didn't keep their promises and I shouldn't want to, either. A world of—God, I don't know."

"Football."

"Football," he says, and they both smile because this is almost fair. "Anyway, that's when she took medical leave. And—there she will remain. Until her parents stop paying tuition. Or, you know, she goes back. Her *sabbatical*. And, until then, I'll just, you know, run into her everywhere I go." He sighs. "It's my own fault. I should have known she'd be here tonight. I wasn't even going to come—but Hal insisted. Mustn't waste *Henry Upchurch's season tickets*."

"God forbid."

There is a busker by the Lincoln Center fountain. Louise knows him. He plays every night, after the opera, and every night he plays something from the opera that people will recognize; that's how he gets his tips. He is practicing, now: *ah, je veux vivre dans ce rêve*.

"You know what's funny?" Rex says.

"What?"

"Sometimes I think she's right." He laughs. "Like—obviously, I don't *wish* I'd done it or anything. I'm not *crazy*."

"Of course not."

"I like my life. Only—" He takes a deep breath. "What can I say? She made a pretty fucking compelling case."

"She's a pretty fucking compelling person."

He laughs. "I mean—people *should* keep their promises. Probably. In a perfect world—we all would."

"It's not a perfect world," says Louise.

"Hers is," says Rex. "That's the problem."

"It isn't," Louise says, so softly he doesn't hear her. "Trust me."

Rex leans on the railing. "It's nice to talk to someone who gets it. Maybe that's selfish."

"You're not selfish," Louise says. Rex shrugs.

"You should tell her."

"What?"

"That I told you. I mean—I don't want to be the cause of any secrets." He sighs one last deep and expansive sigh. "I've done enough damage. I don't want to ruin her for you too."

You don't understand, Louise thinks, *it's too late, now.*

"Spoiler alert." Hal is behind them. "They both die."

"Jesus—Hal!"

"How long were you going to be out here? You missed the whole second half!"

Rex doesn't say anything.

"Philistines. You ran out on me, young Louise. I never got to give you your book!"

"I'm sorry," says Louise. "We left in a rush."

"Women." Hal rolls his eyes. "Educate yourself, sometime."

Everybody is spilling out into Lincoln Center: in their black tie, their silk dresses, their velvet trousers, their heels.

Mimi is falling over.

She's half-lurching, half-kissing Beowulf Marmont.

He hails a taxi. He hauls her in.

"Someone's getting raped tonight," says Hal.

"Jesus, Hal!"

"Christ, Rex, I'm not making a rape joke."

He puts his arms around both of them.

"I take rape very seriously," he says. "I'm a very, very good feminist."

Nobody says anything.

"Now, if I said he was taking her home to make love to her in a very gentle and assured and consensual manner," Hal says, "now *that* would be a rape joke."

Louise and Rex exchange looks.

"Besides, all men are rapists. Just read *Rolling Stone.*" Hal straightens his dinner jacket. "Poor Michelle. Lol."

"Michelle?"

It has never occurred to Louise that Mimi has a real name.

"She was fun," Hal says. "I miss her putting on a show at parties. Remember New Year's 2014, Rex? Wasn't that great? We walked in on Lavinia and Mimi making out in the bathtub at the MacIntyre, didn't we, Rex?"

"Stop it, Hal!"

"What was the theme, Rex? Do you remember? Was it *The Great Gatsby*? It's always *The* fucking *Great Gatsby*. But it was a good party—not like this year, don't you think so, Rex—they're getting worse and worse."

And Louise thinks *this, too, was for them; this, this, too.*

"I have to go."

Rex pushes past them both.

"Oops," says Hal. He looks at his watch.

"By the way, young Louise," he says. "Lavinia's looking for you. And she's not happy."

"Shit."

"I told her you were hanging out with Rex."

"Shit—*shit!*"

The square is full. The party's over. The busker's playing *ah, je veux vivre* at full forte.

There are so many people in sequins and not a single one of them is Lavinia.

"Chop chop, Cinderella," says Hal.

Louise runs.

Between waves of champagne and whiskey and the coke comedown Louise thinks all the thoughts she always thinks, except this time they're louder and clearer and more true.

This, *this* is how she's fucked it up; Lavinia hates her, now—Lavinia will be so angry—and now she has no money for rent and she doesn't have the keys and her subletter has moved in, already, because an empty rent-stabilized place doesn't even linger five minutes in this city, and Louise thinks *oh God oh God* and she thinks *just let her not be mad* and she thinks *I will even let her fuck me, just please God don't let her be mad.*

She doesn't even have the fucking keys.

Lavinia isn't anywhere. She's not on the landing and she's not on the Grand Tier and she's not on the balcony or in the box or anywhere in the orchestra, and Louise tries to call four or five times but Lavinia has turned off her phone, but somehow that just makes Louise try to call more times, even though it goes straight to voicemail, because if there is a definition of insanity it's trying the same thing over and over, expecting a different result.

And Louise tries so hard not to panic or to cry or to scream and she tries to focus on the next steps she can take: she can go back to the apartment and wait by the buzzer (what if Lavinia never comes home? What if Lavinia is already home and won't let her in? What if the neighbors who come in and out see her and think she is loitering like a criminal and call the police?).

She could call a friend (she has no friends). She could get on Tinder and hook up with someone, but then she would have to explain to her supervisor on her shift at the bar (oh God, her shift) why she has shown up to bartend brunch in a taffeta dress that makes her look like Shirley Temple, because everything she owns (her clothes, her clean underwear, her laptop which she needs for her GlaZam job; fuck, *fuck*, her GlaZam job) is all with Lavinia, who now is furious with her.

Then she sees her.

Lavinia is passed out on the side of the fountain.

"Christ, Lavinia—"

Louise runs so fast she loses a shoe and has to carry it, limping, across the square.

"Jesus Christ!"

Her eyes are open.

She reaches down to help her.

Lavinia grabs her so violently she drags her down, instead.

"Where were you?"

It's a snarl.

"I'm sorry."

"Where. The Fuck. Were you?"

"I'm sorry—I had to pee."

"You left me *alone*."

"I know. I'm sorry."

"I needed you."

"I'm sorry."

"I do everything for you—fucking *everything*. And you left me alone!"

She's sobbing so hard she chokes.

"Were you with *him*?"

"No! I mean—I had a cigarette—I gave him a—"

"Did you fuck him?"

"No! Of course not."

"You fucked him! You fucked him and you laughed about it, the two of you, you laughed behind my back!"

"I would *never*!"

And even as she's saying it she thinks *almost, almost*. Even as she's saying it she thinks *maybe*.

"You're so fucking ungrateful!"

Lavinia sits straight up.

"After everything, what more do you want from me?"

"You're tired." Louise is so calm. "You're drunk. You're tired. That's all. You want to go home."

"I let you live in my house."

"Please!"

"Give you—give you a fucking *gorgeous* dress to wear, buy you booze, give you—give you a fucking *free room* and you can't even sit through a whole fucking opera with me?"

"It's not like that."

She does not know if Lavinia has forgotten fucking her, or only wants to forget, pretend it didn't happen.

"What more do you want from me?"

"Lavinia, I—"

"What—you want *cash*, too?"

Lavinia throws her purse.

It hits Louise square in the chest.

She doesn't even think to catch it.

She lets it fall, clattering, to the ground.

Wordlessly, Louise kneels and picks it up.

Lavinia is sobbing; she tucks her knees under her and bites her own palm, just to stop from screaming.

Louise just watches her.

Louise can't get upset. Louise can't get angry.

Louise doesn't have the keys.

"It's okay," Louise says. "You're fine. You're fine. You're okay. I'm here. It's okay."

Here's the thing: she's lying.

You'd never know it. Louise is so good, wrapping Lavinia's coat around Lavinia's shoulders, smoothing Lavinia's hair out of the way of Lavinia's collar, whispering Lavinia's name. She is efficient, in the way that she holds Lavinia's hair back, when Lavinia throws up, when Lavinia wipes her mouth on the beautiful, unsullied taffeta. It is like Lavinia never fingered her in an opera box to make Rex jealous. It is like Lavinia never called her a whore.

The busker has started playing "New York, New York" on his violin.

Lavinia tries to sing along, but she's too drunk, and her voice cracks, and all she can manage is *I want to be apart.*

I want to be apart.

"We should tip him," murmurs Lavinia. She lies back down on the ground. "Do you have any money?"

"No," says Louise. She's lying now, too.

"We should give him some money! He's so good!"

"We should get you home."

"No!" She drops her purse again. She picks up the credit card and drops this, too.

"You can't stand."

"Please, Lou—*please*. Get some cash out, okay?" She's smiling so helplessly now. "My PIN number is 1-6-1-9. Just—give him a hundred, okay?"

Louise starts to say *we have to get you home,* but then Lavinia starts screaming and Louise realizes she doesn't have a choice now, either.

So she gives the busker a look, a significant, pleading, humiliated look that she hopes to God conveys *I'm getting you your hundred dollars, okay? So just make sure she doesn't choke on her own vomit until I get back,* and then she goes to the Duane Reade across the street.

It's not that she means to hit the *balance* button. But it's not that she doesn't mean to, either.

Lavinia has 103,462 dollars and forty-six cents.

Lavinia lives in an apartment her parents own, and she has 103,462 dollars and forty-six cents.

Lavinia lives in an apartment her parents own, and has 103,462 dollars and forty-six cents, and fingered Louise in an opera box just because she could.

Also, she made Louise pay for the cab.

Louise takes two hundred dollars out of Lavinia's account.

Lavinia has jumped into the fountain. She's standing with her arms outstretched, with her hair dripping and the violinist watching her and still playing "New York, New York" on his violin, over and over. Louise puts six twenties into his case.

The final twenty is from her.

"Look at me!" Lavinia cries. "I'm Anita Ekberg."

"Of course you are," says Louise.

"Take a video of me." Lavinia makes such a big splash. "But make it black-and-white."

Louise does.

"I'm the worst," Lavinia murmurs, when at last Louise gets her into bed. She held back her hair for an hour or two or three while Lavinia sweated out all the coke and Louise apologized, not for the first or last time, to Mrs. Winters who lives next door, who is a friend of Lavinia's parents and has had it up to here with the loud music and the banging at all hours and has half a mind to write the Williamses herself and tell them to come home and take care of the problem. "I'm the worst; I'm the worst; I'm sorry."

"Don't worry about it."

"I shouldn't have—I know, I *know* you really like me."

"Good," says Louise.

"And I'm sorry we—you know."

"It's fine. It happens."

"It didn't mean anything, you know. It was just—you know, the opera."

"Of course."

"Like—I'm *straight*."

"I know."

"I'm sorry. I'm sorry. I'm too much. I know—I know I'm too much."

"You're not too much."

"I *am*."

"You're not."

"Don't leave me, Lulu," Lavinia says. "Please—*please*."

"I won't leave you."

"I love you, Lulu."

"I love you too, Lavinia."

Here's the most painful part: she still does.

Louise waits until Lavinia falls asleep. She extricates herself so gingerly, so that she won't wake Lavinia, and then goes into the other room, the one that is nominally hers, with Lavinia's closet overflowing with Lavinia's dresses and Lavinia's jewelry and makeup overflowing all over Lavinia's vanity, in this apartment where she isn't on a lease, where she doesn't even have a key.

She goes to the dining-room table.

She opens up her purse.

She counts them: the four crisp, inalienable twenty-dollar bills.

Not even half a ClassPass membership.

She opens up her laptop. The light is so bright it hurts and she has to close her eyes, just for a second, which only reminds her how tired she is.

She has two more hours of work to do for GlaZam tonight. She has a shift tomorrow at noon. She has a lesson with Paul right after.

Louise goes to Lavinia's drinks cabinet, which is so full of good booze. Louise never noticed how good it was, before, but she notices it now—the Talisker and the Laphroaig and Hendrick's and Rémy Martin and she fingers the labels on all of them and thinks *this, this is where you live now.*

She pours herself a glass of whiskey.

She gets to work.

4

"QUEEN MAB HATH BEEN WITH ME."

That's all Lavinia ever says about that night.

She says it once, in the morning, clicking through all the photos Louise has taken of her. She changes her profile picture to the one that made *Last Night at the Met*. She sits at the dining-room table with her feet up on either side of the stale croissant she's photographing atop turquoise china she had shipped all the way from Uzbekistan.

"You know, Lulu?"

Louise clears the table. Louise pours the tea. Louise sets down the eggs that she has made.

"Yes, Lavinia?"

"I think I saw the fairies last night."

Lavinia leaves it there.

So Louise does, too.

"It's a good video," Lavinia says, of the one in the fountain. "I'm going to send it to Cordy—just to annoy her. She's always telling me I go out too much."

Louise gets dressed in silence.

"Where the hell are you going?"

"Work."

"*Work?*" Lavinia gives a little laugh. "Jesus, how are you *up*?"

"It's eleven."

"Exactly! Just call in sick!"

"I can't."

"You shouldn't go out. You look like hell." She stretches out on the table. "Come on—let's pull a sickie. It'll be great—we can watch every single episode of *Brideshead Revisited*—we'll do tea and scones and—like, I think I have a teddy bear somewhere we can carry around."

"I'm sorry."

"I don't want to do it alone."

"I'm sorry," Louise says. "It's work. I can't miss it."

"Of course," Lavinia says. "Of course—you're right. I'm being self-ish. I'm selfish. You're right. Don't let me stop you."

Louise buttons up her top button. She pins up her hair.

"Hey, Lulu?"

"Yes?"

"Can you pick up dinner on the way home? I don't want to cook. Just, you know, whatever they have at Agata's. Like—a roast chicken, maybe? And, like, a few—fuck it, I'll text you a list. I'll pay you back."

Lavinia's grocery list at Agata & Valentina comes to $61.80.

Louise pays for it with the money she has taken out of Lavinia's bank account. Lavinia doesn't pay her back.

Louise does such a good job, being Lavinia's best friend.

She sews Lavinia's dresses. She mends their hems because Lavinia is always tearing them. She cleans the house. She buys the groceries. She does the laundry. She irons. She sweeps crumbs off the steamer trunk.

She apologizes to Mrs. Winters, again, when she sees her in the hall.

She is very careful to emphasize—Lavinia has made this explicit—that of course she doesn't *live* there (the co-op board, Lavinia says and says and says again, is very strict). She's visiting.

She reads Lavinia's novel (it is always the same novel; there are only twenty thousand words of it and Lavinia never writes any more) over and over, and tells her every time how great it is, and when Lavinia starts to cry and say that she is *too much* and the book is trite and that nobody could ever like a trite book written by such a terrible person as her Louise says *no, you're beautiful* and holds her hand.

They don't do their cowriting sessions anymore. Lavinia has stopped asking for them.

It's just as well. Louise doesn't really have the time.

Louise saves three thousand dollars a month, being Lavinia's best friend.

She works it out, one time, on the back of a napkin.

Lavinia buys Louise at least two drinks a night (*$20 each, including tax, including tip*) (*$40 x 30 = $1,200 a month: entertainment*).

Louise saves eight hundred dollars a month (*nine with utilities*) (*more if you take into account location, location, location, but Louise is being conservative, here*).

(*$900 a month, rent*)

Lavinia also gets all their Ubers (*$900 a month, transport*).

That's before you count the clothes, which are castoffs so don't cost money, exactly, but are still more beautiful than anything Louise has ever worn before, even if Lavinia slams a car door on her hem, even if Lavinia spills something on it, even if Lavinia insists they break into Central Park after a black-tie function and so the skirt becomes covered in grass stains and Louise can never wear it again. That's before you count the Seamless meals (Lavinia doesn't really cook, so most of the groceries she has Louise buy she throws out). That's before you count the enormous oil portrait of a naked courtesan Lavinia buys at the Flatiron flea market one day, and puts above Louise's bed as a gift without asking her.

That's before you count the Adderall.

Of course, there's also the question of expenditures.

There's ClassPass. Lavinia is always too hungover to work out, and usually Louise is too tired, but she insists they enroll for another month, anyway, and this time, she says, it's Louise's responsibility to make her do it.

Also, the time Lavinia sent her in the middle of the rain-soaked night to a sketchy street corner in East Harlem to buy some shrooms that weren't even hallucinogenic, anyway. Also the cash tips for the bathroom attendants at the Met, at Trattoria dell'Arte, at Shun Lee, at all the places that Lavinia and Louise either surreptitiously snort coke or throw up.

Also the shifts that Louise misses, because sometimes not even the Adderall works, when Lavinia swoops in last-minute and says she has tickets for an aerialist performance that Athena Maidenhead's friends are doing at this multipurpose space full of mirrors called House of Yes. The GlaZam work, because that's so easy to say *I'll do later*, and then the shifts she's too sick for, sometimes, and then sometimes she even misses a lesson with Paul, even though he's just a couple of blocks away.

So the second time Louise takes money from Lavinia's bank account, when Lavinia is passed-out drunk on the sofa (because she's been sobbing because they saw Rex and Hal, again, at the Mr. Morgan Spring Gala at the Morgan Library and neither of them looked at her but Rex raised his glass to Louise and smiled, and she is so angry that he has done this, and yet so glad), Louise doesn't even think of it as stealing. She's just balancing the books. Just a hundred here, a hundred there. Then another fifty. Then another hundred.

Somehow, she's still always broke.

Here's the other, funny, horrible thing: Louise has never looked better. She loses six and a half pounds. Mostly this is the Adderall, and the coke, although she and Lavinia actually make it to FlyBarre exactly twice before Lavinia loses interest and declares working out a Calvinist abomination. Lavinia does her makeup. She gets her hair done by professionals. This is at Lavinia's insistence.

Lavinia knocks on her door, one night. Louise doesn't answer, at first, because by now she's learned that the only way to avoid dealing with Lavinia is to pretend to be asleep, but Lavinia knocks again.

"You've dyed the bathroom grout," she says.

She sits on the bed.

"I *what?*"

"The tub. It's yellow."

Louise has been so careful. She has spent hours scrubbing.

"I'm sorry," she says. She turns over like she's falling back asleep.

"And the bathroom smells like bleach."

"I'm sorry," Louise says again.

"Look—I don't care," says Lavinia. "You could dye the house purple, for all I care. But my parents—you know—I'm not *really* supposed to have guests. And they're very particular about making sure the place is, you know. In case they decide to retire back here. Or sell it. And, you know, it's not ordinary grout." She tightens her stained dressing gown around her shoulders. "It's Italian or something. I don't know. You're not even really supposed to get it wet."

She lies down next to Louise in the bed.

"You know what? I think you should go to Licari. That's where I go."

Louise is very, very good at sussing out people's natural hair color. It's one of the things she used to do on the train. It has never occurred to her that Lavinia's hair is anything but perfectly natural.

"I've already made an appointment for us both," Lavinia says. "Besides, I get a discount for bringing in a new client."

She curls up against Louise. She leans her cheek against Louise's back.

"I wish my hair were straight like yours," she says. "It's so shiny. God, I hate you."

Lavinia falls asleep next to her in the bed, with her arm flung over Louise's breast.

The color costs four hundred dollars.

She takes half of it out of the ATM the next day.

———

Other people *notice* how much better Louise looks. Her mother, of course, who for the first time in five years doesn't bring up Virgil Bryce, but instead makes a comment about how all those nice young available men in their early thirties in New York must be lining up around the block. Paul actually checks her out during their sessions, which would feel violating if he didn't start to stammer and blush and look so astoundingly ashamed of it that Louise almost pities him. Beowulf Marmont Facebook messages her at three in the morning to tell her he really liked her piece for *The Fiddler* and maybe they could have a coffee to talk about it sometime.

Also: that guy who ghosted her.

In May, he sends her a Facebook message.

Looks like you've been having fun!

Winking face.

Maybe we should take another stroll through Prospect Park,

sometime.

I feel so bad we never got to do that again.

He doesn't even apologize. He doesn't have to.

Sure, Louise says.

Blushing face.

She carries this knowledge all day in her heart. She scrubs Lavinia's countertops and she beats Lavinia's carpet and she sews Lavinia's fur collar onto Lavinia's vintage opera cape and she spends the whole day smiling.

She doesn't tell Lavinia.

Not until Lavinia has them go, one morning, to the King Cole Bar, at the St. Regis, which might be the most expensive bar in New York. But they're famous because of their murals, and also because they apparently invented the Bloody Mary, and they charge like twenty-five dollars for them (before tax, before tip). Even though Louise doesn't like Bloody Marys, Lavinia does, so there they are, hogging a table.

"You know what, Lulu?" Lavinia says. "I've just had the most incredible idea." They've had two drinks each. Louise feels sick.

"What?"

"Tomorrow," Lavinia says, "we're going to go on a *pèlerinage*."

"A what?"

"A pilgrimage. It's French."

"No, I know—" Louise hasn't slept in three days. "But—"

"To the *sea*, silly! Let's get up really early tomorrow morning and watch the sun rise from the Cloisters and then walk all the way to Coney Island."

"Why?"

"To prove our mettle! To prove we can! Like—like the medieval pilgrims, you know—have you ever listened to Liszt's *Années de pèlerinage*? We can recite 'Ulysses' again, can't we?!" She points at the tattoo. "MORE POETRY!!!" She says it just like that.

Tomorrow Louise and the guy who ghosted her are going to Prospect Park to take a walk. She has suggested an afternoon date, especially, for a Sunday afternoon, because she knows Lavinia never gets out of bed before dusk on a Sunday afternoon.

"I'm sorry," Louise says. "I have work."

"What work?"

"I have a shift."

"Why don't I come by, then? I'll come by the bar—I'll sit and be very quiet, just like a mouse, and then when you're done . . ."

"No," Louise says—too quickly. "Not a shift. A lesson. Um—Flora, in Park Slope."

"I thought you have Flora on Tuesdays and Thursdays."

"It's a makeup session. She's—she's going on holiday next week."

"Where?" Lavinia signals the waiter. She orders a bottle of Chablis without asking Louise.

"I don't know—why?"

"She didn't say? I mean"—Lavinia laughs—"It's the middle of

the school year. Believe me—Cordy won't shut up about her mid-terms; she's been blowing up my phone . . . who'd let a student go on *holiday*?" She shrugs. "Well it's fine. I can meet you in Park Slope."

"Actually," Louise tries again—she tries so hard. "I have plans."

"It's not a *full* walk, but it's still a few miles from Prospect Park to the sea. We can go through Midwood—look at all the Hasidic men with their, you know, hair-things."

"I have *plans*," Louise says again.

"With who?"

"I have a date."

"A *date*?" Lavinia's laugh is sharp. "With who?"

"This—this guy I used to go out with. Nobody important."

"Why didn't you just say?"

"You're right," Louise says. "I'm sorry. I should have. I was embarrassed."

"*Why*? It's *wonderful*." Lavinia pours herself a glass.

"I know I should have checked with you, I'm sorry."

"Checked with me? Don't be ridiculous, Lulu—you're not my *prisoner*! You can go anywhere you want to!" She downs her glass. "It's probably good for us to, you know, have a little time apart. I mean, I know I can be a bit much sometimes."

"It isn't that!" Louise starts, and then stops, and then tries again. "I mean, it's just a date. That's all."

"Wait," Lavinia looks up. Her eyes are shining. "This is The Ghost, isn't it?"

"No," says Louise, automatically, before saying "Yes."

"What does he want?"

"No—we just started, you know, talking again."

"Did he explain why he ghosted?"

"I'm sure he will," Louise tries. "In person. We'll talk about it tomorrow."

"You're very forgiving, Louise," says Lavinia. "If somebody did that to me—I'd never speak to them again." She pours Louise a glass.

"You really shouldn't let people treat you like that." She smiles a sad and sympathetic smile. "He probably just wants sex."

"We're going to the *park!*"

"Where?"

"Brooklyn."

"He's making you come all the way to him?"

"I mean—we just wanted to go to Prospect Park, that's all."

"I'm just saying, be careful. Men like that, you know. They like to see how far you'll jump. Don't be surprised if he just wants to sleep with you. Only—"

"What?"

"You'll probably have to go through with it."

"*What?*"

"I mean—don't come back, like, late or anything. I want an early night's sleep. I don't want to wake up to buzz you in. So, you know, if you're coming all the way from Brooklyn, you might as well spend the night." Lavinia is editing a photo on her phone.

She doesn't look up when the bill comes.

$220. Four Bloody Marys. A bottle of wine Louise has barely touched.

Lavinia keeps playing on her phone.

And Louise thinks *say something, say something, say something.*

Louise doesn't say anything. She puts down her credit card. She signs.

"I think you should sleep with him," says Lavinia. She's still looking at her phone. "You really need to get laid."

Louise doesn't: not really.

She used to (all the time: she used to). Virgil (when Virgil would), and then when she finally (for once, for once) changed her number she'd have so many one-night stands and she fucked the male feminist, the night they met, in a bar bathroom in Crown Heights. She used to crave it (the touch; mostly the touch, but also the laughing and the biting and the *God, you're beautifuls*).

Louise hasn't had sex in four years.

Not unless you count what happened at the opera, but it's hard to put a label on what happens between two straight girls when they're drunk and neither of them comes.

Sex, Louise thinks, is probably a waste of time, anyway.

Louise tells Lavinia her date bailed.

"Men." Lavinia shrugs. "I told you. Fuck them all."

Louise skips her work for GlaZam. *I am a little bit Concerned that you R Not taking this Project seriously?* writes the woman in Wisconsin who runs the business. *We need to Step things up OK??*

"You're just too good for everybody," Lavinia says. "There's nobody in the world who deserves you."

That evening, Louise takes three hundred dollars out of Lavinia's bank account at the bodega on the corner of Seventy-sixth and Lex, while she's supposed to be at Agata & Valentina at Seventy-ninth and First, buying expensive cheeses Lavinia will never eat.

She takes a walk.

It is late, she knows, and she should be getting sleep (she has so much to catch up on; she has so much left to do), but she is afraid if she goes back to the house she will wake up Lavinia. If Lavinia wakes up she'll want to talk to her, or do her hair, or take photos, and Louise can't deal with that again, not right now.

She goes to the park (everything is in bloom; everything is pink), not Prospect Park but Carl Schurz, which is that little sliver of green by Gracie Mansion where you can see the East River and also there's a statue of Peter Pan. Because everything is in bloom and in pink everybody is out, at sunset, and the people who love each other are holding hands, and leaning in. Every single person in New York City except Louise is out there kissing and being in love. And Lavinia is asleep or watching *Fortunes of War* in bed for the umpteenth time and all of a sudden Louise feels so lonely, so goddamn lonely, even though she shouldn't, even though to be lonely is ungrateful, because Lavinia has given her so much (*the room, the booze, the drugs, the parties, oh God the parties*). And to steal money (*it's not stealing; it's insurance; it's reparations; she's still flat broke anyway*) is ungrateful. Maybe that's just who she is, maybe, just the most ungrateful person in the world, that she could have all this and still wish she were in Prospect Park, holding hands with some guy who didn't care enough about her to break up with her by text.

Louise isn't angry. She can't get angry.

She Facebook messages Rex.

Nice to see you at the Morgan Gala.

Nothing loaded. Nothing treacherous. Just pleasantries.

Haha, you too.

I hope I didn't cause any problems?

To which Louise responds: No more than usual.

Good.

How are you doing?

You holding up okay?

To which Louise responds: The usual.

Is that a yes or a no?

I'm not sure, she says. It's been a long day.

I saw.

Of course he saw. All the photos Louise posts are for him.

You two looked like you had fun. Very glamorous.

They were in vintage bathing suits. They had perfect flapper makeup on.

It's the makeup, Louise says.

I don't believe that.

I swear.

Prove it, says Rex.

How?

Take the ugliest photo of yourself you can manage.

She does.

She is afraid, but she scrunches up her face and sticks out her tongue and bugs out her eyes and takes a selfie.

Hm, Rex says.

The little box that shows he's typing stops, and starts, and stops again.

It's not the makeup, he says.

Then: I'm sorry.

Am I allowed to say that?

You're allowed to do whatever you want, says Louise. Makes one of us.

Laughing face.

It is dark by the time Louise comes home.

She puts the groceries down on the table.

"What took you so long?"

Lavinia is sitting in the dark, staring into space.

"Nothing," Louise says.

Then: "I picked up some flowers for you."

Lavinia looks so happy.

"I went all the way to Jerome—I thought you'd like them."

"They're beautiful," Lavinia says. She puts her arms around Louise.

Louise has gotten so, so good at this.

It's easy, so long as Louise thinks of it as a game.

She takes a couple hundred dollars out, every couple of days.

She takes ten milligrams of Adderall a day.

She takes so many photos.

She sleeps in Lavinia's bed.

She stops sleeping.

She keeps it together.

In June, Louise gets fired.

It is not from GlaZam, although her work has suffered. It's not from the bar, although she's always late there, too, and out of it.

It's Paul.

She arrives to do one of their thrice-weekly sessions, which at eighty dollars an hour and three hours a session and three sessions a week (Paul really wants to go to Dartmouth) is her best-paying gig by far. She is late, but not by much. She and Paul go over the difference between *assent* and *assuage*. Nothing is wrong.

Then Paul looks up.

"So," he says. "It turns out I don't need you anymore."

He's been quietly assured by somebody at Dartmouth that he will be able to go as a squash recruit.

"I mean, I've probably gotten everything I'm going to get out of these sessions, anyway."

He gives her an extra fifty.

He's on his phone before Louise even leaves the room.

Louise is fine. Louise can work with this.

Louise just has to take out a little more money from Lavinia's account (Lavinia won't miss it, anyway). Louise just has to make sure she doesn't lose any of her other jobs.

She just has to be out of the house at the same time, every day, so that Lavinia won't know (nine hours a week, there are only nine hours a week where she can be out of the house and Lavinia knows not to ask after her).

She can take walks.

She can get work done at cafés.

She can see Rex.

Not that Louise sees Rex regularly, or anything like that.

It's just that they had one text message conversation, then another, and he asked her about the stories she was writing and told her he thought the one about those runaways from Devonshire Academy was pretty moving, and she asked him how the second year of grad school was going and he told her it was a lot of work, especially Classics where there's a lot of language classes, but that it was rewarding to do something you really loved. Louise said sure, and said something about wanting to go to the Met to see the Greek and Roman sculptures and he said it's a shame, I'd love to go with you some-time, I haven't been for ages and she said haha that would cause WWIII and he said haha and she said I'm going Wednesday at like four wouldn't it be funny if we ran into each other haha and he said well that would be a coincidence and then they do.

"It's nice," he says, as they walk from hall to hall, and from statue to statue. "I always feel peaceful in museums."

Louise has three whole hours to feel peaceful.

"I used to come here all the time as a kid." Collegiate was just across the park. "Whenever, like, I needed to get away."

"Not exactly the Devonshire Mall," she says.

"Was it weird?" he asks her.

"What?"

"Growing up in a campus town."

It strikes Louise, suddenly, that Lavinia has never asked her any-thing like this.

She shrugs. "I guess it's a bit like growing up next to a museum," she says. "It's nice to have it there—but, you know, it's not, like, *real.*"

She tells him the story about the time she was sixteen, and spent a whole week in the dining hall before anybody noticed, and when he hesitates she's afraid she sounds crazy, but then he laughs.

"Did you go to any classes?"

"No!"

"Why not? You should have!"

"They'd have noticed."

He shrugs. "I don't know," he says. "People are pretty oblivious."

They stare awhile at an armless Aphrodite.

"It's a good story," says Rex. "Even so."

"No it's not," says Louise. "If it were a *really* good story, I'd have gone for the whole year."

Rex sighs. "I think being in a really good story is overrated," he says.

They both focus very hard on Aphrodite.

"I just want a quiet life," Rex says.

They say goodbye on Eighty-sixth and Lex, because Rex is taking the subway home to the East Village, and they stand for a little too long by the station stairs.

"I had fun," says Rex, and Louise says *yes, so did I.*

"I hope—you know." He takes a breath. "Is she *okay?*"

She doesn't know why it stings that he cares.

"She's fine," Louise says.

"Don't let me—"

"Of course not," Louise says.

They shake hands awkwardly and then he vanishes underground.

"Lulu!"

Louise's head snaps up.

"Lulu!"

Lavinia is across the crosswalk.

It's the only time Louise has seen Lavinia out of the house on her own.

For a second Louise thinks *she has seen everything;* her gut plummets. She did not know it was possible to be so afraid. She can taste her own heartbeat.

"I thought you were teaching!"

Lavinia's arms are laden with shopping bags.

"Christ, I was so *bored,* all afternoon!"

She is smiling, Louise thinks. *Thank God, thank God, she is smiling. She doesn't know.*

"Why aren't you at your lesson?"

"It ended early."

And Louise thinks *how close will you come to fucking it all up.*

"I've got a present for you," Lavinia says. "I was so bored I went to Michael's—it would look *perfect* on you."

She hands it to Louise in the middle of the street.

It's the most beautiful dress Louise has ever seen.

It's bias-cut. It has a halter. It has sequins all the way to the hem.

"I told Mimi, *this dress would look perfect on Lulu*. I just had to buy it for you! Don't you love it?"

"You went with *Mimi?*"

Lavinia shrugs. "You were out! And she was available. Come on, Lulu, don't be mad."

"I thought you hated her."

"Anyway—let's go home and change. I want you to wear this tonight."

"Tonight?"

"It's *The Fiddler*'s spring fling—didn't I tell you?"

Lavinia is already half a block ahead of her.

"You might want to take an Adderall now," Lavinia calls out. "It's going to be a late one. Ugh—it's going to be a shit-show. Beowulf Marmont has an interview with Henry Upchurch in the next print issue and he's telling everyone who will listen he's going to be one of their Five Under Thirty. God, I fucking hate these people."

They go to the party.

They do lines with Gavin Mullaney's quasi-feminist girlfriend. They do shots with Gavin, who tells Louise she should pitch another story to them, maybe for print this time, and Louise says *yes, of course, when I have time.*

They dance until dawn, because Lavinia has the keys, even though Louise is in heels.

The next morning, Louise sleeps through her shift at the bar, and then she's fired from there, too.

"Just as well," Lavinia says, when Louise tells her. She is painting her nails and doesn't even look up. "That job was beneath you. You're supposed to be a Great Writer. Besides, it's not like you have rent to worry about."

Louise stops texting Rex after that.

She figures it's probably for the best.

He just wanted information about Lavinia, anyway.

Louise is fine. She is still fine. Everything is fine.

Louise is so fucking good at keeping it together.

Even without half her SAT income. Even without the bar shifts. Even without Rex.

She just has to take out a little more money, that's all, just a little more often.

It's not like she has to pay rent.

It's not like she'll ever need a deposit for a new place.

I can do this, Louise tells herself. *I can do this.*

Until the night Louise comes home from teaching Flora in Park Slope, and nobody lets her in.

She stands for a while in front of the door—idly, stupidly—like maybe Lavinia's just in the shower.

Nobody answers Lavinia's phone.

Louise stands like that for almost an hour, even though it's raining, because her bag is heavy with SAT prep books and her laptop and her charger and she has no idea what else to do, and it's only when she sees Mrs. Winters coming down the stairs through the glass in the door that she bolts, because—of course—she does not live there.

I can do this, she tells herself.

So Louise goes to the Carlyle.

She walks so slowly. She walks with her head high. She walks in like she belongs; maybe she does.

Her dress—it is Lavinia's dress—is beautiful. Her hair is impeccable. She has Lavinia's cash in her wallet.

She sits at the bar. She keeps her hands in her lap.

She orders a drink—just like Lavinia would—without betraying the slightest sense that her world is falling apart.

She sips her champagne very, very slowly.

"Thank *Gawd, hunny.*"

It is Athena Maidenhead.

It is the first time Louise has seen Athena here alone.

"I got stood up—*can you believe it?*"

She always talks with an exaggerated New York accent, like she's chewing gum.

"That's the last time I *evah* make a date on OKStupid—that's what I call it, yannow? *Okaystupid.* Get it?" She laughs a mannish, throaty laugh and smacks Louise on the arm.

Louise smiles, like Lavinia isn't missing, like her world isn't about to end.

"From now on," Athena says. "I'm sticking with What'sYourPrice."

She orders herself a glass of champagne, too.

"You looked cute the other day. At the opera. *Whaddya* see?"

"*Roméo et Juliette.*"

"The opera. *Gawd,* I would die!"

She leans in real, real close. "I would *love* to go to the opera, *yannow.* You should get Lavinia to get *me* a ticket, sometime."

She laughs like this is a very funny joke.

"You think, maybe, sometime, you can get a plus-one?" There's lipstick on her teeth.

"Maybe," Louise says.

"Smart girl," says Athena. "Keep your cards close." She gives Louise another playful shove. "Girls like us," she says, "we gotta stick together. You ride it out while you can. Just—you know—be smart."

"What do you mean?"

"How long you known her?"

"Six months. Give or take."

"Yup." Athena taps her wrist. "Thought so. Right on time, too."

"What do you mean?"

"I mean, I wouldn't panic, yet. You probably have another coupla months." She raises one painted eyebrow. "But if I were you—I'd have a backup plan." She gestures for another round of drinks, even though Louise hasn't finished the first one. "When she kicked Mimi out, she had to move back home for, like, two months just to get a deposit together—it was so sad. And the one before her—Lisabetta, God, I think she just packed up and left—"

"Before Mimi?"

Athena shrugs.

"I'm just saying. Sell up while you can." She brays a laugh. "The meek don't inherit shit." She downs her glass. "Get me an opera ticket, sometime."

She leaves Louise with the bill.

It is midnight by the time Louise gets home. It is still raining. Lavinia is still not there. She doesn't answer her phone.

Louise waits across the street, on the stoop of one of the brownstones, so that if Mrs. Winters comes, she will not see, even though there is no awning there and it's still raining.

Louise does numbers in her head to keep herself calm:

First and last month's rent: sixteen hundred dollars—no, that's a lie, she won't find a studio for eight hundred—that one was rent-stabilized—she'll have to find another roommate—*oh God, one with a second set of keys*—somewhere so much further out; *oh, God, the commute.*

She has sixty-four dollars in her bank account.

She has three hundred dollars of Lavinia's cash in her pillowcase.

She barely even has a job.

I can do this, she thinks—she makes herself think—*I can do this.*

Here's the thing: Louise can't.

Lavinia gets home at two.

She stumbles out of a taxi.

She falls over in front of the building.

Her stockings are torn. Her dress is inside out. She's bleeding from the lip.

"Jesus!"

Louise is there, so fast, to help her up.

"Where the fuck did you come from?"

Lavinia's eyes aren't focusing.

"I've been waiting for you (*don't get angry; don't let yourself get angry*). I don't have keys."

"Oh." Lavinia drops them. Louise picks them up. "Okay."

"Where were you?"

"Nowhere. Out."

They go into the lobby. They go up the stairs.

"Your dress is inside out."

Lavinia doesn't say anything. She climbs up the stairs on her hands, on her knees.

"I was worried about you."

"No, you weren't!"

Lavinia tries to pull herself up on the railing, but she falls over again.

"You were glad—weren't you? You were glad—you had the *whole night* to yourself, didn't you?"

There are tears in Lavinia's eyes. There are tears streaming down Lavinia's face.

"I mean, I was locked out of my house, so—"

"*Fuck you,*" Lavinia screams. "Fuck you—it's *my* house! My house—mine and Cordy's!"

A door opens at the end of the hall.

"*Really.*"

Mrs. Winters is standing in the doorway.

Louise mouths another apology.

Lavinia just starts laughing.

"Can you believe it?" she says, right in Mrs. Winters's face. "This bitch thinks it's her house, now."

"I'm just putting her to bed," Louise says. "I'm just taking her home—that's all. Then I'm going."

"I should hope so," says Mrs. Winters.

She raises her eyebrow. She closes the door.

Lavinia keeps laughing when Louise forces the door open, pushes her inside.

"Christ—don't *touch* me! What's wrong with you?"

"Just get inside," Louise says. She's so tired. "Please."

"Don't fucking touch me!"

"Just tell me what happened!"

Louise sits her down. Louise gets some ice for the lip.

"Did—did someone do something to you?"

"What, you *jealous*?"

Lavinia tosses that long, unnatural hair.

"What—you want to make another pass at me, is that it?"

"I'm going to bed."

"Fine! Go to bed! I don't care—I don't fucking care *what* you do."

Louise can't sleep.

She stares at the ceiling, for a while; at Lavinia's chandelier, at Lavinia's painted gold moldings, at Lavinia's ten-foot oil painting of a naked Parisian courtesan that's probably fake, anyway.

She gets up.

She goes into the living room.

She opens the door to Lavinia's bedroom.

Lavinia is lying there, with the light from the moon falling on her in slanting rays. Her hair is golden and billowing and haloed all around her, like a Rossetti angel, like Ophelia drowned. She's wearing a nightgown.

She still sleeps with a teddy bear.

And Louise thinks *oh, God, don't let it be true.*

She goes to the bed. She sits on the edge. She is so careful. Lavinia is clutching the teddy bear so tightly.

Maybe there was a Lisabetta, she thinks, maybe there was a Mimi.

She'll do anything, whatever it takes. She'll lie about the novel.

She'll stay up late no matter how many shifts she misses. She'll stop taking out money. She'll never speak to Rex again. She'll take photos for Lavinia, however many photos Lavinia wants, of Lavinia looking beautiful and glamorous and maenad-ish and world-destroying, whatever Lavinia needs. Just as long as she is not like the others. She won't even ask for love; she doesn't even know if Lavinia can love. Just as long as Lavinia needs her.

Louise gets into the bed and Lavinia's back is still to her.

She is so careful, putting her hand on Lavinia's shoulder. She is so careful, sliding her arm against Lavinia's arm.

Lavinia doesn't move.

Louise lies, so stiffly, against her.

"I love you," she whispers. "I love you; I love you; I love you."

Lavinia doesn't say anything.

They lie there a little longer, in silence, and then Louise gets up and goes back to the other bedroom, and then the next day this is just another thing that never happened, and also Louise sleeps so late she misses her last GlaZam deadline and she's fired from there, too.

The next morning, Lavinia sends Louise out for croissants from Agata's, and it's like nothing ever happened.

The last party Lavinia ever goes to is at a sex club that's not a sex club.

It's called the P.M., which is supposedly short for *petit mort*, and it's bottle service only. It's housed in an old theater that looks like a bordello and it's impossible to get in unless you know somebody (even if you pay six hundred dollars for prosecco; even if you pay eighteen hundred for champagne). One of the sideshow acts is a little person taking a dildo up the ass, and another is a woman who covers herself in shit, and someone who can whistle show tunes with her cunt.

Lavinia isn't even supposed to be there.

It happens like this:

There is a special party that night. Athena Maidenhead is performing her fan dance except with a cat-o'-nine-tails, but they're short-staffed and they need more girls and so she does Louise a solid and hooks her up.

"How wonderful!" says Lavinia, when she hears. "I've always wanted to go. I heard they have orgies onstage—do they have orgies onstage?"

"I mean—I'll be *working*!"

"But you're a bottle girl! All you have to do is stand around and look pretty and hold a tray, right?"

"It's *work*." Louise tries again.

"I see." Lavinia's smile turns sharp.

"I just don't want you to feel obligated," Louise says. She is so careful. "I don't want you to come to keep me company and be miserable because I'm stuck, like, pouring some finance bro champagne—I'm not going to be much fun for you."

"Don't be stupid, Lulu," says Lavinia. "You're always fun for me."

"We can do something else that day." Louise's smile is so much wider. "The Chelsea Flea Market, maybe? Or jazz brunch at Hotel Chantelle—you love jazz brunch."

Lavinia doesn't say anything.

She rises, goes to the dining-room table.

"Hey, Lulu?"

"Yeah?"

"I left a couple of rolls of cash on here. Not a lot—just a few hundred dollars, or so. I could have sworn there were five, but . . ." She looks very evenly at Louise. "You haven't seen them, have you?"

Louise's heart is beating so quickly again.

"No, of course not."

"I figured." Lavinia gathers up the rest. "I just wanted to check."

"I'll keep an eye out."

"Maybe there were four," Lavinia says. "God knows I never remember these things."

And Louise casts about so desperately for that thing, the one thing, that she can do—that she can *always* do—that will make Lavinia happy again.

"You know, the light's really good right now."

"Is it?"

"Let me take a picture of you. Just—you, on the couch, with the dressing gown, and the light on your hair."

"No, thank you," says Lavinia.

Now is the part you've been waiting for.

You and I both know what happens now: Lavinia doesn't make it.

But the thing you have to understand is: why.

Now you and I, we've been to parties before. We've done this a few times before already.

But here's the thing: you've never been to a party like this.

That's the whole point.

When they hire the fire-eaters, the midget who takes the dildo up his ass, the guy who rolls around in buttercream, the conjoined twins, the glitter-eater, the woman who queefs show tunes, they do it because the most important thing in a party like this is that it should be unlike any party you've ever been to before, and if you throw up or cry or run screaming then so much the better, because at least you've felt something.

The bouncer is short and the drinks are watered-down and the only people who pay for them are assholes, anyway, but the line goes all the way to the end of Chrystie Street, some nights, even though none of those people will ever get in (except Lavinia; always, always, except Lavinia), because it is the sort of place that finally, finally surprises you.

Here is a girl who was the villain on *Survivor* one time.

Here are some bros drinking frozen rosé.

Here is the guy who invented this app that's like Uber, except it's for helicopters, except it goes to the Hamptons, except it's five hundred dollars a person.

Here is a former child star who does stand-up now (that's the joke).

Here is a guy who is getting married tomorrow, and doesn't want to be.

Here is Louise in a miniskirt, serving shrimp.

It is hot. It is sweaty. Everything sticks to everything else. Two guys, already, have felt Louise's ass (she isn't allowed to object). Another guy has gone straight between her legs. Athena Maidenhead is completely naked except for these little pasties in the shape of Greek columns, jiggling the tassels in perfect figure-eights. The dwarf is in makeup.

"Spoiler alert." It's Hal, in black tie. "The fire-eaters fuck."

Louise puts on her most docile and most flattering smile.

"Shrimp, Hal?"

"You know, they do horrible things to girls like you in places like this."

"I hadn't noticed."

"It's not a bad thing. You should go for it. Some illustrious Great Men around the place." He considers. "Who knows, you could make a decent wife for somebody, one day. You seem like a nice enough girl."

"Another shrimp?"

"What, you embarrassed to be here? You shouldn't be. Nobody gives a fuck about you. You're a complete nonentity."

She's still smiling.

"I'm not being an asshole, by the way. That's a good thing."

"Tell me more."

She grits her teeth so hard she thinks they'll break.

"It's freeing. Nobody expects anything from you." His tongue lolls, like it always does, and he goes on nodding long after he's finished talking. "I bet nobody cares whether you're a Great Man in New Hampshire."

She starts making eyes at strangers, hoping someone will signal her.

"Are you a Great Man, Hal?"

"Fuck, no. I'm just a humble insurance executive. Just give me a classic six and a Filipina woman to iron my shirts and Wagner on my sound system and I'll happily be first up against the wall when the revolution comes. *Me ne frego.*"

"Sounds lovely."

She's craning her neck now, looking so desperately at the guy who five minutes earlier grabbed her ass and wanted to know if she'd gotten butt implants.

"You know Rex is crazy about you, right?"

"What?"

"It's really fucking pathetic. I told him so. He's a pussy."

"I'm Lavinia's best friend."

"Sure you are," he says. His teeth are yellow but they glint with the strobe lights. "You're such a good friend."

"Is—he here?"

"You think Rex would watch some girl get fucked by a robot?" He snorts. "He'd probably rush the stage and leap to her defense." He takes the last shrimp off her plate. "If it makes you feel better, he feels super-guilty about it."

"It doesn't."

"He's got a hair shirt on, under all that tweed."

"Don't tell me," says Louise. "I don't want to know."

"All property is theft," says Hal.

He tips her a fifty and pats her on the ass.

Louise keeps smiling at strangers. Louise does whatever Louise has to do to keep the wolves from the door.

She smells Lavinia before she sees her. That same, familiar perfume: even here where it smells like bodies and sick. That cloying, heady smell of lavender and fig somehow gets through. Then she sees Lavinia's hair.

She's worn it long and down tonight, and she's in a dark velvet dress; she's leaning back on the banquette and laughing and flashing her teeth.

Mimi is with her.

"Lavinia?"

Lavinia looks up so idly. "Oh, hello, Lulu." She leans back on the banquette. "You're out of shrimp."

Mimi is smiling her dog-like smile.

"Isn't this place *insane*? There was one act—I swear to God—if that dildo thing was a trick . . ."

"Mimi, darling?"

"Mhm?"

"Can you get me another glass of prosecco?"

Mimi trots off happily.

"God, this place!" Lavinia fingers the cocktail toothpick like it's a cigarette. "God, Lulu, everything's so *filthy*. It's disgusting. Don't you love it?" She laughs. "Isn't it, like—what you imagine Pigalle was like, during the fin de siècle. Like, the *real* Moulin Rouge—was it shocking, do you think? Come sit."

"I'm working," says Louise.

Lavinia shrugs. She sips the remnants of her prosecco.

"So," Louise says. "Mimi's here."

Lavinia smiles, too, like nothing's wrong. "Oh, I *know* you don't like her," she says. "But she's all right in *small* doses."

"I never said I didn't—"

"She's just intense, that's all. But then again, so am I—don't you think?"

Louise doesn't say anything.

"Don't you think so, Lulu?"

"I mean," Louise has already lost, "a little, I guess . . ."

"God, you must be so *bored*—"

The woman who rolls in her own shit is rolling in her own shit onstage.

"Poor Lulu. It must be a very great burden on you, putting up with me."

"Don't be silly," says Louise. "I love every minute of it."

"So—how's Hal?"

Louise freezes. "What?"

"I saw you over there—chatting."

"He wanted shrimp."

"You like him, don't you?"

"God—Hal!" Louise doesn't even think Rex likes Hal. "Of course not."

"I mean, it's fine if you do. You should fuck him. I mean—he's an idiot. But he's a rich idiot. And he's, you know, funny."

"I don't want to fuck Hal, Lavinia."

"You should fuck *someone,* Lulu. It'd be good for you! You need a boyfriend. It's not good for us, you know—spending, like, *all* our time together."

Out of the corner of her eye, Louise can see Mimi, raptly applauding the woman rolling in her own shit.

"I want to spend all my time with you, Lavinia," she says.

She keeps her eyes down. She is so good at this part.

"We're best friends, Lavinia."

She has always been so good at this part.

"You were so good to come tonight, Lavinia. You knew—you knew I really wanted you here, deep down."

"I know."

"I wish I could be watching the show with you."

"I know."

"I know—I was stupid—I shouldn't have taken this gig."

Lavinia just looks at her phone.

"No," she says. "You really shouldn't have."

At ten-thirty, Mimi falls asleep on the banquette. She snores.

Lavinia keeps dancing alone, under the neon lights that bathe her in red, blue, green.

"Lulu," she murmurs. Two more men have felt up Louise's ass, by now, and it hurts so much to stand in heels. "My Lulu."

Louise hates how relieved she is.

Lavinia sidles up to the bar.

"You're my favorite, Lulu. You know that."

"I know."

"We should get a picture. Just the two of us."

The aerialists are so high above them.

"When I'm off shift," Louise says. "We'll take a photo. I get off at four."

"We should break into the green room! See if the dildo-fucking is real!"

"When I'm off shift," Louise says again, in exactly the same tone of voice, like it's going to do any good.

"We should break in and take photos with the robot!"

"Please," Louise whispers, "please, Lavinia, don't—"

But Lavinia is so certain and determined. "Mimi promised she'd do it with me. But she's—well, you know Mimi—she can't hold her drink; she isn't like you; she's not like *us*, Lulu."

"I don't want to get fired," Louise says. *"Please."*

"Christ, Lulu." Lavinia rolls her eyes. "You used to be so *fun*!"

She gets up.

"I am fun!"

Lavinia picks up her arm, points to it. "More poetry, remember? More fucking poetry—what the *fuck* did I get this tattoo for?"

Louise can't stay like this. She can't talk to a customer (worse: a female customer); there's the guy who tapped her ass already looking pissed, and Hal enjoying himself with one of the other waitresses in the corner, and if this job goes well they said there would be others, and sure she gets her ass squeezed but the tips are so great, and she doesn't have time for this—*fuck,* she doesn't have time for this— and if she could only explain—

"Fuck it," says Lavinia. "I'm going. Come or don't come. I don't give a shit."

She spits out a cocktail toothpick.

"You can't rely on anybody."

She turns.

———

Things always turn.

You pack up, push off; you get in a beat-up Chevy or a moving van; it doesn't matter. You read poetry on the water or smoke a joint on a railroad bridge; you say *I love you* on the top of the High Line or in the middle of the Devonshire woods.

It's the same, either way.

There's the day you pick up the keys to this railroad one-bedroom in Bushwick and you think *today, today is the day everything changes.* You think you will never see Devonshire and its fading strip malls and its railroad tracks and its squat unhappy houses ever again. You swing the door wide-open and stretch out your arms and dance through the emptiness of every new inch of the space, with your hair short and dark and your eyes closed. When you open them Virgil Bryce is standing there, on his spindly legs, with his arms crossed, and he is telling you: *don't get too excited, dearest, who knows how long you'll be able to make it work here,* and even though you've argued on the way over, even though you've spent the whole six-hour drive arguing, you think *no, no, this time is different, this time I've outrun it; this time I've won.*

Even when he comes so close to you. Even when he runs his fingers through your hair.

Even when he says *I just don't want you to be disappointed when the world doesn't see what I see.*

There're the days you don't believe him, not deep down. There're days you do.

"Lavinia!"

Louise catches up to Lavinia in the green room.

She's out of breath. She's covered in other people's sweat. There's a drag queen putting on fake lashes who doesn't even look at them.

"Lavinia—*please.*"

"Go back to work, Lulu. I don't want to put you out."

"That's not what this is!"

"I get it. You know what? I get it. I'm a *lot*. I'm a lot to fucking deal with—" She strides past a ballerina with pierced nipples. "You—Louise—you must be a fucking *saint*."

She is all the way to the backstage area, now, and Louise keeps thinking somebody is going to notice them, or stop them, but everyone is so drunk and the performers are looking in the mirror and the bouncers are dealing with a brawl, and so nobody does.

"Jesus, Lulu, quit following me!"

They pass ropes and red velvet curtains and lights and sandbags and everything smells like grease paint and cigarette smoke.

Louise doesn't even know why she's following her anymore.

"Christ—leave me alone."

Lavinia presses through a dark red door.

Louise follows her.

"Jesus—you want to watch me pee, now?"

They're in a mirrored bathroom, just between the stage and the dance floor. They are the only ones there. There are art nouveau naked ladies painted onto the ceiling. There's a red velvet chaise. There's a chandelier. Of course there's a chandelier.

Louise locks the door.

"Can you just listen to me for a second?"

A different Lavinia laughs in every mirror.

"Fine," Lavinia says.

She hikes up her skirt.

She takes a piss right in front of Louise.

"I'm listening. Are you happy?"

She bursts out laughing.

"Are you fucking happy now?"

She wipes, flushes.

"Go ahead."

"Please." Louise is doing such a good job. "Can we just talk about this?"

"Go back to work, Lulu." Lavinia has gone to the mirror. She is reapplying her lipstick. "God knows, you need the money."

Louise takes a very deep breath.

Louise is very calm.

"I'm sorry," she says, in such a small, clear voice. "I miss you. Things have been weird, I know, I'm sorry."

"You want a raise?" Lavinia spins around, and all the mirrored Lavinias spin, too. "You want overtime?"

She grins. She's got lipstick on her teeth.

"One card not enough for you? You want the Amex, too? God—how stupid do you think I *am*?"

Louise's heart is in her throat and her stomach is in her feet and nothing in her body is where it is ever supposed to be and she cannot think except to think *it is all over, now.* She tries to focus on just the practical things (*a place to sleep, a place oh God to sleep, don't let me go back home please that's all I want don't make me go back home*).

"I'd have just *given* it to you," Lavinia says. "If you'd asked."

I will go anywhere, Louise thinks, *I will never go back home.*

"Am I really that awful—that it's so hard just to *pretend* you like me?"

"I do like you."

"You hate me!"

"I love you."

"Don't lie to me!" Lavinia's voice goes so high. "Like I don't know—like I don't know how much I fucking *disgust you.* I remember—I fucking remember the opera, okay? God, you couldn't *wait* to get out of there—it's not like we even *did* anything!"

Louise can't even breathe; Louise thinks *make this better fix this do anything say anything make her happy calm her down make it right make it right* and so she blurts it out, among the no's:

"I'm in love with you."

She doesn't mean it. She doesn't know if she means it.

It is the only thing that will make Lavinia stop shouting at her.

"What?"

"I—the opera. I—*like* you, okay? I freaked out because I liked you. I'm sorry. I'm sorry—I know you're straight—I *know.*"

God, listen to yourself, Louise thinks. *Not even Lavinia can be this dumb.*

But Lavinia is smiling.

"Poor Lulu," she whispers. She puts her hand on Louise's cheek—so magnanimously, now—*God, this makes her so happy*—"Poor, poor Lulu"—*of course everybody dies of love for Lavinia; she is just that beautiful; that is how it goes.*

She laughs a little bit.

"It's not your fault," Lavinia says.

She takes a deep breath.

"Come on," she says. "The light is beautiful in here. Let's take a selfie."

Louise can breathe again.

It's worth it, she thinks. *It has to be worth it.*

Louise has been this desperate before.

She has wandered the streets of Bushwick at three in the morning, covered in blood, with a credit card and a driver's license and a sweater and a bus ticket back to New Hampshire on her phone with four percent battery life, and nothing else. She made it work then.

Just go to an all-night diner. Just go to a nightclub where the lights are real low. Just go to a shitty bar and wash your face in the bathroom. Fuck a stranger, just to have a place to stay that is not a night bus to New Hampshire.

It's not pretty, but it works.

She'll make it work now, too.

Lavinia puts Louise's lipstick on. Lavinia wipes the mascara off Louise's face. Lavinia smooths back Louise's hair.

"Give me your phone," Lavinia says.

She moves the candles from the toilet tank to the sink to give them better light.

She turns the camera inward.

That's when Rex texts Louise.

I miss our Met outings.

Another one soon?

Is it weird that I miss you?

Lavinia doesn't even get mad. That's the worst part.

She doesn't rage. She doesn't throw things.

"You're moving out," she says. She shrugs. "You're moving out—*now*."

"Lavinia, let me explain—"

"I don't care." Lavinia is carefully, very carefully, putting her lipstick back in her purse. "Whatever it is—I don't care. Here—take the keys. Get your shit. By the time I come home I don't want to see you."

"I don't have anywhere to—"

"All that cash," Lavinia says. "And you don't have enough for a hotel room?" She shrugs. "Stay with Rex. I don't give a shit."

She throws the keys on the floor.

Louise bends down to get them.

She's already on her phone.

"What are you doing?" Louise can't even think *please, please* anymore. Everything is so still. Movement in the room stops with the finality of it all.

"I'm telling everyone," Lavinia says. She closes the toilet, sits down. She types with both fingers. "I . . . had . . . the . . . most . . . *ridiculous* night." She looks up. Just for a second. "Period. I found out that my crazy roommate stole my money and fucked my ex and tried to fuck me in a nightclub bathroom."

"That's not what happened."

Lavinia keeps typing.

"My *crazy dyke roommate stole a shit-ton of money from my bank account while she was hooking up with my ex-boyfriend and trying to convince me she was in love with me*—how do you spell *deceitful*—is it *i* and then *e*—come on, Louise, you're a fucking SAT tutor, you should know!"

"Don't," says Louise. "Please—please—I'll go, just—"

"It's fine. I have AutoCorrect. My *deceitful psycho dyke roommate I felt fucking sorry for stole four thousand dollars out of my bank account while I was letting her live rent-free in my sister's bedroom.*" She raises the camera. "Come on—fucking *smile,* Lulu!"

Louise grabs the phone.

"Jesus Christ, what the *fuck* is your problem!"

Lavinia yanks it back.

And Louise, all she can think, all she has left, is *let them not know; let them not know;* and she doesn't know who it is that she cares about knowing, because she doesn't care about Beowulf Marmont and she doesn't care about Gavin or Father Romylos or Athena or Mimi or Hal and she doesn't even like them, anyway, but in the moment she isn't considering that. All she's thinking is that nobody can know what she has done, and so she pulls harder, so much harder than she means to, and then she and Lavinia are on the floor, grabbing for it, and the stupid thing, the really stupid thing, is that the phone clatters under the sink, anyway, so that by the time Louise is pulling out Lavinia's hair, by the time Lavinia is scratching at her shoulders, by the time she is yanking her up against the mirrored and the mirrored and the mirrored walls, by the time she hits her head on the sink, the phone isn't even there, not the first time she hits her head, nor the second, nor even the third.

This is how Lavinia dies:

Putting a hand to her head. Looking down at her forearm: at the MORE POETRY!!! that is covered with droplets of blood.

Looking up at Louise.

Falling, with all the other Lavinias: against the mirror, against Louise, onto the floor.

This, this, is how Louise fucks everything up.

5

LOUISE IS ALWAYS RIGHT.

She has known, for years, that you can fool some of the people all of the time, and all of the people some of the time, but you can't fool everybody forever, no matter how good you are at this, no matter how hard you work at it. If you are a deceitful psycho dyke who steals money and also your best friend's ex-boyfriend, no matter how thin you are, or how pretty, or how good that one piece you wrote for *The Fiddler* blog was, the truth is that everybody, sooner or later, will know.

Anyway, it's over now.

Lavinia's dead.

The bass is thumping. People are screaming applause. Somebody's knocking at the bathroom door.

Lavinia's phone rings.

Whatever Louise does, she can't scream.

She puts her hand over her mouth.

There are three hundred people in this club, right outside the door.

Louise tries to breathe in that very calm and mindful way she practiced once, during therapy, that's supposed to put things in perspective.

It doesn't work.

Lavinia's phone keeps ringing.

———

Somebody keeps knocking on the bathroom door.

Mimi's face is glowing on Lavinia's phone.

Just breathe, Louise thinks. *Just breathe.*

The phone goes to voicemail.

Mimi sends so many texts.

where r u???

i woke up all alone

Sad kitten emoji.

Crying fox emoji.

Weeping deer emoji.

r u still here?

Louise breathes.

Louise wipes the blood off the floor. Louise washes blood off Lavinia's forehead. She uses a hand towel and very expensive basil-smelling liquid soap. Louise hides this in the bottom of the trash.

Louise pushes Lavinia's long, loose hair over her shoulders. Lavinia's hair is so long and luxurious that it covers her face. She takes off Lavinia's necklace, which is enormous and glittering and bloodstained, and pins it to her hair so that the medallion falls over Lavinia's forehead, like she's wearing a crown, so that you cannot even see the blood.

The banging on the bathroom gets louder.

"You *cunt,*" cries somebody. "You fucking *cunt!*"

There is nothing Louise can do.

She opens the door.

Twenty people are in line for the bathroom.

There is no way, she thinks, *that this is not the end.*

———

Lavinia is propped up in Louise's arms.

Lavinia is dead, and her eyes are open, and she is propped up in Louise's arms, and a very skinny girl with fried blonde hair and a 1980s dress is staring straight at them both.

She takes them in.

She stumbles to the floor.

She starts throwing up in the toilet.

People swarm in around her—the girl's even skinnier friend, who is holding back her hair, and some guy shouting *gross, Jesus Christ, I've got to take a piss* and then the drunk girl who is holding back the other drunk girl's hair is getting in a fight with the drunk guy who just wants to take a piss and at some point he unzips his fly and gets his cock out and starts pissing on the wall and because everyone is watching him nobody notices Louise haul Lavinia, like she's stumbling, like she just needs her hair held back, back toward the dank and narrow corridors that lead toward the stage.

And still it is only a matter of time, and maybe, *maybe* Lavinia is not dead but only stunned (Louise has watched a lot of *Law & Order* but even so she's not sure how much effort it takes to kill somebody because murder doesn't really feel like a thing that actually happens in the real world), and it is so loud and so crowded and so dark that Louise just hauls Lavinia against the wall (which is sticky, and provides friction) and hides her body with her own, pushing her up, like it's just the two of them, like they've gone in seclusion to some corner so they can make out, so Lavinia can finger her again, so that Louise can kiss her neck.

"Get a room!" somebody is shouting, and Louise doesn't even know if it's at her, because there's a guy getting a blow job out of the corner of her eye.

There is an aerialist's globe abandoned in one corner of the corridor. The fire-eaters have used it, already, and it smells like gasoline still.

Louise lays Lavinia down there, under the skeleton of the globe, under the lights, under the fake chandelier jewels, which shine every time the house lights strobe.

She feels Lavinia's face. She kisses it. She feels her throat and her neck and her heart and nothing, nothing is beating, but still this cannot be real, because people do not die like this, because she is not a person who kills people, she is not a person who does anything wrong, ever, and killing a person is about the worst thing you can do, and also there is a God and He sends down lightning bolts at this sort of thing, and so if Lavinia were dead a judgment would be made and Louise would turn to ash.

Except that the guy who smears himself in buttercream is up for an encore.

This time, he's making balloon animals, except they're not made of balloons.

Lavinia is so beautiful, under the aerialist's globe.

Louise leans over her. She tries to arrange Lavinia's hair, again, so the blood stops showing, and she thinks that Lavinia would love this because Lavinia looks just, just like Ophelia right now and then she starts to feel sick because what kind of sick person justifies killing someone on the grounds that they have always wanted to be Ophelia, a little bit, or at the very least the Lady of Shalott.

Then everyone starts screaming and the lights are blaring and some guy she has never seen before says "CROWD SURF" right in her face and the skinny girl (one of them) screams like this is the first time in her life she's ever heard of crowd-surfing and then everybody is looking at them, *straight at them,* at this beautiful dead blonde white woman and this slightly less beautiful blonde white woman who is still alive and breathing and on top of her and everybody is screaming, screaming, like they are gods, and then they start rolling the globe with the two of them inside and everything is spinning and Louise thinks she is going to be sick—she is sick, and she thinks *now, now is the moment they realize* but they don't, because the lights are pulsing and the sound is blaring and they're crossing the orchestra pit, crossing the main hall, and then glitter falls from the ceiling, in a big grand-finale burst, and it falls thicker and harder than any blizzard Louise has ever seen and in this thickness it sticks to both of them: to the sweat and whatever that clammy thing is called that makes you a little bit wet after you die, and then they are both so covered in silver you cannot even see the blood, you cannot see (how is it that everybody cannot see?) that there is a dead girl with long blonde hair and open, confetti-sliced eyes.

Louise pukes.

Everybody cheers at that, too.

As they roll the globe toward the wings of the stage, Louise catches a glimpse of Hal. He's sitting with the ballerina with the pierced nipples.

He raises a glass at them both.

Now they are in the shadows.

Now Louise is pushing, so desperately, against the wall.

Now Louise finds the service door.

She hauls Lavinia into the service alley. It smells like rotting fish, and sweet wine, and cooking fat.

Lavinia isn't even the only girl prostrate in that alley.

She hauls Lavinia into a splintering wooden trolley. She pushes the crates out of the way. She avoids the rats.

She cuts herself on one of the screws holding the wheels on. She looks down to see if she is bleeding, but Lavinia's blood has stained her calves, too, and so Louise can't even tell.

———

Mimi is still fucking texting.

Where are u? I'm upstairs? Are u here??

And Louise thinks: *I am not myself.*

This is not real life, Louise thinks. Police sirens are blaring, and they aren't even for her.

Louise decides.

Louise grabs Lavinia's phone. She calls an Uber.

She pulls Lavinia's arm over the back of her neck.

"Come on," she says, loud enough for everybody on the street to hear. "Come on, sweetie! Let's get you home."

She is so chipper.

She is just another overworked waitress, helping just another drunk girl to a cab.

They are both covered in glitter. They're both covered in puke.

It's one of those nights: in the city.

It's a Friday night and everybody's screaming, and no matter how late it is it's like daylight out; and it's so uncanny but also it's a relief, because it means you're not alone.

You can walk past so many nightclubs with blood on your face and nobody will even notice.

You can walk down a city street, on the Lower East Side, in Bushwick, with blood on your face and nothing but a driver's license and a credit card and a phone with almost no battery life, and your knuckles bruised from when you have hit a man (you are not even the kind of girl who would lose control and hit a man) (you have always been that girl) (he always told you you were that girl), and nobody will even notice, or care.

Louise has done this before. It didn't feel real then, either.

Louise waits for the Uber in the alley outside the club.

There are so many people out there.

A lot of people are drunk-crying, and so Louise gets on her knees and holds Lavinia real close, and real tight, and murmurs into Lavinia's stiffening neck *I know, honey, I know, I'm sorry, I'm sorry, I love you* and she doesn't even know if she means it.

Another text from Mimi.

Questing exploring fox emoji.

I'm all alone.

did u go off w/ luis?

are u ok????!!111

Louise did not want to hurt Lavinia, when she hurt Lavinia. (She wanted to hurt Lavinia.)

She did not want to hurt Virgil Bryce.

(She is not that kind of girl.)

It's just that when you've had the same conversation over and over for a year, in a tiny little railroad apartment in Bushwick, and once again a man you love is saying *I love you* but also *this is a benediction and a mercy, because I know you better than you know yourself and I have made the choice to love you anyway, and nobody else who knows you will,* and he is both kissing you and also telling you you'd be hotter if you just lost a little weight. He is both fucking you and also telling you it'd be better if you both moved somewhere a little quieter, where you'd have a better chance at *making it,* because then you wouldn't be disappointed, maybe, just maybe one time—instead of nodding, instead of sighing, instead of saying *yes, yes, you're right,* you hit him so hard he falls backward, the way men hit women in films, the way men aren't supposed to hit women in life.

(Maybe you do this, once, and then you know he is right about everything he has always said about you.)

That is when you see that he sees that you are the crazy bitch he always knew you were, and that, that is the only way you can leave.

You are the crazy one, now. You always were.

"I was right about you," he says, in this priggish way that almost,

almost, sounds like he's glad to be able to say it, and mops the blood from his cheek, "you're a fucking psycho, Louise" and he grabs her by the back of her neck, like a dog, and pushes her out the door, and he is right, and it is the last thing he ever says to her.

It's so easy, hauling Lavinia into the Uber. (*Thank God, thank God she's so thin.*) It's the only time Louise hasn't hated how thin Lavinia is.

"Your friend okay?"

"She's seen the fairies," Louise says. She holds Lavinia on her lap. Lavinia's eyes are still open. There's blood on Louise's miniskirt, on her legs (*thank God, thank God I'm wearing black*).

"What?"

"Nothing."

"She smells like shit."

"I know."

"It's a hundred-dollar fine, you know, if she does it again."

"She won't," says Louise.

Lavinia's nipple is showing, where the dress has slipped down. The driver is staring at her in the mirror.

Louise lets him.

There's a joke Louise has always liked, about these two men who find a bear in the woods. This is the joke: You don't have to be faster than the bear. You just have to be faster than the other guy.

She's thinking about that joke now.

Louise has done the next part before.

Getting Lavinia out of a cab. Getting Lavinia onto the stairs. Getting Lavinia into the bathtub. Putting the water on.

Washing that long, tangled, glorious golden hair.

Washing the blood off.

———

should i just go home?

This is Mimi's twentieth text.

lol I'm so drunk I'm getting blackout.

And Louise thinks: *this cannot be real.*

Nothing is real.

Lavinia's eyes are still open.

This cannot, cannot be real.

Lavinia's phone won't stop ringing.

Louise will get through this, too.

I just need time, she thinks. *I just need a little more time.*

"Darling!"

Louise can sound so much like Lavinia, when she wants to. She knows her voice so well. "Darling—Mimi—I'm so terribly sorry!"

"Where are you?"

"Are you still at the P.M.?"

"Hal said you left. He said you got sick."

"Just for a second—darling. Needed a moment's respite, that's all."

"Where are you?"

And Louise thinks *fuck, fuck, fuck.*

And Louise thinks *just let the world stop, just for one second, just long enough for things to start making sense.*

"I'm so drunk!" Mimi wails. "I can't even see straight. Come *party* with me!"

Louise taking an inert Lavinia across the dance floor.

That cannot be the last thing Hal sees. That cannot be the last thing anyone sees.

She just has to keep Lavinia alive a few hours longer.

———

"Just meet me at the Bulgarian Bar," says Lavinia. Lavinia is always, always up for another adventure. "I'm in an Uber right now. I'm on my way, darling, I *swear*."

"You'll come?"

"Yes, of course, I'll come."

"Is Louise coming?"

It's such a sour, pathetic little sneer.

"God no," says Lavinia. "To tell you the truth, I'm a little sick of her, anyway."

It is not as hard as you'd think, getting Lavinia's dress off. It is not as hard as you'd think, rinsing it off, putting it on, covering the back with a fox-fur stole. Lavinia is so stiff, but she resists so little.

The hair is trickier—for now she can back-comb it, then put it up, so it looks like Lavinia's tried to pin it up nicely and failed (Lavinia never pins her hair neatly, not once).

She puts on Lavinia's lipstick.

She puts on Lavinia's perfume.

She closes the shower curtain.

Lavinia posts their selfie in the cab. Best friends.

It gets fifteen Likes in four minutes.

Lavinia introduces herself by name to the Uber driver. She chatters so splendidly about art and life and how if you want it badly enough, you can make yourself into a work of art. You can create yourself.

"I don't think people realize the freedom they have," she says as they pull up on the corner of Rivington and Essex. She tips in cash, even though you don't normally tip your Uber driver, so that he will remember her, and fondly.

Lavinia uploads another photo to Facebook: of Rivington Street, of the sky, of the stars, of the lights. Forget it, Jake, she captions it; it's Chinatown. Technically, it's the Lower East Side, but Lavinia wouldn't let that stop her, because Lavinia believes that Art is nobler and more important than truth. She checks in at the Bulgarian Bar.

Mimi has sent her so many emojis: Lions. Tigers. Bears.

Be there in a sec, Lavinia says.

You should go in the ice cage.

Here's how the Bulgarian Bar works:

Take off your clothes, get a free shot. Have sex on the bar, get a free bottle. Thirty bucks and you can enter the Soviet ice cage, put on the real vintage Soviet military uniform they give you, and also the Soviet fur hat, and then a bartender will take your phone and take pictures through the glass while you drink as much vodka as you can from a shot glass made of ice before it melts.

Now Mimi is in the Soviet ice cage. Now she's naked, except for her underpants, and a Soviet military jacket. Also: the hat.

She's pressed up against the glass, and a man Louise has never seen before and will never see again is kissing the back of Mimi's neck and sliding his fingers through the triangle of her underwear.

Lavinia puts Lavinia's card behind the bar.

She explains that she wants all of that drunk girl's drinks on her tab, too.

She takes a photo of Mimi. She posts it. She tags it. Beowulf Marmont Likes it.

When Mimi stumbles out, Lavinia catches her.

"Darling!"

"Lavinia?"

Lavinia is whispering in her ear, with her hair falling on Mimi's shoulder, with her perfume, standing right behind her. "I'm so sorry I made you wait."

"WherewereyouImissedyouImissyousomuch."

Mimi can't even stand.

"I brought you another drink."

She presses it into Mimi's hands.

"Down it!"

Mimi does. Mimi sways.

Mimi puts a hand over her mouth, like she's going to throw up.

"IwassoscaredLavinia."

There are so many people. It's dark. They're dancing.

"Iwassoscaredyouweremadatme."

"I could never be mad at you," says Lavinia. "I love you!"

"I missed you," Mimi is murmuring. Her eyes are unfocused. Lavinia is always just out of her field of vision. "You have no idea."

"Selfie!" Lavinia says.

They do.

Lavinia is leaning in, kissing Mimi's cheek, features obscured by the flaps of her Soviet fur hat, so you can't really see her face.

Lavinia posts this, too.

"We're going to have a good night tonight, right?"

"The best," says Lavinia.

She sails them both into the crowd.

She leaves Mimi in the arms of the man who was fingerbanging her earlier.

It's four in the morning. Lavinia is still alive.

Whatever happens to her, next, tonight, is not Louise's problem.

Not so long as she, too, has an alibi.

That is the logical next step, Louise thinks, once you've killed somebody. At least, she supposes it is.

Louise texts Mimi from her own phone.

Where are you guys?

Is Lavinia with you?

I need the keys.

Mimi doesn't answer. She's probably in bed with the stranger by now. But in the morning, wherever she wakes up, you will never get her to admit—not for a second—that she and Lavinia Williams didn't have one of those gorgeous, epic, once-in-a-lifetime nights, or that they did not stay out until dawn.

At four in the morning, Louise calls Rex.

"I'm sorry," she says. "I'm so sorry. I didn't know who else to call."

"Are you okay?"

He sounds so awake, for four in the morning.

"It's just—I don't have the keys."

"What?

"Lavinia—she went out with Mimi, after this burlesque thing we— it doesn't matter."

"She has your keys?"

"There's only one set," Louise says. "I don't have it. She's not picking up her phone."

"You didn't go with her?"

"She didn't invite me."

She can hear Rex exhale on the line.

"Come have a coffee with me," he says.

Lavinia goes into a bathroom at a twenty-four-hour diner. Louise comes out.

She has her hair up in a ponytail. She's wearing a miniskirt similar enough to the ridiculous miniskirt they made her wear at the P.M. (there's no use thinking about that job, now; she's lost that one, too), a sweater over the top, which is slutty and sequined and makes her feel like Athena Maidenhead, but she needs to be able to argue that she never made it home.

She packs Lavinia's dress so neatly, in a plastic bag, in case she ever needs it again.

Louise astonishes herself, sometimes.

Louise meets Rex near his place, in the East Village. They go to a 24/7 pierogi place called Veselka, with murals of people doing old New York things, and they sit by the window under the halogen light and watch the darkness fade, moment by moment.

Rex has bags under his eyes. He's wearing a blazer.

"You didn't have to get dressed up for me," Louise says.

They've been sitting in silence for ten minutes, eating greasy pierogis, drinking burnt coffee, staring at each other.

"I didn't," Rex says. "I mean—I mean, I didn't *not.* I mean—" He takes another sip of his coffee.

He sighs. Louise doesn't say anything.

"Look," says Rex. "I'm sure she'll be home soon. Has she done this before?"

"Sometimes." She looks up at him. "Not this late." She swallows. She has to be so careful, now. "I mean—you don't think something's happened to her?"

Maybe Lavinia will get mugged in an alley. Maybe she'll trip and fall in the park stumbling home. Louise can't think about that right now.

All Louise can focus on is not screaming.

"Have you heard back from Mimi?"

Louise shrugs. "Not yet."

"You don't have the keys," Rex says. He says it like he feels so sorry for her.

"It's some co-op board rule."

"Sure it is," he says.

"Sure," says Louise. "I'm sorry—I'm sorry—I shouldn't have woken you up. Not for this. It's just—I didn't know who else to call."

"I'm glad you did," says Rex. "I like talking to you."

"If she finds out—"

"We're dead," Rex says, and Louise has to work so hard not to flinch.

The light is just starting, outside, and rosy fingers claw shadows out of the diner floor.

"I hate that I'm getting you into trouble," Rex says.

"You're not," says Louise. "No—it's my fault. Believe me."

"I know it's wrong," says Rex. "I know that." He exhales. "She's a good person—deep down. Isn't she?"

Louise doesn't even know, anymore.

"Maybe."

"It's just—she's so—"

"Much?"

"Yes," Rex says. "Just—too much." He sighs. "It's not fair of her—to ask so much from you."

"It's fine," Louise says.

Just a couple more hours. Just until morning. You can do this.

She'll find a way to kill Lavinia in the morning.

"You're smart, and you're funny, and you're *nice*."

"Stop it," she says quietly.

"And you're a good friend—you *are*—and, I'm sorry, but you shouldn't *have* to be here at five o'clock in the fucking morning—I'm sorry."

"Stop," she says again, "please stop," but he doesn't hear her.

"You deserve so much better," he says. He takes her hand.

Here's the thing: Louise doesn't.

Louise has promised herself she wouldn't cry. She has been so good at not crying. She hasn't cried picking Lavinia's body off the floor, and she hasn't cried dragging Lavinia out of the theater, and she didn't cry in the Uber or putting Lavinia in the bathtub or posting that photo of the two of them and so Louise doesn't know why she is crying, now, but Rex is looking at her with such kind and magnanimous eyes. All Louise can think is that every terrible thing everyone has ever seen in her is true, has always been true, that there was no universe in which she would not end up doing this.

"I'm sorry," Rex keeps saying, like this has anything to do with him, looking at her like nobody should ever look at her again, and if he keeps looking at her like that another second she will not be able to stop herself from telling him everything, "God, I'm sorry, I shouldn't have— it's not my place."

"It's *fine.*"

She throws down a twenty on the table.

"I have to go."

Here's one way this night can end: Louise turns herself in.

Rex keeps looking at her—with those wide unblinking eyes, with his perfect faith—and Louise thinks *in a perfect world people do the right thing,* and although it is not a perfect world Louise decides it should be, and so she goes to the police and tells them, unstinting, everything that she has done.

For a moment, at dawn, Louise is sure she will.

Rex follows Louise onto Second Avenue.

"Louise, wait!"

He's out of breath. He's forgotten his blazer.

Louise waves for a cab—frantically, wildly, tries to work out where you're supposed to go, exactly, when you've killed somebody: if there's a head office or if you Google your local precinct or just go up to the first cop you see and say *there's a dead girl in my bathroom, sorry*?

Rex sprints the crosswalk so fast a cyclist nearly hits him.

"What do you want from me?" she asks him, and then he kisses her.

Rex isn't kissing her.

He is kissing a girl with fine, blonde hair and docile eyes who is as good as he is. She is shy, clever and witty and kind, and she suffers so terribly and she means so well. He is kissing a girl who does not complain when her friend locks her out at four o'clock in the morning, and who goes to the Met when she is lonely. He is kissing a girl who never killed anybody.

She kisses him back, anyway.

They take that cab back to Rex's place, even though it isn't even ten blocks away, because they can't keep their hands off each other, and Louise pays with all the cash in her wallet and leaves a ridiculous tip because it is Lavinia's cash, and now she can't even stand to touch it.

They climb on top of each other. They annihilate each other. Rex gets his scarf tangled in Louise's tacky, ridiculous sequins and although she doesn't even realize that she's crying at first her tears stain his face. He keeps kissing her despite this and he keeps whispering *it's not your fault; it's not your fault; I'm sorry.* They kiss in front of his apartment building and they kiss again in the lobby and they kiss again on the stairs and on every landing, which is a lot of landings, as it happens, because it's a walk-up and he lives on the fifth floor, and they kiss again by his front door and Louise hasn't even been drinking but she feels drunk. Or maybe it's Lavinia that is drunk—Lavinia who is still alive, Lavinia who is having the greatest night of her life with Mimi, Lavinia whom Mimi only just now has tagged in another incoherent status with every word misspelled about Baudelaire and wine and virtue, Lavinia who is going to get mugged tonight, Lavinia who is going to die—and maybe they are still tethered together because of that one night by the sea and Louise feels everything Lavinia feels and so she is drunk, too, or maybe it's just that somebody is warm and kind and kissing her and whispering her name, *her name,* into her ear, and telling her just how good she is.

"I'm ruining everything for you," Rex whispers, "I'm ruining everything; I know; I'm sorry; please make me stop." But they just cling to each other harder, and he takes off her sequined top and that ridiculous cunt-high miniskirt and then her bra (she realizes, too late, that it is one of Lavinia's, but he doesn't seem to notice). He runs his hands up and down her body and looks at her, I mean really looks at her, and says *Jesus Christ you're so beautiful* like he means it.

"Tell me to stop," Rex says. Louise doesn't. Not even when he kisses her neck; not even when he goes down on her; not even when he asks if she has a condom and she says "don't bother" because the risk seems so insignificant now.

She closes her legs around him and her arms around him and he's on her and around her and against her and inside her. But here's the thing: all Louise can think about is this one time in January that Lavinia decided they hadn't had one of *those nights* in a while, so Lavinia locked all the doors, turned off all the lights, and lit all the candles in the house. She put on Liszt's third *Liebestraum,* which Louise had never even heard before, and in the candlelight explained that the song was all about love in death, how *der stunde kommt, der stunde kommt* where everybody dies. Lavinia was leaning back on the divan with the moonlight on her breasts. But maybe Rex is the only reason Lavinia listens to that song in the first place, Louise thinks *yes, that part was real,* and she doesn't know, now, kissing him back, whether anything will ever be real again. Louise doesn't know whether she's terrified or terrible or triumphant, whether she is in love or just surviving. All she knows is that the world has ended but that it is also still turning.

All Louise needs to know right now is this: Rex is inside her, and she needs him to stay inside her; she clings to him, too, tightly, so tightly, still breathing, because if she does not hold on, if she stops holding on for a single second, Lavinia will sweep her out to sea.

6

LOUISE WAKES UP HAPPY.

This surprises her.

She can't remember the last time she's woken up like this: with somebody's arms around her; with somebody pressing his chest against her, or stroking her hair, or brushing her forearms softly with his fingertips. She's not sure she ever has.

Not with somebody kissing her neck. Not with somebody's lips on her shoulder. Not with this much light streaming in.

It streams through the shutters. It makes a lattice on the wall. She marvels at it, and although she's seen a thousand shadows in her life just like it this one is the one she presses her fingertips to, because she is half-asleep enough to think she can catch it.

"Morning, beautiful," he says.

It astounds Louise that he has spent the night with her—the whole night—and never once suspected the kind of person that she is.

"Want to know a secret?"

He's kissing her shoulders quickly, now, it tickles and Louise laughs without meaning to.

"What is it?"

"I don't want to get out of bed."

He blinks a lot without his glasses.

"Don't tell anyone."

"I won't," she whispers.

———

The phone rings.

Then Louise remembers.

"Shit—shit!"

"What's wrong?"

He smooths her hair back from her face. He is so sweet with her.

It's Lavinia's phone. It blasts the prelude from Wagner's *Tristan und Isolde* all through Rex's apartment.

She is afraid he will recognize it but he reaches into her purse for her and hands it over.

It's Mimi calling. Five missed calls.

Louise sends it to voicemail.

"Is everything okay?"

Lavinia has fifty-six Facebook notifications.

"Nothing." Louise turns the phone off. Louise has just killed somebody. "It's fine. Everything's fine."

"Was it . . ."

"No."

She takes a deep breath.

"Just Mimi," she says.

"Have you heard from her?"

"No."

Now he exhales.

"It's probably fine," he says. "She's probably at Mimi's. Or—you know—dancing on a table. Or in Paris. You never know."

"You never know," says Louise.

He gets up and goes to the window.

He is thinner than she expected, now that she sees him without clothes on. His chest is waxy, and a little concave. She can see his ribs. He is so handsome to her, anyway.

"So," he says. He rubs his eyes. "What do you want to do?"

"About what?"

"About Lavinia."

"What about Lavinia?"

"Do you want to talk to her, or should I?"

"About what?"

"About us."

Maybe Louise is still dreaming.

"What about us?"

You've fucked me, she thinks. *What more is there to say?*

He sits at the edge of the bed. "I mean—if we're going to keep doing this—we can't keep it a secret."

It has never occurred to Louise that Rex would want to do this more than once.

People want to fuck you, sometimes. This is natural, if you're pretty; or if you're not pretty, then at least if you're blonde. People want to fuck you once. Then they leave early for work, and tell you they'll text you in a few days, and they don't.

"You want to do this again?"

(This is not the relevant point, maybe, with a body in a bathtub uptown, but Louise can't think about that right now.)

"Don't you?"

"Of course I do," Louise says, before she can even think about what she's saying. "But—I mean—we—we *can't.*"

"Because of Lavinia?"

"Yes," Louise says. "Of course because of Lavinia."

He sighs. "Maybe, you know—maybe it won't be so bad. I mean—maybe, you know, it'll be hard, at first, but—"

She marvels at how stupid he is.

"She burned your handkerchief."

"Christ," he says. He laughs—just a little. "Of course she did."

He says it with something like admiration, and Louise hates that even now, even now, this gnaws at her.

"Look—Louise." It has been so long since someone has called her by her actual name. "I know it's selfish." He is so quiet. "How much I like you. I know that."

Instinctively, she reaches out. She puts her fingertips on the back of his neck.

"It's not selfish," she says, "to want to be happy."

It is automatic: how she does it. Touching his shoulders. Massaging them.

"I should do it," says Rex. "I'll talk to her. This is on me. I'll explain that you said no, at first, that I pursued you. I'll be the bad guy. I don't mind . . ."

"No!"

She is so loud.

"No—no, I'll talk to her. When she comes home."

"Are you sure?"

"I'm sure."

"I can wait outside?"

"I'll be fine," she says.

"Look—if you need somewhere to stay for a couple days . . ."

"What?"

"Like, if you need some space. I mean—it's a studio, you know. It isn't much. But I *do* have two sets of keys."

He kisses her knuckles, like she is precious.

That's when it hits Louise.

This part would have been true no matter what.

If she'd called him at the P.M.—in tears, hysterical—it all would have happened the exact same way. He'd have kissed her. He'd have taken her home. He'd have let her stay.

Lavinia has died for nothing.

"What is it?" Rex asks her.

Louise can't stop laughing.

The tears run down her face and still she can't stop laughing.

Louise takes the bus home from Rex's place. She wears his Columbia sweatshirt over her sequined top, her skirt. It's a long, slow route up First Avenue, but Louise doesn't mind. When Louise gets home, there will be a body in the bathtub, and, she will have to decide *how to kill Lavinia.*

It is summer. The sun is out and the sky is a deep and inimitable shade of blue and were it not for the body in the bathtub, Louise could almost be happy.

This cannot last forever.

Louise knows this.

She will have to find a way to kill Lavinia. She will have to get out of town before they realize that whatever a mugger uses to brain you isn't a sink at a Chrystie Street nightclub; she has no money, anyway—once they cancel Lavinia's cards she will have nothing, because she doesn't have Paul or GlaZam or the bar and she definitely doesn't have bottle-girl shifts at the P.M. any longer, but how much is a one-way bus ticket back to Devonshire, anyway?

She turns on Lavinia's phone.

Forty-three new Facebook Likes on the selfie of her and Mimi.

Twelve texts from Mimi. A Facebook message from Beowulf Marmont, asking her for a drink (it is, Louise notices, uncannily similar to the Facebook messages he sent *her,* asking for a drink).

An email from Cordelia about an upcoming history test at summer school.

She checks her own phone. Nothing.

Then, when the bus passes Seventy-second Street, a text from Rex:

I'll be thinking about you today, he says. Good luck. Whatever happens.

And Louise thinks: *if only, if only, if only.*

And just a small part of her thinks: *what if?*

The smell is so much worse than she expects.

She is sure that she remembered to close Lavinia's eyes, before leaving, but she is here and they are open and glassy and they stare straight up.

Louise sits on the toilet for a while, staring at the body.

She has never seen a dead body before, but she imagined it would look more like a dead body than it does. It just looks like Lavinia, only less so, like somebody has made a prop of Lavinia for a play.

She opens a private browser (she knows *Law & Order*; she knows your search history is the first thing they check).

She Googles *what do I do with a dead body*.

She doesn't really expect a useful answer, but she scrolls through the results anyway, because she can't think of what else to do.

Turns out, *Urban Foxes* did a listicle on it, once, as a joke. Turns out, there are a lot of bodies in the Gowanus Canal.

This doesn't surprise Louise, thinking about it.

Louise continues to stay very, very calm.

She runs through her options.

She has sixty-four dollars. She has a set of keys. She has a driver's license.

She has an ATM card with the PIN 1-6-1-4 and a hundred thousand dollars in it. But she cannot think about that right now.

She can leave Lavinia in a park, somewhere, late at night (she is never home; she never finds Lavinia; somebody finds Lavinia in Sheep Meadow; she comes back to Rex worried, so worried, she hasn't found her). Maybe it is a mugging. Maybe, maybe it is a suicide (maybe she is found in a paddleboat on the Lake in Central Park, like Ophelia, like she always wanted). She can leave Lavinia in an alley.

On TV, they can always tell the time of death.

Louise isn't sure how that works in real life. She Googles this, too. Apparently there's a window of a couple of hours, which means she is probably safe, but then again, you are never, ever safe.

Maybe it is better, she thinks, if they never find the body.

Another text from Mimi.

I had the best night with you last night.

Let's do it again soon!
Two capybaras holding hands.

And Louise thinks *you can't fool all the people all of the time.*
And Louise thinks *maybe you can.*

It wouldn't have to be for very long, she thinks. Just long enough for her to get a little more money together out of Lavinia's account. Just long enough for her to come up with a plan.

There is a plausible story, now: Lavinia is brokenhearted over Rex. Lavinia doesn't want to live, knowing Rex is dating somebody else. Lavinia takes too many pills. Lavinia writes a brilliant suicide note. She posts it.

Everybody misses her. Nobody is surprised.

Maybe, Louise thinks, this is exactly what Lavinia would have done, anyway. Maybe Lavinia was always supposed to die, and Louise has done nothing but help Fate along.

I had the most wonderful night with you too, darling!
Lavinia writes texts in very long and elaborate and letter-like sentences. Louise knows this.
Sorry to do an Irish goodbye I got mesmerized by the music and then instantly collapsed.
Did you have fun?

It is so easy.

Louise puts Lavinia's body into the steamer trunk.
That's the hard part.
It turns out you can't just make a person smaller by arranging them. You have to break their bones. You have to take a hammer or an axe, or if you're in an apartment like Lavinia's, an antique nineteenth-century neo-Gothic mallet that's lying over the plastered-up mantelpiece, and crush a person's elbows and

their kneecaps until they fit. The sound is a little bit like a cantaloupe. The smell is like nothing Louise has ever smelled before.

When you are done breaking their femur, their forearm, in two or three different places, they look even less like a person than they did before.

Louise will never forget the sound of snapping bones.

She spends thirty minutes with a curling iron, curling and recurling and recurling her hair.

Lavinia rents a moving van.

She wears the exact same thing she wore last time she rented a moving van, the same halter top and palazzo pants, the same scarf in her hair, the same sunglasses. She goes to the same place. She shows her ID.

Lavinia says lots of very memorable things about how she's going on a *very great adventure,* a *pèlerinage,* even, and the woman behind the counter rolls her eyes and slams down the keys, just to get Lavinia to shut up.

Lavinia posts a photograph of First Avenue, of the summer sky, of the Fifty-ninth Street Bridge. She quotes that song by Simon & Garfunkel, which is all anybody thinks about when they see that bridge, anyway. She checks in there.

Lavinia is having such a peaceful Sunday in New York.

Any news? Rex texts.

We're talking tonight, says Louise.

She heaves up the steamer trunk by one handle. She scratches those gorgeous hardwood floors, sliding it out the door.

It is almost midnight. The trunk makes so much noise on the landing, down the corridor. Louise does not understand. Lavinia is so skinny—she's paid so much attention to how skinny Lavinia is. How does a person that skinny weigh so much? The trunk scrapes the walls.

Louise almost pulls her arms out of her sockets, moving the trunk into the elevator.

Down the hall, the apartment door opens.

Mrs. Winters watches as the elevator doors close, and Louise and Lavinia descend to the ground floor.

It takes Louise thirty minutes to get Lavinia into the back of the van.

There are moments, in those thirty minutes, when Louise doesn't think she will be able to get Lavinia into the back of the van, when Louise heaves and gasps and strains. Her muscles ache and her tendons scream and still Lavinia's weight is too much for her, and Louise thinks *it is not worth it.*

She thinks *I will sit here until the police come.*

When they come I will tell them there is a body in the trunk.

They will not believe me. I will show them.

They will take me away and then at last, at last, I will sleep.

Lavinia will win, she thinks.

So what? Let Lavinia win.

She sits like this on the steamer trunk for three, four, five minutes, hugging her knees to her chest.

Lavinia's phone is buzzing in her pocket. Lavinia's perfume is all over her hands.

Lavinia cannot win.

So Louise takes a deep, deep breath.

She practices that breathing: one more time.

She heaves.

She turns herself inside out, heaving. She vomits up acid and it burns her throat and her tongue and even her lips but that doesn't make her stomach untwist.

She does not think she has ever been in so much pain before.

She gets the body into the back of the van.

———

Louise drives all the way up the FDR, along the flank of Manhattan, to where the East River meets the Harlem. She has Googled all of this. She doesn't really know what she's doing but she assumes that most people who are trying to hide a body don't really know what they are doing, either.

She drives all the way up to Swindler Cove, hedging the projects over at 201st Street, in the shadow of the Con Ed station.

Louise has not been up so high, she thinks, since she and Lavinia went to Harlem that one time because Lavinia decided she liked gospel music, but she cannot think about that right now.

They have renovated much of the park, here; but so much is still undone. There are abandoned slats of wood over the marsh, forgotten Coke cans, rotting piers that collapse into the river, one by one.

Louise waits in the van until three. Just in case.

She drives as close as she can to the water.

The funny part is that there *are* people out—one or two—men smoking joints, or on their phones. She has always been so afraid of being alone, at night, with men. Not now.

She pulls her sweatshirt over her head. She has a cigarette. She waits.

They don't even look at her.

When they go, Louise drags the trunk out of the back. It's easier, going down than up; except for the sound it makes when it hits the cement (*is that what it sounds like,* Louise wonders, *the rattling of bones?*).

She drags it by the handle all the way to the waterside. It hurts, but by now Louise has gotten used to the pain.

Then Louise does a very stupid thing.

She opens the trunk.

Lavinia's eyes are still open. They are still glassy. They are still blue.

Her hair winds all around her face, her neck, her broken limbs, like snakes. Her hair, which is long and loose and Pre-Raphaelite, and looked when Lavinia was alive like it, too, was alive, of its own will, that it would grow unfettered and strangle you if you got too close.

They say hair keeps growing after you die. Louise read that once. She doesn't know if it's true.

Louise slams the trunk shut.

She lifts the trunk, one final time, against the railing.

She lets it fall in the water. She lets the water carry it away.

By the time the current has closed over it, it's like it never even happened at all. Maybe it didn't.

It is dawn when Lavinia takes a picture of the sunrise over the East River.

> To sail beyond the sunset, and the baths
> Of all the western stars until I die.

Lavinia takes out four hundred dollars from an Inwood bodega on her way home.

Louise leaves the van parked in Inwood. She takes the subway home.

Louise makes piles of *things*. Lavinia's clothes. Hers. Lavinia's. Lavinia's. Hers. She makes piles of jewelry. She counts up all the cash in the house. Lavinia has left $450.42, in twenties and tens and crumpled dollar bills lying around and coins in the couch cushions.

She charges Lavinia's phone. Lavinia has so many more messages. She sits at Lavinia's desk. She opens Lavinia's laptop. Lavinia is signed into everything.

She checks Lavinia's email.

An invitation from Lydgate to the launch party of his new coffee table book *Sex Toys: An Illustrated Secret History*. Some links from Gavin to gossip-party stories in *The Fiddler* and a request to contribute a diary piece (*you just have the kind of narrative voice that pisses peo-*

ple off and that's great when it comes to engagement numbers). An email from her parents.

> Dear Lavinia,
>
> We are saddened to learn from your Dean that you would like to delay your return to Yale another semester. We believe that this will be detrimental to your future in the long term, and have jointly decided to cease paying to reserve your spot at the end of this academic year (2014–15). If you wish to complete your degree you will have to return in September at the very latest.
>
> We have discussed our decision with the Dean and believe it is for the best.
>
> Your sister is doing very well here and enjoying her summer school. I am sure you have heard she got a 2400 on her SATs—very proud. I think it important that you set a good example as she prepares her college applications as she is still insisting on applying to exclusively Catholic schools . . .

Louise slams the laptop closed.

Louise tries to think of where she will go, when she runs. *Anywhere but Devonshire,* she thinks.

The phone rings.

It's Rex again.

"It's good to hear your voice," he says.

Louise downloads a picture from Google Images of a sunset over a beautiful lake upstate. It's the sort of place a person would go to—say, if they'd just found out their best friend was fucking their ex, and they had the money to just pick up and go upstate.

Lavinia checks in at Beacon, New York. She posts the photo.
Rebirth, she writes.

Rex meets Louise for afternoon tea at the Hungarian Pastry Shop,
near the Columbia campus. His satchel is full of various Loeb edi-
tions. He has bags under his eyes.

"I fell asleep in a seminar today," he says. He's holding her hand.
"Isn't that something?"

Louise stirs the whipped cream into her coffee without drinking it.

"How did it go?" he asks, at last.

She shrugs.

"Lavinia, you know."

"Did she set anything on fire?" He's smiling. A little.

"No. She was calm."

"Really?" he asks. "I can't imagine that—somehow."

"I mean—quiet. Not calm. Quiet."

"You think she's okay?"

Louise holds up the keys.

Like Lavinia would ever be that magnanimous.

"She said she needed space. She's gone away for the week. Upstate."

"And then what?"

"And then . . ." Louise tries not to think about it. "And then she
comes back."

He sighs. He looks up. "Hey, Louise?"

She stirs her coffee. She smiles her slow, kind, sweet smile.

"We're not bad people, are we?"

She pats his hand. She twines her fingers in his.

"Of course not," Louise says.

"You're right," he says. "Of course you're right. I'm being stupid.
Let's do something fun. It's a beautiful day—I don't have class until
Wednesday. Let's go to a museum."

"There's always the Met." Louise thinks of places she knows a
boy who always wears tweed blazers will like. "Or the Neue Galerie—

they've got this whole Ferdinand Hodler exhibition on . . ." It costs twenty dollars to get in.

Rex doesn't say anything.

"They do good Sacher torte at the museum café." (*There is not a body underwater; there is not a trunk at the bottom of the river; there is not blood in the shower drain.*)

"Maybe—"

"What?"

She sees his face. His ears are red.

"Is it—her?"

How, she thinks, *can one person matter so much?*

"It's stupid," Rex says. "We should go—of course we can go."

"But—"

He sighs. "I've been there before."

"Okay?"

"I mean—*we've* been there before."

"What?"

"Like—it was our first date."

"Oh. *Oh.*"

"I'm sorry—that's weird—I'm being weird."

"No, *I'm* sorry. I should have—"

"It's not like you could *know!*"

Louise can't stop picturing them, the two of them, with Lavinia's long and unbrushed hair, with her rapt smile, Lavinia so radiant on his arm, Lavinia in a steamer trunk with her ankle next to her ears.

"Let's just go home," Louise says.

They cab it to Rex's place. Rex pays.

They have sex on the bed, and then again on the sofa, and then they cuddle and order Thai food and watch *The Jewel in the Crown* on Netflix. The weather is so nice outside and there is so much to do on a night like this one in New York but Lavinia has done all of those things, already, and so they just drink beer out of his fridge, because that, at least, Louise is sure that Lavinia has never done.

He is so careful when he has sex with her. He buries his face in her neck, and murmurs things between and underneath her breasts, and rests his head in the crook of her hips, and against her inner thigh.

"God," he keeps saying, "you're so beautiful."

And Louise knows she doesn't deserve it, but she thinks *just one more day like this. Just give me one more day.*

"Hey, Louise?"

He says it to her shoulder blade.

"Yes?"

"How much—on a scale of, say, one to ten—do you hate Hal?"

"Eight? Why?"

"He's having a birthday party this Saturday. Like—a hybrid birthday-Fourth of July type thing, and it's at his father's house, and there will be, you know, people there. And drinks. And food." He's leaning on one elbow. "And if it wouldn't be strange . . ." He exhales. "I told him about you. I hope that's all right."

"It's fine," says Louise. "It won't surprise him." She leans back on the pillow. "He's been giving me shit about it long enough."

"He doesn't mean it. Any of it. When you get to know him . . ."

"He's an angel?"

"You know how it is," says Rex. "He's my best friend."

"Yes," Louise says. "I know how it is."

Louise goes back to the apartment (it feels so good, so strangely good, to unlock it, to fling open the door, to switch on the light). She puts all of Lavinia's clothes back in the closet. She puts all her clothes on the shelf.

She puts on Lavinia's powder-blue dressing gown.

It smells of Lavinia's perfume.

She stares at the hole in the living room where the steamer trunk used to be.

Lavinia posts another photo from upstate.

Everybody Likes it.

Lavinia texts Mimi.

Been having a Crisis of Faith. Long story. Gone upstate to clear my head. But I miss you! LET US GO TO THE ICE CAGE AGAIN SOON yes yes yes?

Mimi responds with an emoji of a spider trying to hug you with all its arms.

Rex texts Louise a photo of the view from his window.

I miss you already, he says.

And Louise thinks *he does, he does.*

She tries not to think about his face when she asked to go to the Neue Galerie (she should have known—it was one of those places Lavinia insisted they go all the time, in Lavinia's opera cloaks, in Lavinia's furs).

She thinks: *there are so many things I should have known.*

She goes through Lavinia's drawers. She throws all of Lavinia's clothes (her lingerie, her thigh-high stockings, her silk blouses, her handkerchiefs) on the floor. She looks through Lavinia's book-shelves. She throws volume after volume on the floor. She looks under the bed, under the Persian carpet; in the little jewelry boxes on the vanity. She strips the sheets.

She claws out the desk drawers. She throws staplers and glue sticks and pens and gets ink on the duvet.

Then she finds it. A stained wood box at the back of Lavinia's bookshelf.

An envelope.

A pack of letters.

There are things it is better for a person not to know. The day and the manner of your own death, that's one, or whether or not you're going to fuck your mother and kill your father. What people say behind your back. The names somebody you love has called some-body else. There's a reason people are able to function, in this world, as social creatures, and a good part of that reason is that there are a lot of questions intelligent people don't ask.

Rex wrote Lavinia two hundred letters in four years.

Most of them are from when they were sixteen, seventeen, eighteen—before they went off to school. He wrote them with quill pens, green ink. He sealed them—the wax is still there, if broken, on some of the edges.

They are awkward. They are pretentious. They are filled with lit-erary allusions Louise already knows, many misquoted. He doesn't even write well.

They are the most beautiful letters Louise has ever read.

She tells herself she will only read one: *My dear Lavinia, what a plea-sure it was to see the Klimt exhibit at the Neue Galerie this afternoon*—she doesn't know why she's not laughing, but all she can think about is walking through the Devonshire woods with Virgil Bryce, holding his hand, smoking American Spirits, staring blankly ahead, until he turns to her and says *well if you want it so goddamn badly . . .*

I didn't know, Rex wrote to Lavinia, the night after they lost their virginities to each other in a Flatiron fleabag, *that people could feel as strongly as this.*

I'm scared, Rex tells Lavinia, the night before he went off to college, *that the real world is going to destroy us.*

I'm scared nothing in the world will ever mean as much to me as this.

Louise stays up all night, reading them.

He wrote her about the places they will go, that they will never go to, and Louise cannot see Lavinia's answers but she can imagine them—they are written on her heart, and in the lines on the palms of her hands.

I want to really live, Lavinia says, in every letter that Louise cannot read. *All I want is to live.*

She falls asleep at dawn, on Lavinia's floor, with the letters spread out in all directions: like a mandala, like a halo.

Lavinia posts a Facebook status about how much she loves the countryside.

Lavinia withdraws another five hundred dollars from her bank account, at a sketchy bodega in Inwood, near the van.

She's wearing sunglasses.

Louise gets through the week.

Lavinia is having the most wonderful time upstate. Lavinia is doing yoga. Lavinia is going to the contemporary art museum in Beacon and posting all about Louise Bourgeois's spider and how it made her think about anger in a new way. Lavinia is learning to embrace what she cannot change. Lavinia is discovering inner peace.

Louise sits in the apartment, reading letters, trying not to throw them across the room.

The night of Hal's Fourth of July party, Rex texts Louise to tell her that the party is black-tie.

Sorry, he says, Hal only just decided.

All Louise has are Lavinia's clothes.

Lavinia has so many dresses. Louise knew this already, of course, but she has never quite appreciated how many. She has never gone into Lavinia's closet and rubbed her face into the silk and the damask and the velvet of every single one. There's vintage and there's black-tie and there are elegant conservative cocktail dresses. Louise has never, ever seen Lavinia wear, short and well-tailored dresses, the kind you wear with pearls.

Louise buries herself in all of them.

Louise lays one dress out on the bed.

It still smells just like her.

She puts on Lavinia's earrings. She puts on Lavinia's shoes.

It frightens her, she thinks, looking at herself in the mirror, how much she looks like Lavinia. She has to touch her face, just to be sure.

She puts on Lavinia's foundation, and it is so strange to be the one putting it on herself, and not to have Lavinia's fingers against her skin, and not to have Lavinia wipe the pouf against her cheekbones, or over her lips, or on her chin.

She puts on the blush, and the mascara, and the eyeliner, and all these things she is so unused to doing on her own.

She puts on Lavinia's wine-dark lipstick. She puckers up. She blows a kiss to the mirror, like Lavinia is on the other side of the glass, like this is the only way to get to her.

Louise's fingers are shaking, but she gets the lipstick perfectly inside the lines, anyway.

Lavinia is reading Thoreau.

She is quoting Whitman.

She is sitting by a fireplace, somewhere.

Henry Upchurch lives in the Dakota. He is in Amagansett, now, and even though Hal has his own place in Tribeca, with this friend of his from Deerfield who works at Goldman, when Hal entertains it's always at the Dakota.

Louise has never been in a home this nice before.

The windows look straight onto the park. The ceilings are so high Louise has to crane her neck to see the chandeliers. There are crown moldings and hardwood floors and a room that is so indulgently full of nothing but books, and there is *space*—so much space to move around in, and Louise has not realized before what a luxury *space* is.

Hal has put American flags everywhere.

He has draped them on the sofas. He has hung them off the portrait frames. He has put tacky paper bunting in every doorframe. They cover every surface in the house except the three portraits along the fireplace wall.

"Jeremiah Upchurch. Henry Upchurch—the third, as it happens. Prince Hal."

Hal on the hall is wearing a bow tie. He is almost handsome.

Hal in the living room is wearing an Uncle Sam hat on top of his pink shirt, his bright-blue trousers. His bow tie has little red elephants on it, which clash violently with everything else he's wearing, his blazer with pink elbow patches. He's holding an unlit sparkler and a red-white-and-blue kazoo.

"Look at you." Hal considers her. "You almost look like you fit in."

Louise smiles.

"So, Rex finally gave in." Hal gulps from a red Solo cup. "What? It's an American tradition!"

He hands her a cup, takes a flask from his blazer pocket. "The swill's on the sideboard," he says. "Henry Upchurch's liquor cabinet is open to a very select few."

"I feel special, then."

She toasts.

"Good," he says. "You should."

"Happy birthday, Hal."

He grins. There is a gap in his two front teeth. "A quarter century," he says, "and I have accomplished exactly nothing with it. Just as God intended. The blood in the race starts to thin." He raises his glass to the portraits. "Or so they say. Can you see the resemblance?"

"I can't say I do," says Louise.

His mouth twists. He smiles. He pours more whiskey into her cup.

The sound system is playing "Dixie" on repeat.

"How about now? Wait—let's ask your boyfriend!"

Rex is in a summer suit.

"Young Louise here questions my paternity! What is it?"

Rex is looking at her so strangely and Louise wonders if this is something Lavinia has worn with him.

"Nothing," Rex says. "You look beautiful, that's all."

He takes her hand. He kisses her on the forehead in front of every-body, like he's proud to be here with her, like he wants everybody to know.

Beowulf Marmont is here; so is Gavin Mullaney; so are so many people Louise hasn't met but whom she has seen, if not at the secret bookstore then at the opera, or the MacIntyre, or the P.M., or so many other places that Lavinia's people—dispersed though they are—seem to go.

"Always a very great pleasure, Louise," says Beowulf. He kisses her on the cheek. A girl with fragile eyes sits very quietly on the couch with her hands folded, watching them. "I didn't realize you knew Hal!" He says it like she's been holding out on him.

Louise just smiles.

"How's your work for *The Fiddler* going? I did enjoy those online pieces you did, earlier this year."

"Thank you. I enjoyed writing them."

"You're not bad, you know. I mean—compared to all the tripe that's out there."

Gavin comes to greet her, too.

"You owe me a pitch, motherfucker," he says. He gives her a high five.

Everybody acts like she belongs.

Hal smokes a cigarette out the window. "Here's the thing I love about house parties," Hal says. "I hate new people. Henry Upchurch always used to say that meeting anybody new after the age of twenty-five is a waste of time." He says it winking, in case anybody thinks he means it. "I guess I'm all out of time. There's only ten people in New York—and I know you all. Everyone else is a garbage fire."

"Only five more years to make Five Under Thirty," Beowulf calls out.

"Please," Hal says. "I'm just a humble insurance executive."

Everybody laughs (and laughs. And laughs).

"I've never been inside the Dakota before," whispers an anorexically thin girl with very clearly defined brows to the girl with the fragile eyes.

Louise fakes it.

She chats with Beowulf Marmont about the opera, about all the productions that Louise has definitely, definitely, not fallen asleep through (that she definitely, definitely, has not spent getting fingered by Lavinia in a private box); about the time the donkey they use for *The Barber of Seville,* who is called Sir Gabriel, took a shit onstage, and this other time that Diana Damrau coughed.

She chats with Gavin Mullaney and the anorexic girl (who is called India) about people they know from Collegiate and St. Bernard's and Chapin and Exeter and Devonshire, of course Devonshire, which Louise knows so very well (she tells the story of the two kids who ran away like she knew them, and Gavin backs her up on what a good piece it was for *The Fiddler*), and then Louise tells a story that Lavinia told her once about this girl at Chapin who masturbated with a lacrosse stick and sent the video to her boyfriend, and how it went viral and she had to withdraw, and everybody laughs because they haven't thought about that story in years, and they're so glad to have a chance to tell it again.

"Aren't you lucky?" Hal's voice is low in her ear. "I told you—so much better to be a nonentity. You could have fucked the entire football team at Devonshire, and nobody would have any idea."

"I *wish,*" says Louise, and everybody laughs, even though, come to think of it, it's probably true.

Louise tells a story about the time the whole campus was snowed in and she (and Virgil Bryce, but she doesn't mention that part) got cross-country skis and made a couple hundred dollars selling hot coffee (and Virgil's weed, but she doesn't mention that part either) dorm door to dorm door.

Everyone laughs.

"She's amazing," Rex says. "She even got away with pretending to be a boarding-school student, once. For a whole year! Before somebody finally figured it out."

Louise rounds on him.

For a second, a horrible sickening second, she thinks he is making fun of her.

But Rex is smiling at her with such affection, and such pride, even the story as he tells it is total bullshit (it was only a couple of weeks, and only in the dining hall, and the only person to ever figure it out was her mother, because she was too afraid to talk to anybody, and her mother had been so ashamed), but everybody is laughing and acting like this is the funniest thing in the world, and even Hal is grinning between his gap teeth, so what can Louise do but cough and swallow her fear and tell the story, the most wonderful story, about the fantastic prank she pulled, and how she even attended Greek classes for a year, and how she even handed in a paper, once, and everybody thinks this is the funniest thing in the world, and also that she is very brave.

Rex puts his arm around her, and kisses her on the cheek, and nobody seems to acknowledge that this means that she hadn't gone to the academy, after all.

Louise goes to the bathroom.

She reapplies her lipstick. She puts on more powder.

She checks Lavinia's phone.

Eleven Facebook messages. Most from Mimi. Thirteen Likes.

A text from Cordelia: where have you been?

Sorry darling! Been having an existential crisis. Things mad. Will write soon!

Lavinia posts a photo of an American flag, flying from a very beautiful colonial house one could very easily think was a charming country inn, where a girl whose best friend fucked her ex might go to get away, for a little while.

She writes: All the past we leave behind;

We debouch upon a newer, mightier world, varied world,
Fresh and strong the world we seize, world of labor and the
march,
Pioneers! O pioneers!
Within a minute, Beowulf Marmont Likes it.

Everyone inside is drunk on sideboard wine, except for Hal, who has
been refilling his flask all evening.

"Christ," Hal says. "How cliché."

"What is it?" India was telling everybody how much better barre is
for your ass than spinning.

"*Fresh and strong the world we seize!*" Hal rolls his eyes. "*World of
labor and the march.* Wow. Such labor." He snorts. "Try coal mining."
He flashes the phone to everybody, so everybody can see.

"Don't," says Rex. He says it very quietly.

"*Pioneers—o, pioneers,* did you dodge a bullet or what?"

Rex doesn't say anything. He has gone very pale. He chews on his
lower lip.

"How'd she take it?" Hal's looking right at Louise now. "When
you told her. Was there a catfight? Did you get naked?"

"She's out of town right now," Louise says. "She's taking a break."

Hal laughs. "Exile. How precious. Diddums. I'd watch your back,
young Louise—she might stick a knife in your ribs while you sleep."

Louise laughs like she can still see straight.

"I mean—you might get lucky. Maybe she'll swallow a fistful of
Mommy Williams's Xanax again!" He blows into his kazoo. "Lock
up all the razor blades. Don't let her near water."

Louise's gorge rises, and she thinks she is going to be sick—she *will*
be sick; she thinks she's going to get hysterical—she will, she *will*—
except Rex is the one to jump to his feet.

Rex is the one to bolt.

That, at least, gives Louise an excuse to go after him.

———

She finds him in one of the bedrooms—a single Spartan bed in the middle of an enormous floor, a frayed rocking horse, boarding-school flags from Devonshire and Andover and Deerfield on a cork-board on the wall.

He's smoking a joint out the window.

"You know." Rex stares so blankly out the window. "I think we really *are* bad people."

"No—no!"

"I shouldn't have kissed you. I'm the worst—I shouldn't have done that."

"It's fine! You're fine!"

"If something happens to her," he says, "if she—Christ—*whatever happens to her,* it's my fault."

"It's not," Louise tries. "I promise you—"

"You don't understand!" It is the first time Rex has ever raised his voice to her. "You don't get it—how long have you known her, what? Half a year?" He exhales so slowly. "She's not your problem—she's mine! You can't just—make that go away because you want to." He puts out the joint on Hal's desk. "I'm sorry," he says. "I'm sorry—this isn't fair to you. None of it is."

"She'll be fine!" Louise puts her hands on his shoulders. She buries her lips in the back of his neck. She takes a deep breath. "I promise—I *promise.* She'll be fine." She forces herself to smile. She forces her heart to stop beating the way it beats. "Things will go back to normal," she says.

He clings to her hand so tightly. He presses it to his shoulder. He looks up at her so gratefully, like she's made this true, just by saying it.

They go back inside. They smile. They toast.

Beowulf Marmont's big-eyed girlfriend breaks a champagne glass, and immediately Rex says "I'll fix it" while Hal just stands there, and then Hal starts laughing.

"That's what they're going to call your biography when you die,"
Hal says. "*I'll Fix It: The Rex Eliot Story.*"

"Nobody's going to write my biography," says Rex, from the floor.

"Probably not," says Hal. "Nor mine, either. Or maybe they will.
Being the life and opinions of a humble insurance executive." He shrugs.
"Oh well. When the revolution comes, nobody will be reading books,
anyway."

He clears his throat.

"We'll burn them all for firewood," he says. "Won't we, young
Louise?"

Louise holds his gaze. "Of course," she says, and raises a glass.

Now they're drinking more champagne. Now they're turning up the
music. Now they're playing *pin the tail on the donkey* with a novelty
set where the donkey is a Democrat and all the pins are flags. Now
they're doing lines off the coffee table, and drinking punch Hal tells
everybody has molly in it although Louise isn't sure.

"What do you want for your birthday, Hal?" asks India.

"A blow job."

Everybody laughs along with him.

"You're disgusting," says India, but she's smiling.

"As it happens," says Hal, "I want absolutely nothing. A true man
severs all attachments."

"Is that what Henry Upchurch says?"

Louise doesn't mean to be cruel. But Hal's mouth twitches,
and he makes a strange little grimace, and then he smiles and he
laughs, which gives everybody else permission to laugh, too, and he
says "That's exactly what Henry Upchurch says" and then he says
"Christ, you're a bitch," but he says it so affectionately, and Gavin
Mullaney claps her on the shoulder and India mimes the dropping
of the microphone and even Rex shrugs helplessly as if to say *is she
wrong?* and everybody is laughing and taking photographs and telling Louise that she's *won the evening* and, in a sense, she has.

———

Now they drink even more. Now Hal proposes a toast that begins "and let us now praise famous men." Now they put on old-school swing-dance music because Hal thinks they should all listen to "Brother, Can You Spare a Dime?" and meditate on its significance for the American manufacturing industry, and Rex lifts Louise high into the air, and Hal catches her legs, and everybody thinks it's hilarious to carry Louise aloft between the drawing room and the library and the kitchen, so she can grab a bottle of Henry Upchurch's hidden, very nice whiskey from the kitchen and pour a whole bunch of it down her throat.

Now Beowulf Marmont is posting a picture of Louise to Facebook.

In it, she sits with Rex on the sofa, under portraits of all the Upchurch men. Rex is kissing her cheek.

Everybody Likes it.

Rex Likes it, too, even though he's sitting right next to her, and when he does Louise looks up at him and he smiles at her and Louise smiles back.

By dawn, everybody except Louise has fallen asleep on Henry Upchurch's couches, even Hal, even though he took a bunch of his modafinil that night, just to stay awake.

Louise flips through the photos on her phone.

She doesn't recognize herself in that dress, that lipstick, happy in the arms of a man who loves her. Borne aloft without Lavinia even there to hold her hand.

Like she belongs.

You cannot do this forever, she thinks.

But when Rex is asleep, and Hal is asleep with India nuzzled up to him and facing into his chest, and Beowulf Marmont is asleep with the fragile-eyed girl's arms slung over his waist, and everyone else is on the floor, Louise slips on her shoes. She goes downstairs, she nods at the doorman, and she walks outside into the barely break-ing dawn.

She calls Rex from Lavinia's phone.

It goes to voicemail, just as she knew it would.

"Darling," Lavinia says, in that light, affected way of hers. Her voice is shaking. "It's—it's been grand, hasn't it?" She swallows. "You're probably asleep right now—maybe—maybe *she's* there. I suppose she's there. That's fine. I mean—" A deep, sincere breath. "I mean: I wanted you to know. I'm fine. Lulu told me everything. And—well, I suppose I raged a bit and set a fire or two but I want you to know—I—I've decided. I—I've got no interest in doing that, now. So—well. I want you to be happy. I've decided that. You and Lulu—both of you. I love you—don't think I don't. I love you both. And I want the best for both of you. Only—you'll understand, won't you? If I prefer not to see you for some time. Anyway. Anyway. Goodbye. I love you. Goodbye."

It's the happiest ending, Louise tells herself, *that she ever would have had.*

7

She posts photographs of sunrises over the East River, of morning skies, of birds in Central Park. She uses ClassPass every single day (you can tell this because the app uploads it to Facebook, when she goes), mostly to go to different iterations of yoga class, and from time to time she uploads a picture of her ever-leaner body—always with her tattoo visible—although you generally cannot see her face. She posts pictures of healthy meals (they are mostly green; many of them are juice). She posts one status about how she's going to give up drinking for a month or two, just to get healthy, just to prove to herself that she can. She updates her friends on her progress every day with an inspirational quote or two.

Nearly everybody Lavinia knows Likes it.

"I'm really proud of her," Louise says, when people ask, which is not as often as you might think, given how many people Liked it. "Of course, I miss her at parties. But I think she's doing the right thing, don't you?"

There are lots of places that Lavinia goes that you'd know about: if you look at Facebook (if you follow the paper trail). She takes out cash two or three times a week, always her max. If you were ever to go look at the camera footage, for whatever reason, you would always see a very beautiful girl in vintage clothes and sunglasses and wine-dark lips get cash out at the ATM. She goes every morning to her ClassPass classes, like every other rich blonde white girl in New York City nobody ever scrutinizes too closely, and the record of this attendance, too, is synchronized with the app and goes on Facebook. She goes to brunch, sometimes, and to bars where she orders seltzer (you cannot be too careful) and always, always, pays with a credit card, and always, always, leaves a memorable tip. She texts Mimi, from time to time, to say I miss you let's hang out soon, and Mimi always says—immediately!—yes, when? but there's always a scheduling conflict, and they say next week and then never make concrete plans.

If you found her on Facebook, too, you'd know she made so many new, wonderful friends, many of whose profiles are locked or whose photographs are blurry, but who frequently check in with her at vegan bars or health-food spas or meditation centers on Jefferson Avenue in Bushwick and post long, thoughtful comments on her wall about how good it was to see her the other night, and how they can't wait to hang out again soon!

There are the photos of her on Facebook, too.

These are, admittedly, not as frequent as they once were (Photoshop, it turns out, is actually very difficult to learn), and a lot of photos are blurry or vague, or involve her turned away from the camera at a distance while in a very elaborate costume (you can ascribe that to a natural flair for drama; even sober Lavinia wears the same clothes drunk Lavinia always did). But they come at intervals, and when they come everybody Likes them, and comments on how great she's been looking lately.

Lavinia tells her parents she is doing very well, too.

Dear Mother and Father (she writes),
I hope you're well. You're right. I think I'll be ready to go back to school, soon. My novel is almost finished. If there's any way I could have just a little more time, I'd love to be able to

complete it and submit it to agents and I'm happy to supply pages of a sample chapter to show you to give you confidence in my abilities and dedication (Louise hopes Lavinia won't have to do this, but she's prepared to make it happen if she does).

Lavinia points out very cleverly that a large gap on her collegiate CV will be much better explained by a sold novel than by nothing at all.

This seems to mollify them. They tell her she can have one more semester, but that's all.

They tell her Paris is very pleasant, this time of year.

They remind her, vaguely but firmly, not to embarrass them at parties. They hope she's not wearing any of her ridiculous clothes again. They remind her how beautiful she is—too beautiful, they say, to waste *that* body and *that* hair and *that* face on outlandish and grotesque creations that will only have other people mocking her.

They remind her how important it is for her to be a good influence on Cordelia.

After all, they do not say directly, but heavily imply, Cordelia still has a future.

Sure, there are challenges.

Like the fact that Louise can only leave the house very early in the morning, or very late at night—times Mrs. Winters, or any other less-perspicacious neighbors would be less likely to open the door, or look down the hall. Lavinia has taken to ordering from Seamless with her credit card—a different restaurant every time—and opening her door just a crack for the delivery guy when he comes. Like the fact that a few times a week Louise has to take selfies where her face isn't visible, and that means spending several hours with the curling iron, wrapping her hair into tiny strands around her fingertips and setting them so that they look long and savage and untamed. Like the texts Louise has to keep sending—to Mimi, to Cordelia—keeping things so wonderfully vague, coming up with such bohemian and adventurous reasons why she doesn't want to come to Paris for the tail end of summer, or to Cordelia's starring role in *Antigone* up at Exeter in September, or to this amazing taxidermy-and-wax museum hidden in a Brooklyn cinema that Mimi wants to go to in October. Or the time the pipe bursts, and Louise stays up all night to fix it herself, with instructions she has found on Google, so that Lavinia will not have to call the super.

But Louise meets every single challenge.

She tells herself, at first, that this arrangement is only temporary. She saves almost all of the money she takes out of Lavinia's account. She buys a fake ID from a bodega near NYU that gives her name as Elizabeth Glass (*twenty-three*) and has a photo of a middling-pretty white girl with red hair she could almost look like, and keeps it, along with a duffel bag and a change of clothes, at the foot of her bed, for the day that everything goes wrong. But here's the thing: that day doesn't come.

In fact, Louise has never been better.

She is writing for *The Fiddler* again (she has so much free time to write, now that she does not have to worry about teaching, or ghostwriting, or tending bar, now that she takes so much of Lavinia's money). She writes book reviews and essays about Devonshire. Gavin talks her into writing about the time she faked being a student, because it was such a hit at Hal's birthday, and she does, and everybody on the Internet thinks it's hilarious, too. And then she starts writing for print because after Hal's party Louise goes with Gavin to India's birthday at Soho House and that's where she meets the print editor who is actually India's father, as it happens, and he gives her his card and says "email me, sometime." She is writing for both *The New Misandrist* and *Misandry!*, even though the editors don't speak. She writes a short story about an art thief who steals a painting but becomes convinced it's a forgery, which is an idea she and Lavinia talked about, one time, while blasting Wagner, and Louise can't remember whether it was she or Lavinia who came up with the idea, or maybe both of them, but she supposes it doesn't really matter now. She sends this short story to a literary magazine called *The Egret,* where Beowulf Marmont interns.

She tries not to think of the nights she and Lavinia decided to cowrite on the divan; the nights Lavinia grabbed her wrist and said "we will be *great,* Louise, *both of us*" and Louise said *yes, yes,* and believed it.

Louise starts reviewing opera for *The Fiddler,* because she asks Gavin if she can, and so she gets free press tickets.

Sometimes, it's like Lavinia isn't even dead.

Sometimes, Louise forgets.

Sometimes, in Rex's arms, with Rex kissing her and inventing new, sweet names for her, Louise lets herself believe that everything Lavinia posts is true.

Now Lavinia is reading Edna St. Vincent Millay, she thinks.

Now she is making chocolate-hazelnut-coconut-saffron tea and spilling it.

Now she is out with her wonderful friends, not-drinking at a wonderful party.

Now she is smiling: that beautiful and world-destroying smile.

Louise can see it when she closes her eyes.

In the mornings, if Rex doesn't have class, they go to Mud down the street for breakfast and eat enormous plates of eggs and hold hands and talk about their plans for the day. Louise invents some SAT clients and they walk through Tompkins Square Park and point out all the dogs they think are adorable and Rex talks about what he's studying. She spends at least four nights a week at his place (of course, he can never come to hers), and she frames it as *giving Lavinia space* but the funny thing, or maybe not the funny thing but the thing that shakes her most, is that he believes her.

———

There's just one little thing.

Rex never mentions the voicemail.

In fact, he never brings up Lavinia again.

Louise goes to great syntactical lengths to avoid saying her name, and often says things like *oh, you know* when describing her day. Rex never asks.

She thinks that it is so strange he would *not* mention it, after how guilty he has felt, even though sometimes she tries to bring up the subject without bringing up Lavinia. "Getting closure is so *good*, don't you think," she says, after she tells the actually-very-funny story of this guy who ghosted her, once, only for her to stand him up at Prospect Park two years later, and he smiles and nods and squeezes her hand but doesn't say what she wants him to.

Come to think of it: the only time Lavinia comes up at all is when Louise is riffling through her purse, one night, and the keys fall out.

"She let you have them?"

The way he says *she* frightens her, a little, because it's so reverential. Even now.

"She finally copied me a set," Louise says, like it's nothing, like Lavinia is just an ordinary normal slightly flawed somewhat-neurotic human being who has gone to a lot of therapy, lately, and who cannot hurt them.

There's another thing, too. Also very small.

Rex has unblocked Lavinia on Facebook.

He hasn't friended her, but he shows up on the People You May Know sidebar, which means he's taken her off his banned list, so she could see him, and add him, if she wants to.

She doesn't want to.

Louise isn't jealous. She doesn't need to be. She and Rex are so happy. She is the perfect girlfriend. She knows because she has read every single letter Rex has ever written Lavinia that Rex loves picnics, and they have gone on so many picnics that summer, and in September, too. She knows that he loves jazz and so they have gone to the Jazz Age Lawn Party, and to Zinc Bar in the West Village every couple of weeks. She knows he loves Korean food and she surprises him for his birthday in October by taking him to this wonderful high-end place in Hell's Kitchen. She even pays, even though the place is very expensive—she *insists* on paying—in cash, as it happens, because it has been so long and Louise thinks probably she will not have to run tomorrow, or this week, or the next.

She tries not to think too much about the expression on his face when she asked him to go to the Neue Galerie with her, or the way he looked at her when she came to Hal's party, wearing Lavinia's dress.

It's just that sometimes—not often, just sometimes—Rex will do something or say something that makes Louise wonder if he is still thinking about her. He'll say something idle—like at the Chelsea Market, one time, he mentioned he liked peach jam—and then Louise will get to thinking (because she has read every letter he has ever written) that he and Lavinia once had peach jam at a French café called Bergamot in Chelsea, sometime, and Louise will wonder whether right now, with his hand in hers and his mouth on her cheek or forehead or shoulder, he is thinking about her.

Like this one time, in early autumn.

It's a beautiful Sunday in October and Rex has just started the second year of his degree. They are sitting in Rex's apartment, and they are being boring (they have already had sex, and drank beer, and watched *The Third Man* on Netflix), and Rex is looking out the window and half-working on a seminar essay, and Louise is flipping idly through records for something to put on.

They listen to classical music, because Rex likes classical music, and Louise has started to appreciate it, too.

They listen to *La Traviata* and Berlioz and Chopin. Louise does the dishes in Rex's sink. Louise wipes their take-out kimchi off his kitchenette counter.

She isn't even thinking about Lavinia. If she lets herself think she lets herself think only of Lavinia the way everyone else thinks of Lavinia (into her fourth month of sobriety, now, getting really into the mystical writings of Simone Weil). She is so good at not thinking about what she has done.

So when the music comes on, and it is slow and dark and mournful and romantic, and there are those sustained three notes which sound a little like a wail, Louise thinks at first that the song sounds familiar without remembering what song it is, and even when she realizes, slowly, more certain with each bar, that it is Liszt's third *Liebestraum,* she does not panic. The piano stumbles higher, and lower, and softer, and darker, and Louise does not think *Rex and Lavinia lost their virginity to each other in a Flatiron motel, thinking about this song* (or maybe, maybe, maybe she does), but she doesn't think it out loud until she sees Rex's face.

He is very, very pale. He is biting his lip.

He looks, Louise thinks, like he has seen a ghost.

"Hey, Louise?"

He does such a good job pretending it doesn't bother him. Louise can see right through him.

"Do you mind turning that off?"

"Sure," says Louise.

She stands in the kitchen doorway. She watches his face. She watches him fidget and stare down at his laptop and his Loeb copy of *Medea* and then look up again at the speaker and turn paler, and even though Louise feels the adrenaline so sharp in her she thinks she may never sleep again, she doesn't move.

She feels a strange, sick power in not moving. She feels like she's proving something to him.

"For Christ's sake!"

It is the only time Rex has ever been annoyed with her.

"What is it?"

"Nothing. Nothing. It's just—I'm trying to work, okay?"

Louise is impeccably swift, sailing to the speakers.

"Okay," she says. She kills the music.

Of course, Rex does not love Lavinia. Rex has spent so much time not loving Lavinia, escaping Lavinia, moving on from Lavinia.

That is precisely why he has chosen Lavinia's roommate, who has nothing to do with Lavinia, to love.

"Thank you," says Rex, when the music stops.

He kisses her forehead.

"You're wonderful," he says, and she says, "You too."

You'd be surprised how easy it is for time to go by: just like this. When you don't work, except for your pieces for *The Fiddler* and *The Egret* and the various iterations of *Misandry!* When you spend your nights holding someone. When you take early morning fitness classes in the name of the girl you've killed.

Except that you know, you know the thing about Louise. It's this: she always, always, fucks it up.

Here is how:

Louise uses Lavinia's credit card, sometimes. You know that part. She goes to the places Lavinia goes and makes her presence known, there, in Lavinia's clothes (just in case), in makeup, in sunglasses.

But one night in December Louise gets lazy. She is tired and she wants a drink and she is upset because Rex has asked her to watch *Brideshead Revisited* even though he must know Lavinia well enough to know how much she loved it, and so instead of going to a vegan bar or a place that does very expensive tea Louise goes to Bemelmans, again, to wait until it's late enough that she doesn't have to worry about Mrs. Winters seeing her come in, and slides Lavinia's credit card to Timmy (it has been four months, remember, and nobody has even noticed that Lavinia is dead, so maybe, maybe, nobody cares at all).

Louise sits alone at Bemelmans. She drinks a glass of prosecco, and then another. She wears Lavinia's 1940s dress, the little black crepe one, the one she wears with a little '40s velvet bolero with gold embroidery on it and angular shoulder pads, and a black wicker fascinator with a daffodil on it, and Lavinia's burgundy lipstick, which looks so beautiful on her, and also Lavinia's perfume—even though there isn't an alibi in the world that necessitates smelling like a dead person, even though the bottle is running out. She drinks until she's drunk enough to face going home.

"Well, *hunny*." Athena flings a white fur coat over a barstool. "Fancy seeing *yew* here."

She sidles in next to her without even asking.

"It's been a *million fucking years*." She leaves a smear of foundation on Louise's cheek where she kisses her.

Louise stammers something vague.

"You here with *her*?"

"I wish!" Louise shrugs, like shrugging is an easy thing to do (to be fair, it has gotten so much easier, with time). "Now she says she's not drinking until the New Year."

"Jesus Christ—I'd *die*! I hope you told her to drink at the MacIntyre party."

"Maybe she'll make an exception," Louise says.

"Jesus, look at you—fuck—you look so skinny I'm worried about you!"

"Thank you," says Louise.

"My life's shit," says Athena. She orders them a round. "I dated this guy a couple months. Turns out—he's shorter than me! Can you believe that?"

"I mean—"

"Men," announces Athena. "They're all the same. Every last one."

Then the bartender brings the bill back.

"Williams?" he says, as he slides the card back across the table.

Now, Louise thinks. *The world is ending now.*

———

Athena and Louise look at each other. They look down at the card, which is black and has LAVINIA WILLIAMS branded on it.

Athena is smirking.

"Well," she says.

"I can explain—"

"Aren't *you* clever?"

Stay calm, Louise tells herself. *You can get through this, too.* She always, always does.

"Actually," Louise says, cocking her head at Timmy (she doesn't look at Athena). "Why don't we have two more?"

She slides the card back across the table.

"Let's make it Taittinger," she says.

Athena smiles so broadly she gets lipstick on her teeth.

"Look at *you*," she says.

"Hey." Louise downs her glass, the way Athena downs hers, without grimacing. "Lavinia's not using it." She toasts when the champagne comes. "I told you. She's off the sauce. She goes to bed at eight."

Athena snorts.

"You know," she says. "You'd better be careful. She'll notice—sooner or later."

"You think she checks her statements?"

"Her parents might."

"It's not my fault," says Louise, very calmly. "She keeps losing her wallet. If I didn't hold on to her cards she'd leave them at every bar in town. Just the other night, she left her Amex at Apotheke."

"Even sober?" Athena raises an eyebrow.

"Exactly," Louise says. "Even sober." She raises her glass. "To the girls who hustle," she says to Athena. "Enjoy."

Athena tilts the entire glass right into her mouth.

"To the girls who hustle," she says.

"Which reminds me," Louise says. "You wanted to go to the opera, didn't you?"

Athena's smile spreads across her face.

"I'm going with Rex and Hal tomorrow. We have an extra ticket" (they don't, but Louise has a credit card). "Hal needs a date."

"Of course he does," says Athena. "His mouth is weird. And he's retarded."

"You don't want to go?"

"I'll be there," says Athena.

Louise swallows as she asks for the bill.

Louise pays.

She thinks *now is the time for you to run.* There is no way, she thinks, she can keep this up any longer (if they start to worry they will trace the cards; Athena will talk; she will *always* talk). But her print piece in *The Fiddler* is coming out so soon, and Gavin has been talking about inviting her to the Five Under Thirty benefit that's every winter, and there's a Halloween party happening at the MacIntyre Louise wants to go to and also Rex has gotten them a reservation at Babbo and also has texted her to tell her he misses her because he hates not spending every single night by her side.

Just a few more days, Louise thinks. *That's all.*

A last-minute orchestra seat to *Carmen* costs $260. Louise pays it, anyway.

Lavinia posts an extended meditation on her yoga poses: just in case.

Rex and Louise and Athena and Hal go to the opera.

They meet at Boulud Sud, an hour before curtain. Athena sticks her hand straight out when she meets Hal and shakes his hand so hard he grimaces.

"I'm Nathalie," she says, and grins.

She doesn't even speak with her New York accent, when she says it.

Louise doesn't think she's ever heard Athena's real name before.

"Pleasure," says Hal. He does a double take. "Have we met before?"

(They have, actually; she was performing at the P.M., but Athena is wearing so much less makeup, now, and so many more clothes.)

"So, Hal?" Athena orders a bottle of champagne before anyone can say anything.

"You got any phobias?"

"*What?*"

"Like—heights or snakes or something?"

She leans her chin on her hand. She stares straight at Hal.

Hal shrugs. "I don't like the Eurostar," says Hal. "Going underground for too long dehumanizes a man. It makes us into animals."

"What do you think of the subway?"

"I don't take the subway."

Athena brays.

"All I'm afraid of is the two *D*s," she says. "Death and death."

"You're a charmer," says Hal.

It's almost nice, Louise thinks, to exchange the kind of looks she exchanges with Rex, that night. Like the two of them are in on a secret.

Rose photographs the four of them that night for *Last Night at the Met.*

In the photo, they're standing together, four abreast, on the grand stairs, and all four of them look beautiful.

Louise knows the mezzo now. She has seen this Leonora do Rosina in *The Barber of Seville.* She knows when to say *bravo,* and *brava,* and *bravi.*

Her hand is in Rex's hand. Her hair tumbles over his shoulder. The music is so beautiful, and so dark, and so sad, and every time it swells Louise wonders whether he is thinking of the time he has heard it before.

Afterward they go back to Henry Upchurch's apartment in the Dakota, because Hal wants them all to try this very special whiskey

Henry Upchurch bought once, which Louise is reasonably certain Henry Upchurch wouldn't want them to drink.

"You really should meet him, sometime," Hal says to Louise, as they all gather under the portraits. "He'd love you. He loves bootstrap stories. He was the great chronicler of bootstrap stories. I mean—other *people's* bootstraps, but still." He grins. "It'd be good for you, young Louise—if you're going to stick to this whole writing thing."

Athena gives Louise a significant look.

"Well, look at *you*," she murmurs.

She downs the whiskey like it's meant for a shot glass. "Nice place you have here, Hal."

"I know," says Hal.

The four of them drink so much. They drink Hal's whiskey and Henry's whiskey and also scotch and also gin because the drunker they get, the sloppier they are, and even though they're not celebrating anything in particular and even though they're not drinking to forget anything in particular, somehow they get so drunk that Athena lets on that she performs onstage, sometimes, and then Hal leaps to his feet.

"That's where I know you." He grins. "Fuck it—I knew I recognized you. I've seen your tits."

Louise gasps.

"The P.M., right?"

"Fuck, no," says Athena. "I don't work there anymore. Fuckers tried to stiff me on tips."

She pours herself another drink.

Hal just laughs.

Rex and Louise laugh, too.

Hal brings out the modafinil at three, so that they can stay up late. Hal shows them all photographs he's taken on his phone of dinner parties he's attended, the labels on the bottles of wine.

No people. Just wine.

"I'm going to ask out India," he says, to nobody in particular. "I'm going to invite her to Miami, next week." He puts his feet up on the coffee table.

"Look at you," says Rex. "Getting serious."

"Please," Hal says. "I never want to get married." He crushes another pill and snorts it.

There is snot dripping out of his nose where he has snorted. He doesn't wipe it.

"Do you know what I want in a wife?"

He turns to Athena. He puts his arm around her.

"We will discuss the morning paper and the children's education and absolutely nothing else. How does that sound?"

Snot is still trickling so slowly out of his nose.

Rex takes a handkerchief out of his breast pocket. Hal ignores it. He lights an enormous Cuban cigar and blows smoke in Louise's face.

"Also, she should have a patrician nose. The Upchurches are very big on patrician noses. Jeremiah Upchurch's wife—a fine woman, a Havemeyer—had the most delicate, upturned nose—look!" He waves the cigar at another, smaller portrait. "The age of eugenics is upon us." He goes to the stereo. He puts on Wagner. It's *Tristan.*

"I love this part," he says, and maybe it's the wine or maybe it's the whiskey or maybe it's the modafinil they've been snorting but Louise thinks *everything we do we have done before.*

For the first time, Louise is almost bored.

There is nothing, nothing, Louise thinks, *that does not belong to her.*

Then it is four.

"Fuck," Hal says. "*Fuck!* Everybody needs to shut the fuck up!"

"What ate your ass?" Athena is puffing on Hal's cigar.

"It's three in Beijing."

"What?"

"In the afternoon—Christ." Hal clears his throat very ostentatiously. "I have a work call." He plugs in his cell phone. "My boss is a Very Great Man. His name is Octavius Idyllwild."

Athena snorts.

"Maybe you've heard of him."

"Sure," says Athena.

"He lives between New York and the Cotswolds. He has a classic car collection. He and his wife are the same age—can you imagine that?" He starts dialing. "Listen."

Louise and Rex sit, and Athena sits, and they listen to Hal talk to Octavius Idyllwild about spreadsheets, and at first Louise thinks this is whatever Hal's sense of humor is, and they're all supposed to laugh at Hal performing Hal, but it's only when ten minutes have gone by and they're all still listening in silence to an elderly and very posh British man talking about compliance regulations on speaker, and Hal has shown no signs of stopping, that Louise realizes he isn't in on the joke.

"Don't trust Alex Elias with the numbers," Hal says. "He's fucking incompetent, and he should know better than to think he isn't."

Hal's grinning at them, and winking, and pointing at the phone like they're all supposed to applaud him.

They all stare right back at him.

"Henry," says Octavius Idyllwild. "Language."

"There's nothing worse than an incompetent fucking underling," Hal says. "Nothing at all."

He winks at Louise again.

"Language, Henry."

Hal hangs up the phone.

"Will you look at that," Hal says. Dawn is breaking out the window. "Men like that—I swear." He snorts. "Don't mind me. I'm just your ordinary bro."

He turns to Athena.

"I want nothing in this life," he says. "Isn't that wonderful?" He puts his hand on her knee. "Just a beautiful woman and a nice glass of whiskey and some Nazis on the radio. That's all."

Rex and Louise exchange looks.

"I'm not like Rex," Hal says. "Rex is a romantic. Women *love* Rex. Just look at those big brown eyes—aren't they adorable? Don't you just adore him?"

Athena shrugs. She shows all her teeth.

Hal goes on: "Not me. I know what I am. I'm . . . a Stoic. I don't feel anything." He thumps his chest, just to make this clearer. "What do you think, sweetheart? Which would you prefer?"

He leans in real close to Athena.

"You're not the woman I'm going to marry," he says. "But you're better than a blow job on Tinder."

Athena slaps him.

It's such a forceful, astounding blow that Hal staggers back; he drops the whiskey and the tumbler spills all over Henry Upchurch's perfectly upholstered cream-colored sofa, all over Henry Upchurch's Oriental rug.

"Fuck," Hal says.

"Fuck—fuck—fuck!"

He has gone white.

"Mother*fuckers*!" He throws the empty glass clear across the room.

It hits the fireplace and shatters.

"What the fuck is wrong with you?"

He gets in Athena's face. For a second, Louise thinks he is going to hit her.

"What the absolute fucking *fuck* is wrong with you?"

"Hal!"

Rex is already on it. Rex is touching Hal's shoulder so lightly, like he knows what to do, like he has done this all already.

"Didn't your *pimp* ever fucking teach you anything?"

When Athena stands up, she's taller than he is.

"Don't you know how to behave in *other people's houses*?"

The snot is still dripping from his nose.

Also, he's crying.

"I'm out of here," says Athena. She says it very quietly.

She says it *out of,* without her accent, and it is the first time Louise has ever clocked that the accent is not real.

She turns to Louise. She kisses her on the cheek.

"Next time," she whispers. "Just give me cash."

She takes the rest of the bottle when she goes.

Hal is on his hands and knees on the floor, rubbing so hard the suede flakes.

Rex is helping him.

"Don't touch it," Hal keeps saying. "Fuck you, Rex—don't touch it—you're making it worse."

Louise knows what to do.

Louise gets the white wine from Henry Upchurch's sideboard. She gets salt.

"For fuck's sake—she *was* a whore, wasn't she?"

Louise doesn't say anything. Louise scrubs.

"I'm not the asshole here!"

Louise gets the stain out.

When she does, Hal smiles like nothing has even happened.

"See?" he says. "That's why you need a woman. They know things. You're so lucky, Rex, to have a woman like this."

He sits back down on the sofa. He puts his feet back up on the coffee table.

"I wasn't *really* angry," Hal says. "Actually—I was *performing* anger."

Nobody says anything.

"It's important for a man to perform anger, sometimes. So people know they can't get away with things."

Louise puts the dirty paper towels in the sink.

"You know, I did her a favor," Hal says. "Next time—she's going to spill something on something *actually* priceless. If she's not care-

ful. Now she knows better. Now she can bag herself a rich husband."
He chuckles to himself. "I call it *broblesse oblige*." He nods at Louise.
"You know how it works, don't you, young Lulu?" He pats the stain
where she has cleaned it.

Louise flushes.

She looks over at Rex—waiting for him to say something, to
object, to defend her. But Rex only smiles a sad, soft smile.

"You're going to make a very good wife one day," says Hal.

"Thank you," says Louise.

Louise and Rex take the elevator down, together. It is morning.

She does not know why she is so angry at him.

"What is it?"

He puts his arm around her. He kisses her head. She recoils without meaning to.

"What's wrong?"

She exhales so slowly.

"He shouldn't have said that to her," Louise says, as they walk
down Central Park West.

She doesn't even know why she's defending Athena. She doesn't
even like Athena. Athena has just blackmailed her.

She is angry, anyway.

"It's Hal," says Rex. "What can you do?"

"He called her a whore!"

"He was joking—you know how he is."

"I do know! He's an asshole!"

"You have to get to know him." Then: "You don't just go around
slapping people."

"Why not?"

"I—" Rex sighs. "People just don't do such things."

"Lavinia would!"

Louise doesn't mean to say that, either.

She hasn't said Lavinia's name out loud in so long.

It feels good, strangely, to say it.

Rex looks like she's hit him.

"I'm sorry," Louise says. "I'm sorry, I didn't mean—"

How stupid are you, she thinks, *to make him think of her right now.*

"You're right," Rex says. He says it like it chokes him. "She would."

He hails a cab. He doesn't invite her in it.

"When you get home, tell her." He swallows. "Tell her I say hi."

He leaves her alone on the street as the cab drives away.

Louise walks home through Central Park.

And Louise thinks: *if Lavinia were here, we would laugh at everybody*—at Rex and his cowardice, at Athena with the lipstick on her teeth and her disappearing accent and her *two Ds, death and death,* at Hal ("a mental Habsburg!" Lavinia had called him), just like the night at the High Line, where they set everything on fire, where they shouted names, when they were gods.

Louise hates how much she misses her, sometimes.

Louise and Rex make up, via text, but it's one of those stopgap let's not fight about this texts that nobody feels good about sending *or* receiving, and Rex has finals for this semester so he's pretty booked up that week, and Louise is almost relieved.

She doesn't do a lot that week.

She gets up early to go to 6 a.m. ClassPass classes—yoga, strength training, barre. She peers down the hall. She avoids Mrs. Winters.

Or she doesn't get up at all and stays in bed, answering Lavinia's emails, telling Cordelia not to worry about AP Latin because she's so clever she'll pass with flying colors, anyway, and that she's sorry she won't make it to Paris for Christmas break, either, but she hopes Cordelia has a wonderful time and enjoys the stained glass in all the Gothic churches on the Left Bank, around St.-Germain.

Or she reads and rereads Rex's letters, in bed, in Lavinia's powder-blue dressing gown (Rex writes about this, too; one time, he tells Lavinia how beautiful she looks in it).

Or she answers the calls of her own parents. They're proud of how beautiful she looks, and how thin. They tell her they photocopied the *Fiddler* piece that ran in print and Louise's mother took it to book club, and Louise's mother grunts and says, "Everybody's real surprised."

Still, Louise's mother reminds her, she can't do this forever. At some point she should probably come home, before it's too late to start over.

"You're almost thirty," Louise's mother says, and reminds her that her fertility will soon decline.

Athena sends her a text that week.

Hey hunny, she says.

Turns out I'm a little short on rent this month.

I know you've got such a good thing going maybe you can Venmo me like $200 maybe?

Just to help a friend out!

Xxx

Louise does.

A few days later Louise runs out of Lavinia's perfume.

She tells herself that she needs it. She can't leave anything to chance.

So she goes down to the East Village, one night, to East Fourth Street (she thinks about calling Rex, asking to come over, but that is a thing desperate, clingy girlfriends do and Louise is neither of those things), to the little fragrance shop where Lavinia keeps her recipe, which she has named Sehnsucht, on file.

The woman behind the counter shuffles through a stack of index cards, down to the Ws.

"Wilson?"

"Williams."

She takes out the card. She gathers up the oils: lavender, tobacco, fig, pear. She mixes them.

They are so much stronger, here, than they are at the bottom of Lavinia's vial—aged, distilled. Every jar is overpowering.

"Give me your hand," the woman says, because the whole point of the fragrance shop is that you're supposed to mix them on your skin. She dabs droplets of oils against Louise's wrist, shakes the mixture and then rolls it against Louise's palm, and then her neck, and when she does this the smell is so overpowering that for a second Louise thinks that this has all been a trick, that Lavinia must be behind her, with her hand on Louise's hand and the MORE POETRY!!! tattoo against hers. She has not realized until now how strongly it smells, and how she must have been smelling it all the time. Maybe now she is just inventing it, but Louise bursts into tears in the middle of the store. The woman puts down the beakers and the eyedroppers and asks if she should call a doctor, and it is all Louise can do to shake her head, and close her eyes, and sob.

She doesn't call Rex that night.

She is afraid to go home until she is sure Mrs. Winters is asleep, so instead she walks all the way home up First Avenue, and tries not to think about the fact that this, too, is something she and Lavinia used to do.

She doesn't leave the house the next day. She locks the doors. She starts drinking at noon. She has worked her way through most of Lavinia's liquor cabinets, by now, but there is some cheap gin left, and Louise drinks that, straight. She is hungry but she doesn't even order in because now she is afraid to open the door. She is drunk and loses track of what time it is (she was supposed to write a piece for *The Egret* today, but she hasn't done that, either).

It's dark. That's all Louise knows. It's dark outside and she hasn't even bothered to turn the house lights on. She hasn't even bothered to turn Lavinia's phone on. It's easier to pretend it doesn't exist.

It's dark outside and then the buzzer goes off.

Louise ignores it.

If it's someone else's delivery guy, or a package guy, a Con Ed guy, or any other kind of guy, really, he'll go away eventually.

The buzzer sounds again.

"Jesus Christ."

Again. Again. Again.

She goes to the video screen.

It's Mimi.

Her hair is unbrushed. Her lipstick's smudged. She's sobbing.

"Lavinia!" she's shouting into the intercom. "Lavinia—please, please, *let me in*!"

It's eight o'clock at night. Prime time for neighbors to come and go.

"*Lavinia!*" Mimi screams.

"*Fuck.*"

Louise lets her in.

Mimi is even worse up close.

Her mascara is all over her face.

"I'm sorry," she sniffles. "I've been calling for hours—I can't get through."

"Lavinia's not here," says Louise. "I'm sorry."

"Out with her cool new friends, huh?"

"Yes," says Louise.

"Can—" Mimi swallows. "Can I come in anyway?"

She hops from one foot to the other. Her fishnets are torn.

She makes too much of a spectacle in the hallway.

"Sure," Louise says.

It's Beowulf Marmont.

Mimi has been sleeping with him since the night of the *Roméo et Juliette* premiere, when he took her home, even though she was passed out, and had sex with her ("I mean," she says, so brightly, "if I *were* conscious I would have had sex with him, anyway, so it's not like I didn't consent!"). He'd write her the sweetest texts. At Burning Man, Mimi explains, they even gave him the playa name "Hemingway," that's how good a writer people thought he was. He's dating the girl with the fragile eyes, and he'd been up-front with her about that, which was so good of him all things considered, but, he'd said, it's like that Fitzgerald quote, what was it, *he climbs highest who climbs alone,* and Beowulf Marmont had an Alpine peak to scale. If anyone was at his side, he'd said, it should be someone like Mimi—someone smart, who was beautiful in that rare, feminine way.

"It was stupid," Mimi says. "I'm stupid."

"You're not stupid," Louise says.

Mimi is getting mascara all over the couch cushions.

Louise has poured her ginger-turmeric-pineapple-champagne tea. Mimi drinks it with shaking hands.

"He didn't mean it."

Louise doesn't know whether Mimi means *he did not mean I was special* or *he did not mean to fuck me while I was unconscious* but she nods, anyway, and rubs Mimi's back while she cries.

"I don't know why I keep doing this," says Mimi.

Louise sighs.

"You don't have to," Louise says. "You don't have to put up with it—from anyone."

"Why not?" Mimi says, and Louise doesn't really have an answer for her.

Mimi swallows. Hard.

"I know what everybody thinks of me." She wipes her eyes with the back of her hand. "But what's the alternative? *Not* loving the people you love?" She laughs a little. "Is that really what we're supposed to do?"

"I don't know," says Louise.

"I thought, you know, that there was something beautiful in

being the one left behind. Isn't that how the poem goes? *Let the more loving one be me*? That's not how it works here, is it? Whoever cares least, wins." Mimi gulps. "*Does* she care about me?"

Her eyes are so wide, and they are glassy with tears.

Louise has the strangest compulsion to hold her.

"No," Louise says. "Probably not."

Mimi blinks.

"What?"

"Lavinia doesn't care about anybody," says Louise. "That's why everybody who loves her, loves her."

"She cares about *you*."

"Lavinia cares about Lavinia," Louise says. "That's all." She tries to find some kindness in that. "You deserve somebody who cares about you," she says. "You deserve somebody who treats you like you treat them."

"So does everybody," says Mimi. She shrugs. "I'm not, you know, *added value*. I don't *optimize anyone's experience*—Gavin told me that, once. That I wasn't optimizing Lavinia's experience, and that's why she didn't want me around. I'm sure he thought he was being helpful. Gavin usually thinks he's being helpful." She takes another sip of tea and laughs. "I'm not like you, Lulu" (nobody has called her Lulu in so long). "I'm not smart. I'm not a brilliant writer."

"*I'm* not a brilliant writer."

"But you are!" Mimi spills a little bit of tea into the saucer. "Believe me—I *wanted* you not to be. I remember when your first piece for *The Fiddler* came out I bookmarked it just so I could hate-read it. I thought I could at least enjoy you being bad at something. But that piece about the runaways—it was beautiful! And the one you wrote for *The New Misandrist* about polyamorous men—I loved that one."

"You read it?"

Louise cannot remember Lavinia reading a single one of her stories.

"I read everything you write."

Mimi is beaming.

"I even put a Google Alert on your name," Mimi says, "so I can read them as soon as they go up. Sorry. That probably makes me a stalker."

It probably does, but Louise doesn't mind.

"Do you think you'd ever write a novel?"

"I don't know."

"Because I'd read it. If you ever did. I bet it would get published, too."

"I don't know about that."

"Oh, it would!"

And the way Mimi's looking at Louise, with such wild surety, with such dog-like love, is exactly like Louise once looked at Lavinia, and Louise doesn't know whether or not this means that Mimi is lying, now, or whether Louise was telling the truth, then, but didn't know it.

"You're a better writer than Beowulf Marmont," says Mimi. She finishes her tea. "I'm not saying that because he raped me. It's true, either way."

"Come on," says Louise. She slams the cup down on the saucer. "Let me buy you a drink."

"Really?"

"Really. Let's have one of *those nights.* Okay?"

Mimi's smile spreads like honey. "Okay."

Louise suggests that they go to this swing-dance night over in Hell's Kitchen, because she remembers how much Mimi loves to dance and truth be told she hasn't danced in ages, not since Lavinia, and *Urban Foxes* has an article in this week's edition about a bar themed after the London Underground during the Blitz where they serve cocktails in repurposed pea cans, but Mimi doesn't want to go near Times Square, not so soon after the Paris attacks, and so Louise takes Mimi down the block, to a boxy little gay piano saloon called

Brandy's halfway down a Yorkville side street, where they have wood paneling and ten-dollar well drinks and the guy at the piano plays Frank Sinatra. A stark and lonely sadness has branched into Louise's spine tonight and she wants to be somewhere where there are other people singing.

They sneak out of the apartment.

"It's like we're secret agents," Mimi whispers, when Louise explains about the co-op board, and then: "I remember. We used to have to sneak me all the time."

They take a selfie outside the bar.

Out with my girl, Mimi captions it.

Two dancing bears dancing with each other.

Brandy's isn't really a Lavinia place. It's not elegant or exciting. The only interesting thing that happens to them is that when the waiter pours Mimi and Louise two glasses of house wine there's a little left over in the bottle, and the waiter tells them they can have it for free if they drink it straight from the neck, and everybody applauds them when Mimi does.

"Do you miss her?" Mimi asks. "I mean—with her new friends. Her sober friends." Mimi laughs. "Her *successful*, sober friends."

"All the time," Louise says.

"So do I," says Mimi. She downs a little more wine. "Only—"

"What?"

"Sometimes, like—it's like a *relief*, sometimes, you know, I miss her so much. But at least, you know, I don't have to try so fucking hard anymore." She orders another glass of wine. "I remember, when we were friends, I was so scared she'd figure out I was just, like, this nobody. That she might as well have, like, drawn my name out of a hat. If we hadn't been at the same audition . . ."

"*Audition?*"

"She was an actress, when we met." Mimi grins. "She didn't tell you that, did she? Before she was a writer. She'd taken time off from Yale to pursue her *stage career.*"

In the corner the pianist is singing "A Nightingale Sang in Berkeley Square."

"Who was I to her? A fat failed actress? Every time we went out, we had an adventure, I thought: *tonight's going to be the night she gets sick of me.* And now I have nothing left to be afraid of, I guess."

Another round. Another toast.

"I didn't care about the money. She made you feel so *special.* Until she didn't. I mean—as long as you played the *game,* right?"

"Right," says Louise.

"It's stupid. Sometimes I still feel that way—I mean, no offense. But I feel, sometimes, if I'd just, like, done better, been *better,* she'd have let me stay. If I'd just—played the game."

She starts to giggle.

"Of course, the funny thing," Mimi says. "Is she's the one who fucked it up."

"What do you mean?"

"No!" Mimi clasps a hand over her mouth. "I can't."

"What is it."

"She'd *kill* me."

"I promise you," says Louise. "I'll never, *ever,* tell another living soul."

"It's awful." Mimi's laugh sounds like little hummingbird noises in her mouth. "God—it's so embarrassing. I can't even."

"Say it."

Mimi takes a deep breath. "Okay. So you know—you know Lavinia's big thing about Rex?"

Louise just stares at her a second.

"Of course—of course you do. But I mean, before. Lavinia's whole thing—*I've never had sex with another man.*"

"I remember."

"I mean—there's a lot of loopholes, there. If you think it through."

"You mean—"

"I think that's why she liked us—sometimes. Maybe that's mean. I mean—I think that's an awful thing to say. But—I did wonder, sometimes. If she just uses us to, you know—fill a need, so that she never had to be, like, the person who wasn't so special and so wonderful and so magical and *so in love* that she *never let another man fuck her,* again."

"The two of you—"

"I don't know," says Mimi. "I don't know what you call it. Maybe it was sex. For me, it was sex. But—I mean—I haven't been *straight* since I was twelve. For her—maybe it wasn't."

Louise hates that she's a little bit jealous, even now.

"But—that's not it. I mean—that's not the reason she threw me out. God—she'd have done it indefinitely, I think. As long as I gave her what she wanted. I shouldn't be telling you this, Lulu; I'm *such a bad friend.*" She says it like she relishes it.

"No, you're not," Louise says.

Louise pours Mimi more wine.

"I was working at this bar in Alphabet City. And I had the same shifts, all the time. And Lavinia—she knew them. And one night, I drank too much with this bachelor party that came in and made me do shots, and I started feeling really sick to my stomach and so the bartender sent me home early. You promise you won't tell her I told you?"

"Cross my heart."

"I walked in on her," says Mimi. "On—both of them."

"Who?"

"It's really gross."

"*Tell me who,* Mimi."

"Hal Upchurch."

Louise spits out her drink.

Louise tries to imagine him—his sweat and the snot dripping down his nose and the gaps in his teeth and the smile so much wider than his face—on top of Lavinia, and can't.

"But that's not it," says Mimi. "I mean—that wasn't the worst part." She buries her face in her hands. "Jesus—I'm the worst friend in the world."

"Believe me," says Louise. "You're not."

Mimi takes a deep breath.

"He was..." She bursts into hysterical, tearful giggles. "He was..." She swallows a glass of red wine in one gulp.

"He was fucking her in the ass."

She devolves into a series of helpless giggles, which somewhere along the line turn into sobs.

Louise was not expecting that.

"Wow," says Louise, because really there is nothing else to say.

"I know..." Mimi can barely breathe she's cry-laughing so hard. *"I know."* She swallows her phlegm. "So I guess, like, *technically,* she's only had *vaginal* sex with one man!"

Louise can't help it.

She starts laughing, too.

"I didn't even *care,*" Mimi hiccups, when at last they can breathe again. "I mean—I was jealous, of course I was jealous, but I *knew* she was straight, deep down. I knew—I'm not dumb. And he was single and she was single and, I mean—*what does it matter?* I didn't care how he fucked her. I just loved her."

And Mimi starts to cry again, and laugh some more, and also hiccup, and tell the whole horrible story about opening the door and walking in and then pretending she hadn't, slamming the door and running to her room and turning up her headphones as high as they would go, and never mentioning it again. Never asking *why* even though of course she had so many questions: like *really* and *do you love him* and *is this to piss off Rex* and *this is probably to piss off Rex, isn't it.* Mimi was so good, *so good,* for a whole week after even though Lavinia shouted at her so much more than normal, and made her go to so many more parties than normal, and got angry at Mimi for having gained five pounds and not being able to fit into that taffeta-princess dress Louise wore at *Roméo et Juliette* one time. This gets Mimi to thinking about Beowulf Marmont again and this, too, makes her cry, and anyway, anyway, Mimi got a little drunk one night and felt a little too free, and a little too safe, and a little too loved, and she asked Lavinia, point blank, what the hell was up with Hal Upchurch, anyway. Lavinia didn't even look up—*she didn't even look at me*—but everything warm and fecund and flickering inside her crumpled into ash and she told Mimi to get her things and get out and never come back.

The pianist passes around the tip jar and Louise puts a twenty in, just another one of Lavinia's twenties she's supposed to be saving for when she finally runs.

Then the pianist tells everybody it's open mic night and asks for volunteers.

"You know," Mimi murmurs. "I came to New York to go onto Broadway. Isn't that so funny?"

The world is so full of so many desperate, unhappy, guilty people. All Louise wants is for one person to have something good happen to them tonight and so she says *Mimi you should volunteer* and Mimi laughs and sighs and blushes and says *no I can't I lost my voice years ago.* Louise grabs her hand and holds it up and waves and cries out *over here over here,* and even though Mimi's blushing and cringing she is so delighted. The crowd collectively drags Mimi up onto the little platform that constitutes a stage.

They play "New York, New York." (They always play "New York, New York," Lavinia used to say, but Lavinia loved the song so much and the city so much that she never got sick of it, not even once.) Nothing in this city changes, and every party is the same, and every bar is the same and every Friday night is just like the Friday night that came before it, and the same photographers take the same pictures of the same people at the opera and the same passwords open the same speakeasies like skeleton keys and every single fucking piano bar in the whole fucking city plays "New York, New York" at the end of the night.

Mimi sings it, anyway.

Here's the thing you never knew about Mimi:

She's good.

Mimi's not *good-for-an-amateur,* or *good-for-New-Hampshire,* or even *good-enough-to-make-the-chorus-maybe.* Mimi is the kind of good that makes every single person who is laughing and drinking and taking photos stop and put down their phones and stare.

If I can make it there, she sings, and when she sings it's raw and when she sings her mascara runs with her sweat and for the first time Louise realizes that Mimi is beautiful.

When she sings *I'll make it anywhere* it's like she's tearing her throat apart, and everybody is clapping their hands and screaming her name because *that* is how good she is.

When she finishes, she gets a standing ovation. Even the waiters whoop her.

She looks over at Louise, across the bar, her eyes shining with tears, and even though nobody is done cheering her on Mimi tears across the bar and throws her arms around Louise and says, over and over, *thank you, thank you* and then *I'm sorry, I sniffled on your shirt* and Louise keeps saying *you're okay, you're okay, I got you.*

"This is the best night of my life!" Mimi breathes, and she is so happy and right now all Louise wants is to say *come home with me;* all Louise wants is to make Mimi cardamom-cranberry-cinnamon-elderflower tea and sit with her on the divan and play classical music so loud Mrs. Winters knocks on the door to complain, or fall asleep with her in Lavinia's oversized bed, under that enormous, fur-lined jacquard bedspread, or just *talk,* in that endless up-all-night nobody-will-judge-you way. But of course Louise can't, because Lavinia is *at home* (she has checked in on Facebook at this goddess consciousness group in the East Village but it is past midnight and she is probably home by now) and also because Louise can never be truly honest with anybody ever again.

"You're so *nice*," Mimi says. "You're so *nice*, Lulu. Why weren't we friends?" She grins. "We should hang out sometime."

"That'd be nice."

Mimi stumbles onto Second Avenue.

"I love you, Lulu."

Louise hails her a cab.

She gives her sixty dollars in cash for the fare, because Mimi lives all the way out in Flatbush, because Mimi never has any money.

"I can't—"

Louise closes the car door before Mimi can give it back.

The cab rolls on toward Flatbush.

Louise can't do this anymore.

Anything would be better than faking pictures on Lavinia's phone or Googling motivational quotes just vaguely literary enough for Lavinia to use; anything would be better than sending cryptic, cheery texts to Beowulf Marmont and Gavin Mullaney and chipper, studious emails to Cordelia and Lavinia's parents and hiding from Mrs. Winters and humoring Hal Upchurch and sending Venmo payments to Athena and trying not to make Rex remember her and panicking every time the newspapers report somebody found a body in the East River and pretending to Mimi's face that Lavinia is still alive.

Louise calls Rex, even though it's after midnight, even though he's probably asleep, even though she's not one of those clingy girl-friends who calls her boyfriend after midnight. She lets the phone ring through.

"I need you," she says. "I need to talk to you—*please!*"

"Are you okay?" (She wonders if he is hesitating.)

"I need you," she says again. "Come over."

"But—"

"She's not there."

And Rex says, "*Of course; of course; don't worry; I'll be there.*"

She wants him so badly with her. She wants him in her. She wants him to hold her and stop her shaking and listen to her sobs and her sins, and understand all that she has done and left undone, and maybe then somebody will know her and love her at the same time.

Louise fumbles with her keys in the lobby. She doesn't even remember to look out for Mrs. Winters on the stairs.

The stairs have never seemed so tall before.

She clomps up the stairs—she makes so much noise (*let that old bitch open her door,* she thinks; *just let them come*).

The light is already on.

The door is already open.

Lavinia is sitting on the divan.

Her hair is long and savage. Her feet are tucked under her thighs. She is wearing her dressing gown.

Louise drops her keys in the doorway.

Of course, she thinks, through the wine, through the adrenaline, through all her sleepless nights, *nobody ever really dies.*

Lavinia turns toward her slowly.

They have the same cheekbones. They have the same brilliant blue eyes.

"I've come to see my sister," Cordelia says.

8

LOUISE PICKS UP HER KEYS. She walks inside. She sits down next to Cordelia on the divan.

"I'm sorry," she says. Her voice is not her own. "Lavinia isn't here."

"Where is she?" Cordelia lifts her chin.

"She went away," Louise says. "With some friends."

"Away where?"

"She didn't give me details. Like—a road trip." She thinks so quickly. "A kind of, like, meditation thing. They were going to drive out west."

"When did she leave?"

Louise tries to remember the last thing Lavinia posted on Instagram.

"Just today," she says.

"What friends?"

"Nerissa. Jade—Jade Wasserman. Holly Hornbach." They all have Facebook accounts, too.

"Did you meet them?"

"When?"

"Before she left?"

Cordelia doesn't move.

"A couple of times. Why?"

"Has she been taking her meds?"

"What?"

"Her meds—has she been taking them?"

"How should I know?"

"I went into the bathroom cabinet," says Cordelia. "I'm sorry. I don't mean to be rude—coming in like this. But you see—she hasn't been taking my calls."

"You know Lavinia," Louise says, so lightly. "She can be—"

"Of course I know Lavinia." Cordelia is very calm. "She's my sister."

Cordelia gets up. She goes to the liquor cabinet.

Louise is so numb.

"You've gone through a lot of booze," Cordelia says. She turns around. "I thought Vinny wasn't drinking."

"Oh—she's not. That's all me." That part, at least, is true.

"You shouldn't drink around her," says Cordelia. "Not if she's trying to quit."

"I mean that was from before."

"Why did she quit drinking?"

"She—" Louise decides this is not the best time to bring up the fact that she's fucking Rex. "I think she wanted to make, you know, a clean break. With her past."

"The bottle in the medicine cabinet's still full," she says. "I thought you should know. The prescription's old. She hasn't been taking them. You didn't notice?"

"She seems fine. She's doing a lot of yoga."

"With Nerissa? And Holly? And Jade?"

"Yes."

Cordelia looks up.

"Don't lie to me," Cordelia says.

Louise can't move.

"You think I can't tell when you're lying to me?"

They even have the same glare.

"I was there—remember? The first time this happened."

"The—what?"

"Thanksgiving. 2012. She was—you know—*fine*, then, too. Told everyone she was absolutely at peace with what had happened. She got into astrology—spells, Wicca, tarot cards, that was the big thing. Said the cards had predicted Rex would leave her but that one day when they'd done all the growing up they were going to do they'd get back together. She used to insist on telling my fortune, too. She got into painting. She'd post all sorts of her art online—tell me she was *fine*, back at school, excited to start dating again—she even told me there was someone she thought she might like to date, some TA of hers." Cordelia lifts her chin. "Then she swallowed a bunch of pills over Christmas and tried to kill herself in a boat. So if you're protecting her," Cordelia says. "You're doing a very stupid thing."

"Do your parents know you're here?"

"I'm supposed to be on a flight from Boston to Paris, tomorrow for Christmas. Mother's *very excited* to have at least one of us back." Cordelia's mouth twists into a smile. "Instead I got on a bus from South Station and came here. A homeless man showed me his Johnson outside Port Authority. It was disgusting." She shrugs. "Vinny needs me."

"You need to call your parents," says Louise.

"It wouldn't be fair to them. They've already got one fuckup. That's bad luck. But two looks like carelessness." She kicks off her shoes. "When's Vinny getting back?"

"I don't know," says Louise. "She didn't say."

"Then I'll wait here until she does."

"You really need to call your parents."

"Why?"

Louise gets up, goes to the phone.

"I told them I was invited to Aspen last-minute with some friends from Exeter. They'll like that. You won't tell them I'm here, will you?" She smiles again. "And I won't tell them *you're* here." She cocks her head. "And what happened to Granny's steamer trunk?"

"Lavinia took it to use for some photo shoot she was doing."

"Did she?" Cordelia looks up.

She swings her legs around. She stands.

"You're sure you don't know when she'll be back!"

"I told you—she didn't say. She just said she was going on a road trip—that's all!"

"And you *let* her go!"

Louise doesn't understand.

"Christ—how stupid are you?" Cordelia spins around so quickly the bottles on the sideboard rattle where her dressing gown has whipped them. "Don't you get it? She can't be left alone."

Louise doesn't say anything.

Cordelia draws in breath so sharply.

"I'm sorry," Cordelia says. "I'm sorry—that wasn't fair of me." She sits down on the divan again. She folds her hands in her lap. "She's not your problem," she says. "She's mine. But if she's drinking—I mean, if she's *lying*—I want you to tell me."

"I understand," says Louise.

"*Is* she drinking?"

"No," Louise says. "Not that I've seen."

Cordelia exhales. She closes her eyes.

"Good," she says.

Then: "But she *could* be?"

"All she ever tells me," Louise says. "Is that she wants to stop that kind of life. That she wants to be different."

"But you don't know these *new* friends?"

"Only in passing."

Cordelia nods.

"You know," Louise says, "how Lavinia is—when she's found new people."

Cordelia has softened, just a little bit. "She collects people. Like stray cats." She laughs. "She used to say I was the only one who ever stuck with her."

She goes to the kitchenette. She starts making tea.

"Do you want some?"

"No, thank you," says Louise.

She is so tired, all of a sudden.

"You should have water," Cordelia says.

"I'm fine."

"You've been drinking. You should have some water."

Louise sighs.

"Look," she says. "Lavinia's all right, okay? She's doing well. I know—I've seen her. She's happy. She's—getting over her issues. So—you don't have to stay. She'll—she'll be gone a couple weeks, anyway; there'd be no point."

"But I'm *here*."

"Look, I can rent a car tomorrow. What time's your flight? I can drive you to Logan."

"That's very kind," Cordelia says. "But I don't want you to. I'm going to stay here." She sits down. "I don't want to go to Paris. After all," she says, "this *is* my house."

That's when the buzzer rings.

That's when Louise remembers.

Cordelia goes to the intercom before Louise can think of a good lie.

They watch Rex pacing on the video screen. He is out of breath, disheveled. His blazer is wrinkled, like he's picked it off the floor.

"Bloody hell," says Cordelia.

Then she starts to grin. "I *knew* it."

"What?"

"I knew it!"

She starts to laugh, and it sounds so much like Lavinia's laugh that Louise starts to shiver, just a little. "Of *course* he's come back—I always knew he would—of course he loved her. It was just—it was just—*cowardice*!" She spits the word.

Louise doesn't think she's ever seen someone so happy. She doesn't think even Lavinia could be this happy.

"I can't wait to see the look on his face—"

"Wait!"

It's too late. Cordelia has already buzzed him in.

"If I were a man." Cordelia is pacing. "*Gosh,* if I were a man. I'd—I'd sock him in the jaw for what he did to her."

"It's not like—"

"He ruined her life! He's a miserable, cowardly, sniveling *blackguard*!" She draws herself up to her full height.

"Please," she says. "Vinny's honor is at stake."

She opens the door.

Here's what happens next:

Rex sees Cordelia.

Louise sees him start, because she sees him thinking the exact same thing she thought, seeing that long hair and those wild eyes and those dark, heart-shaped lips—and he goes so pale, for a second, the way people go pale in books when they have seen a ghost, and Louise hates that a person (not a ghost, not a femme fatale, just an ordinary twenty-three-year-old girl) can have that effect on somebody.

Then he gets it.

"*Cordelia?*"

"You're too late."

Cordelia is enjoying this so much.

"*What?*"

Louise catches his eye, behind Cordelia's back, and she shoots him such a desperate, plaintive look, and mouths *please, please.*

"Vinny. She's gone. She's run away. You can't see her."

"I . . . *what?*"

"She's on a road trip. She's gone out west. On an adventure."

"Okay . . ."

"*I'm so sorry,*" Louise says, in such a burlesque of sincerity she thinks Cordelia must be able to see through it, "*I know you're here to see Lavinia. She's out of town.*"

"You should be ashamed of yourself." Cordelia crosses her arms. "Showing up here—after all this time."

Rex just blinks.

"She's moved on. She's over you. She'd never stoop to *lower* herself to your kind again!"

Rex looks over to Louise, who keeps just mouthing *please, please.*

"I'm sorry." He speaks very, very slowly. "You're—you're right, Cordelia."

"Vinny's not interested in your bourgeois, boring, Biedermeier little life." Cordelia spits it. "She's doing *far* more interesting things, now. She's on—she's on Route Sixty-one, right now!"

"Right." Rex's ears have turned red. He's staring straight at Louise. "Right—I can go . . ."

"Don't you *dare* ever come back!"

"You're right," says Rex. "I won't."

He turns and leaves without even looking at Louise.

When they at last see him storm out on the intercom screen, Cordelia bursts into laughter.

"Did you *see* that?"

"I saw it."

"The look on his face!"

Cordelia locks the door. She rounds on Louise. She is radiant.

"God—I can't *wait* to tell Vinny!" She claps a hand over her mouth. "Promise—promise you'll let me tell her, okay?"

"I promise."

Louise's head is spinning.

"I knew it—I *knew it*! Nobody—nobody could ever forget Vinny!" Cordelia kicks up her feet where the steamer trunk used to be. "Nobody!" She lies down on the divan. "Ordinary people—you know! People like Rex. They can't handle her." She sits up on her heels again. "I know my sister's a lot, sometimes. She's silly and frivolous and vain and she thinks about herself too much. But she's not *selfish*, not really."

"Oh?"

"If Vinny was really selfish she'd make herself happy. And—Vinny's never happy. Not really. She can't be—not so long as the world is the way it is." She hugs her knees to her chest. "It's original sin, you know?"

"I don't understand."

"You're like Vinny." Cordelia smiles a little bit. "She hates when I say things like that to her. They give her the creeps, she says. But I think it's the only way to explain everything. Everything's our own fault—and also nothing is." She sighs. "Of *course* he couldn't be enough for her. And still—*what if he had been?*" She absentmindedly starts to braid her hair. "Anyway," she says. "That's why I'm Catholic. That—and Mother hates it."

Louise texts Rex while Cordelia is in the bathroom.

I'm so so so so so sorry.

I'll explain tomorrow.

She'll come up with something tomorrow. Louise always comes up with something.

Can I come over so we can talk about it?

Rex Reads it.

He doesn't answer.

It's three o'clock in the morning before Cordelia at last yawns.

"You're right," she says, so suddenly. "I'm sure I'm worrying for nothing. Vinny's—fine, right?"

"Of course she's fine," says Louise.

"She'd tell us—if things were getting bad again."

"Of course she would."

"The last time . . ." Cordelia puts her chin on her knees. "I *knew*—before. She started getting manic. She'd do card readings for herself and stay up all night trying to work them out and call home from Yale predicting her own death."

"I promise you," Louise says. "Lavinia's getting better. She's—" She tries so hard. "She's even over the Rex thing."

"She'll *never* get over the *Rex thing*. She'll cling to that until the day she dies. Vinny wants to be the sort of person who only loves once." She drinks the tea she has made. "Even if it makes her very unhappy." She rises. "I should let you sleep. I suppose she's not coming back tonight, so there's no point worrying."

"Text her in the morning," Louise says. "I'm sure she'll be so sorry to miss you."

By then, Lavinia will have posted so many photos of her road trip. She will have posted so many, splendid photos. Louise will have worked out the whole itinerary. She'll have Googled the relevant literary quotes.

"Hey, Louise?"

Cordelia stands in the doorway.

"Yes?"

"You'd tell me—if you were worried. Right?"

She looks on Louise with such a pure and unblinking gaze. Like she trusts her.

"Of course," says Louise.

"I suppose you've been sleeping in my room," says Cordelia. "Would it be easier if I just slept in Vinny's bed?"

Louise has slept in Lavinia's bed every night she has not slept with Rex.

"No—please," says Louise. "Take your own room. I insist."

"But won't you have to move all your stuff?"

"You're right," says Louise. "It's just—Lavinia left it a bit of a wreck."

Cordelia giggles.

"She is a bit messy, isn't she?"

"Let me just clean it up a little for you," Louise says.

Louise goes into Lavinia's room. She makes the bed. She takes everything incriminating—the fake ID, the cash, the jewelry Louise has been selling, bit by bit, Rex's letters—and shoves it all into a messenger bag.

Louise checks her phone. Rex still hasn't texted her.

She checks Lavinia's phone.

The missed calls from Mimi, from Cordelia.

That photo she posted of the High Line, yesterday, has gotten twenty-six Likes.

"All yours," Louise says.

Louise goes back into her old room, which is so much smaller than she remembered.

Lavinia posts some photos from her road trip. A car (the license plates are not displayed). Some more Whitman. A sunset over a forest that could be anywhere (some Thoreau). A woman doing yoga from a distance who could be Holly, or Nerissa, or Jade (Louise finally decides that this is Nerissa and tags her accordingly). Lavinia posts a long and rambling meditation about *sitting well in order* and *striking the sounding furrows* and *all the western stars until she dies,* and maybe it is in keeping with who Lavinia is that she has posted that quote so many times before.

Lavinia texts her sister.

DARLING.

Lulu told me you're in town.

I'm so sorry I wish I'd known but you see we're having the most marvelous time out here and we want to see if we can make it all the way to California by hitchhiking (I have long relied on the kindness of strangers).

GO TO PARIS and bring me back some Mariages Freres tea please. I like the Marco Polo best.

Xxx

Cordelia Reads it.

She doesn't respond, either.

Rex finally texts Louise the next morning.

Come over after class, he says; she does.

She explains how Lavinia went off on this hitchhiking-Bob-Dylandiamonds-and-rust road trip without telling her beforehand, and left her alone in the apartment that's not even hers, and how Louise was so angry and so foolish—*I don't even know why I was upset*—that she freaked out and called Rex and won't he forgive her for that?

"Girl stuff," Louise says. "That's all."

Also, Lavinia hasn't told Cordelia about the two of them.

Cordelia is so fragile, Louise says, and so ferociously protective of her sister. She has no idea why Lavinia hasn't just told Cordelia the truth but she feels like it's not her place to do it, because she doesn't want to come between the two of them, either. The important thing is that they convince Cordelia to go see her parents in Paris because they can't have a seventeen-year-old girl just wandering around the apartment pretending to be in Aspen because if Louise gets her upset she can just tell her parents that Louise is living there, which, of course, she's not supposed to be doing.

"So you see," Louise says—so desperately.

"That's insane," says Rex. He's right.

"It's complicated."

"I don't see why you don't just move out," he says, like there's a person in this city who wouldn't live with Goebbels if it meant free rent.

"It's *complicated*," Louise says again.

"Look," he says. "I know—the two of you—have your shit. And I don't want to know what it is. It's between the two of you. But don't make me part of this."

He says it like Lavinia isn't dead because of him.

"I just don't want to cause any more drama," says Louise.

"Well, you've done a great fucking job of that!"

Louise hates it when he raises his voice at her.

She puts her hands on his shoulders. She kisses him.

"It's just for a little while," she says. "Just—to keep the peace."

"So, what? I pretend I'm still in love with her to keep some *kid* happy?"

"You don't have to pretend anything," she says. "We just lay low.

Until we can convince her to go home. So I don't have to live with somebody who hates me."

She waits for him to say *stay with me*. He doesn't.

"And what happens when Cordelia tells *her* I've been *pining*." He doesn't even say her name. Not even now. "Do I keep the peace then, too?"

She tries so hard to come up with a way this can sound less bad than it is.

"But you're not." Louise can't stop herself. "Are you?"

He rolls his eyes.

"It's always about her, isn't it?" he says.

He doesn't say *no*, though.

Lavinia roasts marshmallows over a campfire in Louisiana.

Cordelia sits at the dining-room table making notes in the margins of the writings of Julian of Norwich.

Louise pays Athena Maidenhead another two hundred dollars.

They never discuss outright *why* Louise is doing it. It's just that one day Athena sends her a text to say hey hunny do you have any leads I'm pretty broke right now haha and the guy who usually pays my rent turned out to be an asshole.

Maybe you could ask Lavinia if she knows any way a girl could make like $500 fast?

She's always so generous. (Haha)

Louise pays.

Athena thanks her, and then mentions so casually she'd also like to buy a new dress.

Turns out, she met a guy the night they all went to the opera. He asked her out during the intermission. She wants to dress real classy for him.

Athena sends her the Net-a-Porter link and Louise buys this, too.

———

Lavinia's parents start to put pressure on her to come home for Christmas.

We understand Cordelia has impulsively decided not to return home, they say. We can't help but wonder if this is in part due to your example? Now that Cordelia is getting older we feel it's more important than ever that you be a role model for her, and your current way of living is—your father and I agree—hardly an appropriate one for her to emulate.

We feel it would be prudent for you to come home for the remainder of the holiday season. We can discuss your imminent return to Yale then.

Lavinia writes a very earnest letter explaining that her novel is almost done, and that this road trip she's doing—completely sober, she adds!—is of utmost import for her physical as well as emotional well-being.

Be that as it may, Lavinia's mother says, we cannot support you in this endeavor. We may not be able to alter your course of action at this stage, but we can, at least, play a role in setting an example for your sister.

With that in mind: we'll be cutting off your cards until you return. You have until December 19th to decide.

If you would like to return to Paris we would more than happily purchase a one-way plane ticket for you.

But your father and I are in agreement: we're both unable to justify our bankrolling of your lifestyle choices any longer.

Please contact us with your passport details and details of your proposed flight.

I hope you realize that this is the kindest thing you could possibly do for your sister at this stage, Lavinia's mother adds.

Lavinia doesn't answer them.

Louise starts running out of money again.

She'd planned to save every cent she took from Lavinia. But Louise hasn't worked in so long, and the payments from Athena have started to add up, and also the times she takes Rex to dinner, because it makes her feel like she's capable of giving him some kind of happiness, and also the times they go Dutch, because Louise never wants to admit she can't afford the kinds of things Rex can afford, because Louise can never say *no* to him.

Lavinia doesn't take Cordelia's calls.

Sorry darling! she says. The signal's terrible out here! Last night we went bathing naked underneath the stars and nearly froze to death and it was BEAUTIFUL.

Every day, Louise thinks *today.*

Today will be the day everything ends.

She will run away; she will take Lavinia's passport or the fake ID belonging to the redhead from Iowa called Elizabeth Glass; she will take whatever money she has left and she will walk out the door and she will vanish into the city, but then Gavin Mullaney tells her that he wants her to do another piece for *The Fiddler* in print, and gives her a heads-up that they're considering naming her one of their Five Under Thirty of that year, if she can impress the rest of their editorial board with her upcoming piece. And then Rex texts her a picture of Central Park in the snow, even though they've been fighting so much, lately, and Louise thinks *just one more day; that's all I need; just one more day,* but then another day comes and she needs that one, too.

Truth is, Louise has nowhere else to go.

The twentieth of December is Louise's thirtieth birthday.

Rex knows it's her birthday, because he sees it on Facebook (she tells him she's twenty-six).

I'm sorry things have been stressful lately, he says. *Let's do something special, okay?*

Louise tells Cordelia she has a date with a guy she met online.

"He's probably a serial killer," says Cordelia, without looking up from her work.

Louise dresses up in the only dress she has that Cordelia will not notice belongs to Lavinia, which is too big for her now and also made of cheap polyester and which she bought at Housing Works for twenty dollars two years ago, and which at the time was the nicest thing she had ever owned.

Rex has texted her: an address, a time.

It's a surprise, he says, with a smiley face so she knows he is not angry at her, this time.

It's a secret cocktail bar in Williamsburg with only three chairs, one of which is for the bartender.

He has dressed up for her—his blazer is darker than usual, and less creased. He leaps up when she comes in (even though she is wearing such a frumpy dress, such an ugly and oversized dress) and when his eyes rest on her she wonders if it is because he thinks she is beautiful, tonight, or because he has finally figured out that this is just what she looks like when she is not being Lavinia.

"You look nice," he says, which doesn't clarify anything.

Louise has spent an hour looking in the mirror this evening.

I look thirty, she thinks, and it baffles her that he does not know this.

They don't talk about Lavinia. They don't talk about Cordelia. They talk about the weather and Rex's seminar papers and some of the qualifying exams he'll have to take, soon, and what he thinks of his professors and this amazing living-Latin program he wants to do in Rome next summer. They talk about Hal and how he's dating India, now, and how he's decided already that she is the girl he's going to marry, without asking her what she thinks of it. They talk about Louise's pieces for *The Fiddler* and how Gavin thinks she has a real shot at being one of *The Fiddler*'s Five Under Thirty, which Rex seems to find impressive.

They talk, Louise thinks, like any other boring couple in this city who only have sex two or three times a week.

They talk like Rex has never dated the kind of woman who sets shit on fire, or stands naked at the water's edge at the dawn of the New Year.

They have Korean-Mexican fusion. They have red wine. Rex pays.

After, he asks her to take a walk with him. They do.

It is all very sweet. It is all very ordinary. They walk, hand in hand, through the snow, down Bleecker, then through Washington Square Park, then back down to Chinatown. The stars stud the sky and Rex's ears get red when they are cold, as they do when he is nervous or embarrassed. All of a sudden Louise starts to feel intensely sure that the only reason they're walking so romantically in the moonlight is because he doesn't want to fuck her (not in that dress; maybe not ever).

He hums softly as they pass Doyers Street.

She takes his hand. She pulls him down the alley, which is unlit and dark and cobblestoned and where mobsters used to commit murder, once upon a time (Lavinia once said), because nobody could see you there.

He laughs. He follows her.

She pushes him up against the wall. She kisses him so hard she bites his lip.

She kisses him so hard he gasps.

He looks so confused when she pulls away.

He should not be so surprised, Louise thinks; *he should be used to this by now. This is exactly what Lavinia would have done.*

She kisses him again, harder this time, and slides her hand up the inside of his thigh, feels his cock (it is not yet hard; this is on her).

She draws away. She looks at him.

"What are you doing?" He's laughing as he asks her, but he means it.

"Come on," she says. "Nobody will see" (*everybody wants to fuck the crazy ones, that's the whole point*).

"I want you," she says.

And he's still laughing, a little, like this part is ridiculous. Is it the dress? Is it because she's thirty? Is it because Cordelia has said *nobody will ever forget Lavinia* and because she is right? Louise kisses him harder, so hard, she thinks, that she even means to hurt him, because if she can't make him want her she can at least make him afraid of her, just a little, and because if she cannot be Lavinia she might as well be a whore (*you're not the woman I'm going to marry,* Hal had said to Athena, so easily, like she'd ever fuck him if it weren't for the Dakota), and she kisses him harder and harder and says *I want you to fuck me* in his ear. Finally, he gets hard, and it's only when he grabs her wrist, when his breath gets ragged, that he moans in that sharp and desperate way that means she has power over him, when he gets rough with her in that way that means that she has power over him, that she pulls away.

He pulls her back.

She wants to savor him wanting her like this forever.

He pushes her up against a wall, hikes up her skirt and pulls aside her panties, and now Louise isn't sure which of them is initiating it, whether she has tricked him into wanting her (she has gotten so good, now, at that part) or whether all along this is just what he wants because he's a man. He feels her up underneath the skirt of her dress (*this I have done before;* Louise thinks; *all this, all this I have done before*) and Louise starts to whisper to him all the things that a woman you'd want to fuck would say, and she doesn't know if she means them or she just wants to be the woman who makes men hear them but she tells him, right in his ear, that she wants him, that she needs him, that she is wet and needs him to take her home right now, and he is hers, now, hearing it; he gets rougher, hearing it, and then without thinking she tells him she wants him to fuck her in the ass.

"What?"

He says it like this isn't something every single straight man dreams of.

He pulls away to look at her.

"Nothing," Louise says, "never mind."

"But—"

"Keep going," she says, and they start to stumble over each other and get in each other's way and their bodies don't fit, and then Rex says "Fuck it, let's get a cab" and they cab it back to Rex's place (Louise pays) and Rex fucks her, just like every other time he's fucked her. He burrows into her shoulder and buries his face into her hair like he's hiding from something, like the crook of her arm is his harbor. She clings to him, too, and thinks *this has to be enough,* and he starts getting so rough with her that she thinks *I have driven him mad* and she half-wants him to get rougher, still, just to prove that this is a thing she is capable of doing to a person, but he's not even looking at her—he's thrusting so hard it hurts but he's not even looking at her—and maybe because she means it or maybe to shock him or maybe to make him notice her Louise says *I love you, I love you,* just as he comes.

He kisses her forehead.

He rolls off her.

"I need you," he whispers. He kisses her shoulder.

Louise doesn't sleep that night, either.

"Did you have sex with him?" says Cordelia, when Louise gets home the next day. "Your serial killer?" She's fully dressed at nine in the morning, in a dowdy little skirt and a turtleneck. She's reading.

"That's none of your business," says Louise.

"Why?"

"Because you're seventeen."

"The age of consent in plenty of places is sixteen," says Cordelia. "Anyway, I waited up for you."

"Why?"

"I was worried. In case he *was* a serial killer and he'd chained you up in a basement."

"How would you know?"

"Well, you wouldn't have come home." She raises her chin. "Was that the first time you met him?"

"I'm taking a shower," says Louise.

"I'm not trying to intrude," says Cordelia. "I'm just curious. Can you really have sex with somebody you've just met?"

She follows Louise to the bathroom door.

Louise closes the door. She takes off her clothes.

"Aren't you afraid?" Cordelia's voice is muffled through the door.

"Of what?"

"I don't know. Diseases? Getting hurt?"

Louise steps into the shower. She turns up the heat so it scalds.

Cordelia spends her days studying, and texting Lavinia, who rarely responds.

"You don't have to worry," Cordelia says, three days before Christmas. "I mean—about leaving me alone. I don't drink and I don't do drugs and I don't do anything, really. So you can go home, if you want to. I'll just stay and wait for Vinny. I'm not going home."

"Why not?"

There is such a great space in the living room, where the steamer trunk once was.

"Why aren't you going home?"

"I don't like my parents very much," says Cordelia, so simply.

"Well, I don't like my parents very much, either," says Louise.

"Why not?"

Louise shrugs. "I don't think they really like me."

She says it like it's a joke.

"Why don't your parents like you?"

Back when Louise went to therapy (she ran out of money for therapy, and also didn't really trust her therapist), she spent a lot of time developing mantras like *people express love in different ways* and *concern can sometimes translate into criticism* and *letting your children go out in the world is a difficult process,* but now that she thinks about it that's probably bullshit.

"I don't make enough of an effort," Louise says.

"That's what Mother always says about me, too. But she likes me." She swings her legs up onto the divan. "That's why I don't like her.

She likes me better than Vinny—and that isn't fair. You should love all people equally." She winks. "It's really the only Christian thing to do."

"Are you really religious?"

Cordelia plays with the tassels on the throw pillow. "At the beginning," she said. "Maybe I just liked to annoy Vinny. When she was a very terrible pagan I used to tell her I'd pray for her soul." She considers. "But I think I believe it, now." She leans her hand on her cheek. "The more I read," Cordelia says, "the more it's the only thing that makes sense to me. If God doesn't exist—this world would be too terrible for words."

"Look at this!"

She shows Louise her phone.

Lavinia is at the Grand Canyon. Her shadow fades into the rock.

"Have you ever been to the Grand Canyon, Lulu?"

"No."

"Me neither." Cordelia blows up the photo to make it bigger. "I'm not really very adventurous. Do you know—I've never even disobeyed my parents, before this week? I'm the good daughter, you see. Look—isn't it beautiful?"

"Lovely."

"I tell Vinny all the time—it's not good to be so frivolous. She should go back to school. She'll regret it when she's older, if she doesn't. Only, Lulu?" She takes a deep breath. "How long does it take to drive to the Grand Canyon?"

"Five days" (Louise has Googled this). "Why?"

"You don't think . . ."

"No."

"We could rent a car! And we could go and surprise her! Or we could fly—if we flew, we could be there by Christmas!"

Louise keeps her eyes on the photo, so she doesn't have to look at Cordelia's face.

"We can't do that," she says.

"Why not? Vinny's always doing crazy, impulsive things—why can't we? And look—it's *beautiful* out there!"

"Because she's with her friends, Cordelia."

"So? Vinny likes me better than any friend she's ever had—I'm sorry, Louise, but it's true—there's no *way* she wouldn't want me there! She'd be *thrilled* to see us both!"

Louise closes her eyes.

"We can't."

"Why not?"

"Because."

"Because why!"

"Because she doesn't want you there!"

Cordelia looks like Louise has just slapped her.

Cordelia doesn't say anything.

She puts her hands in her lap. She folds them. She is very quiet for a while.

"Hey, Lulu?"

"What?"

"Do you want to get a Christmas tree?"

Their first and only Christmas in New York, Virgil and Louise bought one of those potted-plant firs they could keep on the kitchen counter, which was the apartment's only real surface, because they didn't have space for anything bigger, except they kept arguing over who would take care of it and the thing died without either of them noticing even though they're supposed to be evergreen and that, Virgil said, was proof that Louise should never be a mother.

Cordelia and Louise go to the guy on Seventy-ninth and Third.

They jack up the prices, so close to Christmas Eve, but Louise pays, anyway, with one hundred of the eight hundred or so dollars she has left.

Louise offers to pay for the guy to deliver it, but Cordelia insists that you haven't earned a tree if you haven't at least dragged it with your own two hands and so the two of them lug it all the way back to Lavinia's house.

They spend the afternoon decorating it. They don't have ornaments so they decorate it with detritus of Lavinia's: tarot cards, crystals, peacock feathers, erotic statuettes.

"I suppose it's not *really sacrilegious*," Cordelia says. "Christmas trees are pagan, anyhow."

Cordelia puts Lavinia's present under the tree.

"I want it to be waiting for her when she gets back," Cordelia says.

That night, after they go to bed, Cordelia calls Lavinia.

She calls her four or five times, and Louise huddles up in bed and watches the phone go off, and go to voicemail, and lets it go, and doesn't say anything either.

Cordelia leaves so many voicemails: *pleasepickuppleasepickuppleasepickup.*

Louise can hear them through the bedroom wall.

On the sixth call, Lavinia answers.

Louise has gone out the fire escape. She's gone all the way up to the roof.

"What is it, darling? Is it *catastrophe*?"

Louise is shaking, doing it, even though she's been doing it so long.

"Vinny!"

Cordelia's voice trembles.

"Vinny—I've been trying to call for days!"

"Darling, *tell* me you're not still in New York. I'm so sorry, Cordy—you should be furious with me; really, you should; it's just that Nerissa wants to make it *all the way* to Big Sur and I really, truly, think we could—"

"I need you!"

Louise can hear Cordelia three flights up.

"Cordy, please, be reasonable—"

"Just come *home*, okay?"

"I'm sorry, darling, you know I'd love to, but—"

"Please!"

"I'm so sorry. Look, Cordy—the others are all here—"

"Please!"

"I have to go."

Louise hangs up the phone.

She tiptoes so quietly downstairs. She sneaks so quietly in back through the window.

She gets so quietly back into bed.

She can hear Cordelia in the other room, quietly sobbing.

Cordelia doesn't mention it to Louise.

She is impeccable, the next morning, which is Christmas Eve. It's like she hasn't even been crying at all. She gets up before Louise does, cleans the house, makes breakfast.

"I'll probably go back to Paris soon," Cordelia says. "You must be quite sick of me."

"Not at all," says Louise.

She forces down some coffee.

"I suppose we should do something for Christmas. Maybe Midnight Mass? There's one I want to go to at St. John the Divine—I know it's Protestant, but I really like the music there . . ."

"I'm sorry," Louise says. "I have plans."

She and Rex planned it weeks ago. Henry Upchurch is throwing his annual Christmas Eve party. He's rented a room at the Yale Club, like he does every year. She and Rex have not gone to a party in so long. They're getting so dull.

"Oh," says Cordelia. "Of course you do. You probably have a lot of friends."

She shrugs. "That's fine. I don't mind going by myself. It's a religious holiday, anyhow. It's good to focus on, you know, God and things."

"I'm sorry," says Louise. "I said I'd go before you even got here."

"Of course," says Cordelia. "I mean—you don't owe me anything." She swallows. "You hardly even know me. It's Vinny who—" She stops herself. She turns back to her book. It's Hildegard of Bingen, this time.

Louise can't stand this.

"Look," she says. "Why don't you come?"

"Where?"

"It's a party. At the Yale Club. It's—it's Henry Upchurch's Christmas party."

"Oh," says Cordelia. "I don't think his books are very good."

Louise has actually never bothered to read any of Henry Upchurch's books.

"Well, don't tell Hal that."

"I don't like him, either. He's got no social skills and he's friends with Rex."

"He's not that bad," says Louise. "I mean—neither of them is. And, I mean, there's going to be a lot of people there. We might not even see them."

"Vinny would be furious if I even spoke to them," Cordelia says. "Anyway, I haven't got anything to wear to that sort of thing."

"You could borrow something of Lavinia's? I'm sure she wouldn't mind."

"She hates it when I borrow her clothes without asking." Cordelia considers. "What were you going to wear?"

Louise hesitates.

"If we *both* borrowed something, she couldn't very well stay mad at us both." Cordelia breathes in. "Besides, if she wanted us not to borrow her things she should have come back and worn them herself—right?"

"Right," says Louise. "Exactly."

"It serves her right." Cordelia smiles. "Rex coming all the way here—and she'll never even know! You kept your promise, right? You didn't tell her?"

"I didn't tell her."

"Good. Don't."

Cordelia goes to the closet. She fingers Lavinia's things.

"I'm going to be *very polite* to them both," she says.

I'm sorry, Louise texts Rex.

I couldn't just leave her alone.

Rex Reads it. No answer.

We can still have fun! We just have to be discreet, that's all.

Blushing Przewalski's horse emoticon.

She sees the ellipses on the screen that mean he's typing. They go on for five minutes.

ok.

That's all he says.

Louise does Cordelia's makeup.

She shows Cordelia how to straighten her hair, to transform the wilderness of her curls into something neat and smooth. She shows her how to put on lip liner, so that the lipstick will stay within the bounds of her mouth. She highlights Cordelia's eyes with mascara (*how blue they are,* she thinks). She puts Lavinia's lipstick on Cordelia's lips.

She helps Cordelia choose a dress.

Cordelia fingers a red one, silk, cut along the bias.

"This one, do you think?" She stops herself. "No, I can't."

"Why not?"

"My breasts are too small. And I'll look ridiculous." She sits on the bed. "*This* is silly—you should just go without me."

"No—no, you should come!"

Louise doesn't even know why it matters.

"I'll look stupid!" Cordelia says. "I don't—I don't even know how to stand."

"I'll show you," says Louise. "Just—put it on."

Cordelia does.

It hangs long and loose on her.

"It looks like a tent."

"You're not standing right," says Louise. "You have to, you know, *pose*. Arch your back a little—right there, good."

"I feel like a cobra."

"That means you're doing it right. And put your tongue behind your teeth when you smile."

"Why?"

"It makes you smile with your eyes."

Cordelia looks dubious.

"It comes out better in photos."

"So?"

"Just—trust me, okay?"

Cordelia's lashes are so dark when they flutter, now.

"Will you take a picture of me? I mean—I don't want to post it, or anything. Just—just for me to have?"

Louise does. She shows it to Cordelia.

"I look ridiculous," Cordelia says.

Actually, Cordelia looks beautiful.

"Will you send it to me?" Cordelia asks.

They take a cab to the Yale Club. Louise pays.

She has $402.63 in her checking account.

When they pull up, Hal is already there. He is smoking a cigar on the steps. Beowulf and Gavin are with him.

Hal does a double take when he sees them.

"I heard you were in town." He looks Cordelia over. "You've sure been causing trouble, haven't you?"

"It's nice to see you again, Henry," Cordelia says. "It's been a while."

She shakes his hand.

"Last time I saw you, you had braces."

"Last time I saw you, you were thin."

Hal grins.

"Are you even legal?"

"Only in New Hampshire."

"Shame."

"No," says Cordelia. Her mouth twists a little. "Not really."

Then: "You're Henry Upchurch's son."

"For my sins."

"What's that like?"

"Go read his books." Hal puffs on his cigar. "That'll tell you every-thing."

"I've read his books," says Cordelia. "I thought *Folly's Train* was cliché and every character in *A Dying Fall* was too easily redeemed."

Louise bites her lip so Hal won't see her smile.

"I'll have you know, little girl," says Hal, "that Henry Upchurch is the greatest American writer of the past fifty years."

"Don't worry," Hal says to Louise, as Cordelia checks her coat. "I've been briefed. I'll be good." He hands her a drink. "It seems like a whole lot of fucking trouble, if you ask me."

"I didn't," says Louise.

Hal reaches out to grab Rex by the arm.

"Now, do you two *know each other*?" Hal's tongue lolls a little to one side. "Or do I have to introduce you."

"Hal, don't—"

Louise squeezes Rex's elbow, just a little, and feels so pathetic for doing it. Rex smiles—or maybe grimaces.

Cordelia sees them.

She walks over. She's measured and unsteady in Lavinia's heels.
"Hello, Rex," she says. Her voice is low.
They shake hands.

"I'm prepared to be civil," Cordelia announces, "if you are."
Hal bursts out laughing.
"However you like it," says Rex.
Hal raises his glass.
"To your sister," says Hal. "Who has brought us all together."
Everybody clinks glasses.
Nobody drinks, except Cordelia, who closes her eyes and drinks her champagne in one gulp, and then makes a face.

The Yale Club is like a wedding cake—white, gold-shot, confectionary: with its curved windows, its white, whipped curtains that seem to flutter up to the sky. There are so many people here who know Henry Upchurch, or don't and want people to think they do, or who have never heard of Henry Upchurch but who want to drink for free.
Louise drinks. Hal drinks. Rex drinks. Cordelia drinks.
She drinks more than anybody else.
"It's not so bad," she says, on her third glass. She hiccups.
She claps Rex on the shoulder.
"You're not so bad, either," she says. "I've decided."
Rex doesn't say anything.
"You're a fool," she says. "But I forgive you. If Vinny weren't my sister, I wouldn't be able to stand her, either." She smiles. "Cheer up, Rex—maybe she'll take you back, after all. If she ever comes back. Who knows, with Vinny? You never know *what* she'll do!"
Rex forces his drink down.
"No," he says. "You're right. You never know."

"Come on," says Hal. He puts his hand on the small of Louise's back. "I want you to meet my father."

———

Henry Upchurch is old.

Also, he's fat.

He looks like a little sphere glued to a bigger one. He has a flap in his neck, like a turkey's. He sits because he is both too old and too fat to stand. He doesn't speak.

Beowulf is stuck to his side, his fragile girlfriend hovering over them both like a mosquito. Beowulf is midway through his discourse on *A Dying Fall*, which Louise has already heard. He's talking about that famous scene where the protagonists get into a fistfight over Latin conjugations, and he is making the point that in today's world, with today's sensitivities, you could never write a scene like that and have it be understood by *hoi polloi* (he is very careful not to use the article) because the *you-know-what* brigade is always turning over rocks to look for homosexuality and there's no time for discussing what it means to be a *man*, in the Classical sense.

Rex stands close by but doesn't touch Louise.

This is what the two of them agreed. It hurts anyway.

"I bet," Hal says into Cordelia's ear, close enough for Louise to hear, "that Beowulf Marmont gets off picturing his girlfriend fucking black men."

"*What?*"

"Exactly."

"You're disgusting."

"I'm honest," says Hal. "Some men are like that, young Cordelia. Better you learn now the ways of the world."

"I know the ways of the world just fine!" She pronounces it *wheyze*.

Hal pours some whiskey from his flask into his champagne flute. "Henry Upchurch just *loves* Rex. Doesn't he?"

Louise isn't sure whether Hal is trolling Rex, or trolling Cordelia, or trolling her.

"It's a good story, actually," says Hal. "Rex has never even read *A Dying Fall*, have you, Rex? But Rex is a good little Classicist. He went on some tangent about Greek verbs when he came over for tea—Christ, ten years ago, now? About how *substantia* and *hypostasis* mean the same thing, etymologically speaking, but are totally opposite theologically speaking."

"It's true," says Cordelia, suddenly. "There's one *substantia* and three *hypostases* in the Trinity." She hiccups. "Or is it one *hypostasis* and three *ousia*? I forgot."

Hal ignores her.

"They're nouns," says Rex, under his breath.

"Henry Upchurch was *so* impressed—he wrote one of your Yale references, didn't he, Rex? Weren't you impressive?"

Rex is looking down at the carpets.

"There's a stain on this carpet," he says, without looking up.

"He always asks about you," Hal says. "Every single fucking time he and my mother come in from Amagansett. *How's your clever friend Rex doing? Isn't he clever?*"

"You would think," Rex says, "that in a place this expensive, they'd clean their fucking carpets."

He jerks his head up.

"I'm going for a smoke," he says.

Louise can't follow him.

"I'm getting another," Cordelia says.

She glides off.

Now Louise meets Henry Upchurch.

Hal steers her to him once Beowulf has been dismissed.

"Louise Wilson," Hal says, in that half-whine whose sincerity Louise still cannot ascertain, "is going to be one of the great writers of our generation."

Henry Upchurch lifts his head with very great effort.

"My name is Louise Wilson," Louise says.

She sticks out her hand. He looks so confused and so she grabs his hand, which is flabby and unsteady, and shakes it firmly. She looks him straight in the eye. "I write for *The New Misandrist* and *The Egret* and *The Fiddler*."

"Ah," says Henry Upchurch.

His head bobbles, just a little bit. He drools. Louise thinks, at first, that he is nodding, but it's only a tremor.

"Louise is looking for representation," says Hal. He's still smiling, like he doesn't even notice that his father's snot has pooled on his tie.

"Ah," says Henry Upchurch.

His eyes are glassy. He doesn't look at either one of them.

"I'm going to send her to have lunch with Niall Montgomery, okay?"

"Ah," Henry Upchurch says.

He dribbles into his tie.

"That's just his trick," Hal says. "Everybody knows really powerful men don't *talk*. It just means everybody has to work harder to engage *him*. Niall Montgomery is his agent. A friend of the family. We're going over there, tomorrow, for Christmas lunch. I'll mention you."

"Why are you being so nice to me?"

"Because," he says. "You're in on the joke."

"What joke?"

Hal grins. "*The* joke." He wiggles his eyebrows at her. "You get it. And I get it. And none of these other poor fuckers gets it. Least of all Rex. Poor, poor Rex."

"I don't know what you're talking about," says Louise.

"There are some benefits," Hal says, "to being the ugly friend. Don't you think?"

Then Louise sees Cordelia.

She's standing in a corridor, talking to Beowulf Marmont, who is leaning in so intently. She is swaying, just a little bit.

They're standing under mistletoe.

"I am nothing," Beowulf Marmont is leaning into Cordelia's ear, "if not a man of tradition."

That's when he leans in to kiss her.

Cordelia starts to put her hands up, but she's too late, or else Beowulf pretends not to notice that she's doing it, and he grabs her by the back of the neck and pulls her in and jams his tongue so confidently down her throat, and it takes Louise yanking him off her and shouting *she's seventeen* straight in his face before he stumbles away.

To his credit, he looks horrified.

Cordelia stands very still.

She doesn't look at Louise.

"Do you have a tissue?" she asks.

Louise hands her one.

Cordelia rubs her mouth raw.

She lets it fall.

"That," she says very slowly, "was my first kiss."

She hiccups again.

"I'm going to be sick."

Cordelia doesn't even make it to the bathroom.

She throws up in a wastepaper basket in the corridor outside the function room.

Louise holds her hair back and strokes her shoulders.

"It's fine," Louise says. She has done this so many times before. "Don't force it. You'll feel better once you've thrown it up."

"I shouldn't have drunk so much."

"It's my fault," says Louise. "I should have been watching you—I didn't realize—" And then she stops herself, because it should be obvious that most people can't drink a bottle of champagne on an empty stomach without vomiting.

"I'm not your fucking problem!" Cordelia says. She chokes out more phlegm into the bin.

It's the first time Louise has ever heard Cordelia curse.

"It's my fault," Cordelia says again. Louise can't tell if she's convulsing because she's sick, or because she's sobbing. "It's my fault—I betrayed her."

"How?"

"I spoke to Rex! And Hal! *I shook his hand*—oh, God! God! She'll never forgive me!"

"She will!"

"I *shook his hand*! I want to burn it off!"

Cordelia starts rubbing it on the carpet, like she can blister off her sin.

Louise tries, so vainly, to shush her.

"I'm awful!" Cordelia cries.

"You're not."

She begins to sob, so brokenly, in Louise's lap.

"It's all right," Louise says, like she knows what to do, like she knows how to handle any of this. "It'll be all right."

"She hates me."

"She *won't*. I promise." Like that, too, is a thing she can assure.

"How do you *know*?"

"Because," Louise says, at last, "she was fucking Hal!"

That's when Cordelia finally, finally looks up, to see Rex and Hal behind them.

Rex doesn't even bother to first ask if it's true.

He punches Hal anyway.

They fight like dogs do.

They roll on the carpet. They smash each other's faces into the wall. Hal forces his fist into Rex's mouth. Rex kicks Hal in the stomach. They roll on top of one another. Rex grabs a fistful of skin from the back of Hal's neck. Hal grabs Rex by the hair. Rex slams Hal's head into the ground.

It takes Gavin and Beowulf (*really, Henry, at your own father's fête!*) to separate them.

When they separate them, Hal is laughing.

"And they say," he wheezes, "that men aren't men anymore."

Louise watches Rex go.

She wants so badly to follow him. For a second she thinks she will.

But Cordelia is sobbing, again, in her arms, and blowing her nose on Louise's skirt which is really Lavinia's skirt, and getting makeup all over her red silk dress which is Lavinia's dress. The only thing Louise can do is take her home, in a cab, which costs thirty of the three hundred eighty dollars Louise has left in the world, and whisper *it's okay, it's okay,* and haul Cordelia up the stairs, and take off her clothes, and put one of Lavinia's crisp nightgowns over her head, and tuck her in.

"I hate them," Cordelia whispers. "I hate them *all.*"

"I know."

"They're all *awful.*"

"I know."

"I hate *her!*"

"I know," Louise whispers.

"I hate her *so much!*" she hiccups. *"I hate her! I hate her! I hate her!"*

"I know."

"Rex should have let her jump."

Louise's breath catches in her throat.

"Don't say that."

"Why not? It's true—isn't it?"

"I don't know." Louise's heart is beating so quickly. "No! Of course not!"

"What has she ever done but lie to anyone who's ever loved her?"

Louise doesn't have an answer for her.

They lie together, in Lavinia's bed, and Cordelia sobs so brokenly, and she curls into herself and there is nothing for Louise to do but hold her so tightly, and so close, tight enough that she shakes when Cordelia shakes, and is racked with Cordelia's sobs.

They lie there together until Cordelia falls asleep in Louise's arms.

Louise goes into Cordelia's room. She sits at the desk, in silence. She texts Rex—she's texted him so many times tonight—telling him she can explain, begging him to let her explain, begging him to let her fix everything she's fucked up, in the service of fixing things.

He's Read every message. He hasn't responded.

Please.

Louise is so clingy, now. She disgusts herself.

She plugs in her phone on Cordelia's desk. She stares at the photographs, awhile, at Cordelia's books: Julian of Norwich, Thomas Merton, Teilhard de Chardin, John Henry Newman, St. Augustine. She stares into the darkness, awhile more.

She goes to bed.

At one, her phone pings.

She can see Rex's name, flashing on the nightstand.

I miss you.

Can we talk?

Thank God, Louise thinks. *Thank God.*

She can taste how relieved she is; she is so relieved, as she grabs the phone, that she starts to laugh out loud, and she starts typing yes, of course, you can call me right now, I don't care what time it is, we can talk as long as you need even though her phone is right there, charging, on Cordelia's desk.

I'm sorry, Rex tells Lavinia.

I hate that I still love you.

9

CORDELIA IS SNORING IN THE OTHER ROOM.

Louise can't feel anything, anymore.

Lavinia Reads Rex's text, so he will know she's read it. She doesn't answer.

Now he will know exactly how Louise feels.

It's Christmas.

Louise goes for a walk. She smokes five or six cigarettes, even though she hasn't smoked since taking up Lavinia's workout regimen (the only good part of Lavinia's being away, she thinks, is that her thighs don't ache so much anymore).

Rex keeps texting Lavinia.

Please.

Just talk to me.

I'm sorry.

I'm the worst.

I know.

I know how selfish I am.

Lavinia posts a public Instagram picture of the Rocky Mountains, just to hurt him.

Can't sleep, Lavinia says. The whole world is just too beautiful to stand.

Rex Eliot Likes it.

When it's late enough Louise calls her parents in Devonshire to wish them a merry Christmas. It's a very formal conversation. They ask how she's doing and she tells them about *The Fiddler*'s Five Under Thirty, which is the closest thing you can get to a big break when you've only written personal essays on the Internet.

"Most people who get on it get agents soon after," says Louise, like this is a thing that still matters. "One girl got a book deal for a memoir within a week."

"Oh," says Louise's mother.

"But you're not under thirty."

"December counts," says Louise, even though that isn't true.

"Does it pay? If you win?"

"No," says Louise. "It's just prestige. And it's not a prize—it's a list."

"Oh," says Louise's mother. "That's a shame."

"Yes," says Louise. "It is."

"You know," says Louise's mother. "You'll never believe who I saw on the street, the other day."

Louise already knows.

"He's gotten very handsome—now that he's cut his hair. He's left the bookstore. He's actually got a job managing the Devonshire Inn. Pretty good, huh?"

"Sure," says Louise.

"Now I don't *presume* to know what happened," says Louise's mother. "But he is a *very* nice boy. It's not like there's a line around the block for you."

Louise opens her mouth to say something about how she has a boyfriend now, actually, and he's very handsome and he goes to Columbia and he loves her, but then she closes it again.

"Anyway," says Louise's mother. "I *know, I know* you'll be mad at me—but he asked for your number, and, well—*I know* what you always say, but it's been *so* long since you mentioned anybody else, and he—he's done so well for himself, lately, and he still always asks after you, and he cares about you *so much* . . ."

Louise hangs up the phone.

When Louise comes back to the apartment, Cordelia is already up. Her hair is pinned in a braid. She's washed all the makeup off her face. She's in pajamas.

She looks, Louise thinks, so young.

"I've been waiting for you," she says. "I wanted to give you your present!"

She hands a wrapped package to Louise.

"I bought it for Vinny," she says. "But I think you'll appreciate it more."

It's an antique miniature booklet of Tennyson's "Ulysses." The binding is split. It's beautiful.

"Vinny told me about your adventure," Cordelia says. "It sounded beautiful."

"It was," says Louise.

"Nobody does that at Exeter," Cordelia says.

"I bet."

"They only do things that look good on their college apps."

Cordelia takes out her phone.

"Do you have plans?"

"No," Louise says.

"Want to order Chinese?"

"Sure."

"I booked my flight," Cordelia says. "I'm heading to Paris New Year's Eve. Mother's very happy. I told her my friend in Aspen had a mental breakdown because she didn't get in early to Brown. I'll be out of your hair, soon enough. I'm sure you'll be relieved."

Louise doesn't know why she isn't.

"I bet she's bathing naked in the Pacific right now," Cordelia says.

"Probably."

"Fuck her," says Cordelia. "I'm getting fried rice."

———

Louise pays for these, too. The order comes to $32.41. Louise even tips.

Rex finally texts Louise that evening, because Lavinia hasn't texted him back.

I'm sorry, he says.

I needed some time.

Do you want to come over tonight?

They sit in silence on Rex's bed, because his apartment is too small for a sofa.

She waits for him to break up with her. He doesn't.

"I'm sorry," he says. "I shouldn't have left you, last night."

He has a split lip.

Then: "How long did you know?"

"Not long," Louise says. "I only found out before she left."

"She told you."

"I saw her phone. I should have told you. I'm sorry. She made me promise not to."

"No," he says. "No—you shouldn't have." He swallows. "It's—you're in the middle." He sighs. "I never should have come between you two," he says.

"Don't say that."

"I put you in an impossible position—I'm sorry. I never should have."

"Don't *say* that."

Like she's begging him.

"It's stupid," says Rex. "I don't even know why I was mad. It's just—Hal being Hal. And her being—"

He can't even say her name.

"Lavinia," Louise says, so quietly. "Lavinia being Lavinia."

"Right."

He keeps checking his phone—right in front of her.

"Cordelia's leaving," Louise says. "She's going to Paris. She's realized that Lavinia's not coming back, anytime soon."

Rex exhales.

"Of course," he says. "Good."

He squeezes her hand.

"Then everything will go back to normal," he says.

Gavin emails Louise that night to let her know she's been selected as one of *The Fiddler*'s Five Under Thirty. They'll be announcing it on New Year's Day, he says. There will be a party. He wants her to read that piece she wrote about pretending to be a Devonshire Academy student. *It was the third-most-read piece this year,* he says.

Louise dyes her hair again. It leaves stains all over Lavinia's bathtub.

Rex keeps texting Lavinia.

Please, he says. Just talk to me.

Lavinia doesn't.

The day after Christmas, Hal texts Louise.

Let me buy you a drink, he says. Bemelmans? 8?

"I talked to Niall Montgomery about you," says Hal. "He likes your work. I told him you'd been selected as one of the Five Under Thirty. He's going to the launch party."

His black eye makes him look more misshapen than ever.

"Really," Hal says. "You should be buying *me* a drink."

Louise can't afford to do that, but she smiles anyway.

"Don't worry." Hal puts his card down. "Henry Upchurch always keeps his word. And you're an Under Thirty. You actually matter, now."

"I'm grateful," says Louise. "Really."

"Good. You should be."

Then: "How's Rex?"

"He's fine."

"He still mad at me?"

Louise shrugs. "I don't know."

"He didn't say?"

"We're trying not to talk about it."

"Good girl," he says. "Poor Louise."

"Why?"

"Don't forget—I've known Rex longer than anybody. Including her." He toasts to her. "I'm his best friend. I know what he was like—about her."

"So why did you do it?"

"She was hot and desperate and I wanted to fuck her. That's all."

"You know that's not true," says Louise.

He looks affronted, but Louise doesn't even care anymore.

"You want to play the bad friend game?"

"No," says Louise. "Not really."

"What do you want me to say?"

"Nothing."

"Rex didn't deserve her," says Hal. "Is that what you want to hear?"

"Not really."

"She didn't deserve anything, either. She wasn't anything special. She wasn't even good in bed. But—she loved him. And he doesn't deserve to be loved like that." Hal drinks. "She wasn't like you," he says. "She never got the joke."

Under the bar, Lavinia's phone pings. Louise doesn't even have to look at it.

"He shouldn't complain," says Hal. "He got *years*. He got love poems and love songs and long walks along the beach and classical music. What did I get? A couple of filthy weekends and some light kink." He stretches out along the bar. "Anyway, she put a stop to it. She was terrified you'd find out."

"I wouldn't have cared," Louise says.

She remembers the night that Lavinia stumbled home, with her dress inside out, and blood in her mouth.

"Oh, you would have. You'd never let yourself be bossed around by a girl who liked to get fucked in the ass."

He wipes his face with a cocktail napkin.

"Fuck it," he says. "I'm getting out of New York. I'm going to quit my job. I'm going to buy a vintage air-cooled Porsche and I'm going to drive it to Big Sur. Maybe I'll see her there. Maybe I'll see you."

"Maybe," says Louise.

"I'm going to become a writer, young Louise. Just like you. I've still got five years to make Five Under Thirty. And I *do* have, as it happens, the first fifty pages of the novel I'm going to write."

"Good luck with that," says Louise.

"Maybe I'll send it to you. Maybe you'll tell me if it's good?"

She can't tell if he means it.

"I'm sure it's fine, Hal."

"It's a piece of shit," says Hal. "I haven't even written it. And I'm never going to quit my job." He pays the bill.

"And *that*, young Louise." He grins at her. "Is the joke."

Please, Rex has texted Lavinia.

> I understand if you need more time.
> Just tell me if I should wait for you.

Lavinia texts him only one word: Don't.

Rex is so good to Louise, that week. He gets her a Christmas present, a beautiful art nouveau brooch he found for her at an antique market on the Hudson and Louise tries not to think, as she admires it in the mirror, whether she was the one he bought it for.

Rex is so good at not letting Louise know. He takes her to Mud, to Veselka for pierogis just like he did the night he first kissed her; he takes her back to the secret bookstore to celebrate her making Five Under Thirty with Gavin and Matty Rosekranz, even though it hasn't even been announced yet, not formally ("I can't wait to see the look on Beowulf Marmont's face," says Matty, who doesn't like him, either).

He goes down on her every single time they have sex.

Guilt's such a useful mechanism, Louise thinks. It makes you a much better person than you otherwise would be.

Lavinia has made it all the way to California.

She posts Instagram photos all the way up Route 1.

She's doing the last phase of her pilgrimage alone.

She posts a photo of her tattoo, against a blue body of water that might be the Pacific but also might be Photoshop.

MORE POETRY!!!

Always, Lavinia says.

Only: Rex has blocked her again.

On New Year's Eve, Cordelia packs her suitcase.

"Big plans?" she asks.

Louise is going to the MacIntyre again. She's meeting Rex there. Mimi is coming over to the house beforehand: officially, to get ready, but really because neither of them can stand to be alone.

Louise shrugs. "Just the same thing as last year," she says.

"I suppose I'll be midair when it happens," says Cordelia. "I don't know which one counts—midnight in Paris or midnight in New York. I don't suppose it matters."

"No," says Louise. "I don't suppose it does."

"I'm sorry to miss your reading," Cordelia says.

"It's fine," Louise says. "There will be people there."

"You know—it wasn't such a bad Christmas," Cordelia says. "I learned a lot. And a first kiss—that's a milestone, isn't it?"

"I mean—sure."

"It's better than Christmas in Paris, that's for sure." Cordelia lifts her chin. "You don't have to worry. I won't tell our parents Vinny's been letting you live here. I didn't tell about Mimi, either—and I didn't even like her."

"Thank you," says Louise. "I think."

"And you won't tell Vinny—I mean, when she gets back. I was drunk, when I said those things."

"I won't tell," says Louise. "I swear."

The house feels so empty, once she's gone.

Mimi comes over a couple of hours later. She's wearing false lashes and a Louise Brooks wig.

"OhmyGod!" she exclaims. *"Ihaventseenyouinforever!"*

She's brought a case of those little Sofia Coppola cans of champagne you're supposed to drink through a straw.

They get dressed for the MacIntyre.

This year's theme is Weimar Berlin. Louise wears a tuxedo jacket she's borrowed from Rex and nothing else, because the idea of wearing Lavinia's clothes one more time has made her nauseous.

She paints her face white. She draws kohl over her eyes.

Mimi is flipping through Lavinia's pictures on her phone.

"I'm so jealous," she murmurs. "I wish I could drive." She looks up. "Maybe I'll give up drinking, too," she says.

"You—I mean—that might not be such a bad idea."

"I'd get so skinny, that way. God, did you *see* the picture she posted of her abs?"

Louise was so proud of that one.

"I saw."

Mimi applies glitter to her cheeks.

"Starting January First," she says. "New Year's Resolution. Don't let me drink. Wait—" She swallows. "I forgot. Five Under Thirty. Okay, *January Second,* don't let me drink. Promise?"

"I trust you," says Louise. "If you say you won't drink, then you won't."

Louise puts on Lavinia's lipstick.

She considers herself in the mirror.

She wipes it off.

She doesn't even want to taste it.

They cab it to the MacIntyre. Louise pays. *January First,* she thinks, *I will reach out to Flora and to Miles. I'll find more clients. I'll get a job. I'll go on SeekingArrangement and find a rich boyfriend, just like Athena Maidenhead*—she can't let herself think about Athena Maidenhead, right now. She can't afford it, but there's a blizzard on, outside.

It's so cold, in the line, and even though it's freezing half the people there are dressed in club dresses and stilettos or jeans, and not in costume, and Louise doesn't know if that was true last year, or whether it's just that the parties aren't as good as they used to be.

The bouncer's rude and everybody's so busy taking photos that they shove Louise clear into the wall, and this one girl steps on Mimi's toe.

At ten-thirty they let them in.

This is what Louise sees:

Red velvet, electric lights, plastic bags, a taxidermied deer, torn upholstery, a spread of tarot cards, speaker cables, a woman in a backless sequined dress singing Peggy Lee's "Is That All There Is?," drunk bros in baseball caps, chandeliers, watered-down champagne.

This is all Louise sees:

Nothing she hasn't seen before.

Louise drinks.

She drinks just like Lavinia used to, getting a whole bottle all at once and pouring it down her throat, and Mimi thinks this is so hilarious that she takes different pictures, all from different angles.

"It's just like Weimar Berlin," Mimi chirps. "It really is."

She starts dancing on the tables.

Louise starts doing shots.

Just one more, she thinks. *Just one more.*

Then you'll start to have fun.

Mimi is kissing strangers.

Mimi is taking photos (she's in one of the asylum bathtubs, pretending to be a suicide; she's straddling the taxidermied deer; she's wrapped around Louise's neck like a mink; she's Liza Minnelli with her legs backward on a chair).

Mimi is having the best night of her life.

You'd know if you checked her Facebook.

Louise sees Rex across the ballroom.

He's wearing black tie. That's the closest thing he's made to an effort.

He smiles when she goes to him.

"Look." She tries so hard. "We match!"

He holds her hand. He kisses it. He looks out into the crowd, like Lavinia might be there.

The lights flash. The music is so loud. Louise can't hear a single word Mimi says.

Father Romylos is there and Gavin Mullaney is there and reminding her *tomorrow is your big day, isn't it?; aren't you so fucking excited you actually leveled up in this life?* and so is Athena Maidenhead, in the dress Louise has bought her, on the arm of Mike from the opera; Rose the photographer from *Last Night at the Met* is there, and so is the girl who was on *Survivor*, so is Laurie the erotic illustrator who drew Lavinia's tarot cards, and so is the Egyptologist Lavinia knows who got kicked off the faculty at Yale for leaving his wife for a student.

Mimi takes a picture of Louise and Rex, holding hands, and they look so goddamn happy in that one.

The lights are so bright. Neon blinds them. Smoke gets in Louise's eyes and makes her sneeze. Some drunk girl spills a rum and Coke all over Louise's nice borrowed jacket and even her collarbones get sticky.

Somebody who isn't Peggy Lee keeps singing Peggy Lee.

"Wasn't she here last year?"

Mimi shrugs. "Of course not!"

She is singing it on a loop, and maybe Louise was just that drunk last year or maybe she's just that drunk this year but in any case it turns out the woman isn't even singing, just lip-synching to the actual Peggy Lee, and she's doing it over and over again.

If that's all there is, my friends (turns out, it's blasted from every single boom box in the place). *Then let's keep dancing.*

"It's even better than last year!" Mimi grins.

She grabs Louise's hand. She makes her dance, and Mimi pulls in Rex to dance with them, too, because Mimi is so extravagant with her love that it has never occurred to her to want to win more than she wants to love somebody.

Louise has to pee.

Rex and Mimi and Gavin and Athena and Father Romylos and Laurie and Rose and the Egyptologist and the girl who was on *Survivor* all promise to wait for her by the downstairs bar, the one that looks like an art deco podium.

When Louise comes out, everybody's gone.

It's eleven-forty-five.

"Tick tock!"

Hal is marching toward her.

He's dressed like a Nazi. Nobody will look at him.

"Get it?" he says, when he sees her. "Because of the theme."

"I got it."

"You know, it's actually real Hugo Boss."

"Jesus Christ."

"I mean, it's not like I'm wearing a mustache or anything."

"Small mercies," says Louise.

Hal's black eye is almost gone. Now he just looks like he hasn't slept in a couple of days.

"Do you know what I gave Henry for Christmas?"

"I don't really care," says Louise.

"A copy of 'The Social and Political Doctrine of Fascism.' One for my mother, too. Plus an Hermès scarf, obviously. I'm not a monster."

"Are you done?"

"We all are. The world's ending. The revolution is imminent."

"Why are you even here, Hal?"

Hal shrugs. "All my friends are here."

He leans against the wall of the corridor.

"Come on, Lulu," he says. "Just be a fucking person, okay?"

"What does that mean?"

"Dance with me!"

The bass is turned up so high the walls shake.

"I should go find Rex."

"Don't."

"It's almost midnight."

He grabs her by the waist.

"Hal, don't!"

"It's almost midnight. I'll come with you!"

"Hal," Louise says, because the last thing in the world she needs right now is for Rex to have another reason to hate her. "Don't."

"Please!" he says.

The light strobes and that's the first time Louise really sees him.

He's been crying.

"Please don't go," he says.

"I have to."

"I want to talk to Rex!"

"You can talk to Rex tomorrow."

"I want to talk to Rex now!"

"Well, you can't."

"Tell him—" Something strangles in his throat. It's like a cat, dying.

It's five minutes to midnight.

Louise doesn't let him finish.

———

Louise stumbles in the crowd. She sees doubles, everywhere.

She sees Athena swaying with Mike (or maybe it is a stranger) and there is Beowulf Marmont, or someone who looks just like him, swaying with a girl who is definitely not his fragile-eyed girlfriend, and she sees Gavin Mullaney with his second-favorite girlfriend and she sees Mimi, Mimi dancing alone, Mimi moon-bathed in some spotlight, Mimi dancing for the first time like she's not desperate for somebody to come dance with her, and this huge deco clock in the shape of the numbers 2-0-1-6 has descended like a chandelier from the ceiling and it's thumping with the bass so Louise can't even tell what part's music and what part's the march of time.

It's one minute to midnight.

All Louise wants to do is sleep.

But that's not the world Louise lives in, now.

At a minute to midnight Louise sees Rex.

He's standing all alone, at the bar, with a martini in his hand.

Louise runs to him.

He looks so happy to see her.

They're counting down, everybody's counting down from sixty, and slurring the numbers wrong, and Louise is so lonely and Rex looks so happy to see her, even though she knows, she *knows,* that there is no way he can be, that he can't possibly be, not if Lavinia is somewhere in the world just beyond his field of vision, but remember Louise is drunk, and Rex is drunk, and both of them have had their hearts broken beyond repair this week, and more than anything in the world Louise just wants to be a person who is held in someone's arms.

Rex takes her in his.

He falls to his knees.

He kisses her stomach, like she's pregnant, or like she's a god.

His eyes are so full of tears.

"I'm sorry," he says. He keeps kissing her, like he knows she knows.

He kisses her hands. He kisses the insides of her wrists. He kisses her palms. "I'm so sorry, I'm sorry; I've been so stupid; I'm so stupid."

She's crying, too. She shakes her head.

Ten—nine—eight

She kisses and kisses him with a hungry mouth.

Seven—six—five

His tears are tributaries into hers.

"I miss you," Rex says; "I need you—*I need you,*" and Louise is standing on a precipice, and the world is vanishing and spinning and flickering all around her and Louise is falling, Louise is falling, and there is nobody else in the world who can catch her.

Four—three—two

"I love you," Rex says.

Maybe he does.

They cab it back to Lavinia's place. They kiss all the way uptown. Rex says *I love you* on every block; Rex puts his hand up Louise's shirt and feels her breasts like the cabbie isn't even listening to every sound they make; it's snowing so hard Louise can't even see the black of the sky; it's snowing so hard the cab radio keeps repeating *haven't seen snow this bad in sixty years* so maybe Hal is right, maybe the world really is ending, but right now it doesn't matter because they are so lonely but they have each other, both of them, because Lavinia is never coming back and this is the next best thing.

Her makeup smears his face. Their jackets crumple on the floor. Their clothes tear when they take them off.

I love you; I love you; I love you.

The door opens.

Cordelia just stands there.

She lets her suitcase drop in the doorway.

They're scrambling so fast—they're rushing—to cover their nakedness, their shame; Rex grabs a couch cushion and Louise grabs Lavinia's dressing gown and they're stammering out excuses and they're saying *this isn't what it looks like* even though it so manifestly is.

"It's—snowing, you know." Cordelia's voice is so calm. "There's a blizzard. Haven't you heard? All flights are grounded."

She walks into the living room. She goes to the kitchen. She puts the kettle on. Rex is so hasty, zipping up his trousers.

"I'm sorry," Cordelia says. She doesn't look at them. "I've intruded."

Cordelia picks up the teapot.

She throws it at Louise's face.

"*Damn* you!"

It shatters just behind Louise's head.

"God*damn* you."

It cuts Louise, a little, grazing her. She doesn't even feel it.

"Wait!" Rex is trying, so manfully, to put his shirt on. "I know this looks bad."

"You sniveling little *coward!*"

"She knows, okay? She knows!" Rex is out of breath. "She's fine with it—she's known the whole time—I swear!"

Cordelia is so pale.

"Don't you *fucking presume* to know my sister. She is *not* fine!"

"She told me! I swear to God—I swear to God—she called me up! She gave me her blessing! Both of us."

Cordelia laughs in his face.

"She didn't!"

"She did—Christ, Louise, tell her!"

Cordelia looks straight at her.

Her eyes are so clear, and so blue.

She looks at Louise, standing in the space where the steamer trunk once was.

"You want me to believe Vinny knows?"

Louise hesitates just a second. "She knows."

Cordelia exhales. Just once. "No," she says. "She doesn't."

"She *knows*."

Cordelia looks so slowly, from the door to the space in the floor, from the space in the floor to Louise.

"Then where is she?"

"I told you. She's in California."

"No she's not. Where is she?"

"You know as much as I do."

"*Where is she?*"

"I swear," Rex says, again, but Cordelia isn't even looking at him.

"Let's call her, shall we?" Cordelia begins, and Louise says *no,* so quickly, and that's when Cordelia starts to scream.

"*Where is she?*"

"I don't—"

Cordelia slaps her clear across the face.

"I said—where the *fuck* is she?"

"Cordelia!" Rex tries, but she's grabbing at Louise, she's pulling at Louise's hair; she's trying to claw out her eyes.

"*I know you know where she is!*"

She is so small, and Rex is so much larger than she is, and still it takes all his strength for him to pull Cordelia off her.

The two of them crash to the floor.

Louise is bleeding.

Cordelia gets up, staggering. She's out of breath. She's bleeding, too.

"You're a fool," she says, to Rex. "God—what a fool you are."

She doesn't take her eyes off Louise.

"God—you *idiot*!"

Rex is helping Louise to her feet. He's scrambling for their coats.

"We should go," he says.

Cordelia is panting. Her gaze is so, so blue.

"Look, I'm sorry," Rex says, like that's even what matters, now.

"Just get out," Cordelia says.

———

"We'll fix it." That's all Rex can repeat, all the way down to the lobby, all the way in the cab. "Look—she's upset. She's just upset."

Louise is shaking.

"You can stay at my place tonight," he says, because now, now he can save her, now this is a thing for him to do. "In the morning we'll go back, we'll explain. We can explain!"

It's stopped snowing. The world is frozen and stark and dead. Even the trees look like bones.

"We're not bad people!" Rex says.

Louise can't stop laughing.

Then she is so hot.

She is so achingly, boilingly, paralyzingly hot that she thinks she's going to die.

"Stop," she tells the driver.

"Louise, what are you—"

"Take us to Coney Island," she says.

"Louise, it's two o'clock in the . . ."

"I said." Louise has never been more sure of anything in her life. "Take us to Coney fucking Island."

The driver does.

Louise pays with the last of her hundred-dollar bills.

They sit in silence.

"Lou—" Rex tries—just once—but Louise kisses him, so hungrily, and does not let him speak.

When they arrive it is so cold, and so dark, and so empty.

Louise opens the car door. She bolts toward the water. She lets her purse fall on the sand.

Rex trails after her.

"Are you going to tell me *what the hell is going on?*"

Louise is just so fucking hot.

She walks so much faster, on her way to the water. She runs.

The water is so cold. She washes her face with it. She washes her face and her neck and her hands and she is still so fucking hot she thinks she will burn up completely.

"You're going to kill yourself, doing that."

Rex is standing with his hands in his pockets, away from the water.

Louise doesn't care.

She rubs her skin until it's raw.

"Look—we'll just *call Lavinia,*" Rex says. "It's not hard. It's not complicated. We just—we call Lavinia and we ask her to explain to her own fucking sister—"

"That's not going to happen," Louise says.

She is knee-deep in the water. She doesn't understand why she is still so fucking hot.

"Of course it will," says Rex. "Lavinia's not a bad person, she's not going to try to fuck with us; she'll tell Cordelia—"

"Lavinia's dead," Louise says.

Here's another funny thing: Rex doesn't believe her.

He just stands there, so stupidly, gaping at her, opening and closing his mouth, like a fish.

"Don't be ridiculous," he says. "Of course she's not dead."

"Believe me." Louise gets deeper and deeper into the water. "She's dead."

"She's in California."

"No, she's not."

"I just talked to her!"

"No, you didn't."

"We just—"

She turns around to face him. Her pantyhose are drenched. Her lipstick has smeared halfway down her chin.

"No," she says. "You really, really didn't."

———

Rex still doesn't get it.

Louise marvels—she can't stop marveling—at just how stupid he is.

"Lavinia's been dead since July," she says.

"That's crazy," Rex says. He says it a few times, as if repeating it will make it true. "Jesus—Lou—are you *on* something?"

"We had a fight at the P.M. I killed her."

"What did you take?" It's like he hasn't even heard her. "Jesus Christ, Lou—tell me what you took! I'm—Christ—I'm calling an ambulance, okay?"

It feels so good, how cold the water is.

"We had a fight. Put your phone away."

It astonishes her how confusing he finds this.

"What happened?"

"I told you. We had a fight. She hit her head. I dumped her body in the East River."

"No, you didn't."

"Why not?"

He's stammering. "People don't *do* things like that."

It's almost funny, Louise thinks, how she could love someone so stupid.

"It's very simple," Louise says. "I dumped her body in the East River. I've been posting on her Facebook every day for six months." It gets easier and easier to say these things. "I get money from her ATM every week. I left you that voicemail. I can do her voice."

"Jesus!"

Rex finally puts his phone down.

Rex finally, finally believes her.

"Jesus."

"Christ," Louise says. "It's freezing out here."

———

Louise is up to her hips in the water.

She lets herself sob.

She lets herself scream.

Here's, no *here's,* the thing:

All Rex has to do is understand her.

All he has to do is say *yes, I love you, I know why you have done this, you are not a bad person; you tried; what matters is that you tried.*

I love you. It's so easy. That's all he has to say. He's said it before.

"Fuck," Rex says. It's the first thing he says in a minute. *"Fuck!"* He looks at her so helplessly. "What do we *do?*"

Louise doesn't say anything.

"For Christ's sake—tell me what to do, Lou!"

"Nothing," Louise says. "There's nothing *to* do. It's done."

Rex takes so many deep breaths.

Rex can't speak. Rex can't deal.

"Look," he stammers, when he can finally get out words. "We'll go to the police, okay? Both of us. We'll go and tell them it was an accident—*Jesus*—it was an accident, right?"

"Does it matter?"

"It wasn't an accident?"

Louise isn't even sure anymore.

"Christ, Lou, tell me it was an accident!"

His eyes are so goddamn wide.

Louise doesn't.

Rex is hyperventilating.

He can't even look at her.

"You need to turn yourself in."

"There's no point," Louise says. "It won't change anything. Lavinia's dead."

"It's the right thing to do!"

"So?"

He's looking at her with such horror.

He's looking at her like he really, really knows her.

Louise keeps her eyes on the horizon, on the point where the water is black and it meets the blackness of the sky. She has not noticed, before, how much salt water stings where somebody has clawed you, or slapped you, or yanked out your hair, how it feels like you are being flayed alive.

It's just nice to feel something.

"I'm sorry," Louise says. "I know you loved her."

Louise doesn't know when she started crying. Maybe she's been crying this whole time.

"Come out of the water," Rex says.

He takes off his jacket. He takes off his watch, his phone. He puts them on the sand.

"You loved her so fucking much."

"Please," he says. "Please—just come out."

"Didn't you?"

"No—Christ, Lou."

"Don't fucking lie to me! Please—please—don't lie to me."

"I love you," Rex says.

It feels so fucking good to hear it.

He goes into the water. He goes up to his waist. He takes her by the shoulders.

"I love you—just please—come out of the water."

Here's the thing: he doesn't.

Rex tries—God, he tries—he tries to pull her out; he grabs her by the forearm, harder, maybe, than he means to, or should—it's forgivable, maybe, if you're trying to bring a murderer to justice; it's the right thing to do, maybe, if you're a hero, or playing a hero, or need to be a hero no matter fucking what; it's not a terrible thing—even if you are playing justice, it isn't the sort of thing you kill a person over.

But it is so stupid of him, to grab her like that, when she is sobbing, when she is screaming; it is so stupid of him to lie to her, when all she has asked of him is to stop lying to her.

He wraps his arms around her, and he bales her up, but here's another thing: Louise is so much stronger than he is, or at least, she's been in the water longer, and she's been in the cold before, and she's used to being cold or wet or just plain in pain, and she can stand pain so much better than he can, so when Rex goes numb he goes weak, and that is enough for her to get her hands around his neck, and that is enough, too, for her to get her legs on his back, and that is enough for Louise to hold him under the water which is so cold that it stuns him and Louise is not sure—she never will be sure—if it is the water, or the cold, that gets him.

He goes under.

He bursts back up.

He screams and his lungs fill with salt water and he kicks and Louise has to push him down again, and deeper, with a strength that sickens and thrills her at the same time.

He goes under.

He bursts back up.

He flails and he writhes and he elbows Louise in the face so violently her nose breaks; he cries out half of her name and Louise has to shove her hand over his mouth until he bites.

He goes under.

He doesn't come up.

Then it is just Louise, in the water, shaking, by the light of a full moon.

10

LOUISE KNOWS WHAT TO DO NEXT. Louise has done it all before.

Louise has Rex's phone.

Once, a girl, by a full moon, took a fistful of pills and said *if the world is not what it should be I want to die,* and Rex did not die with her. Not now. Then.

Now there is a man who has had too much to drink facedown in the water; this happens all the time.

Louise knows how to create an alibi (there's a whole trick to it: getting the right combination of check-ins and time stamps and specificity because that's what people respond to most and if they respond to you that means they think you're alive but also leaving things vague enough that you never have to explain a discrepancy). She knows how to move a body. She knows how to write a frenetic, late-night text from one phone to another, that says *please don't make me live without you.*

Louise gets through things. She always gets through things.

She can take a cab back to the MacIntyre with the cash in Rex's wallet. She knows, she *knows* Mimi will still be dancing there, and she can say that she and Rex had a fight after Cordelia found them; he stormed off (how likely is it that they will ever find that same cab driver again; she paid in cash—she hadn't meant to pay in cash but she has gotten so used to paying in cash when she is not Lavinia, just in case); they might not find his body for days.

Everyone will feel so sorry for her at the funeral.

Rex has killed himself over Lavinia (everyone will hate Lavinia, more), and maybe if Lavinia vanishes somewhere in Big Sur, everyone will think they know why.

Louise can probably move in with Mimi.

Louise sits on the sand, alone, soaked, so cold she can't breathe, and she stares at Rex's body bobbing up and down where the shore meets the sea and thinks *I can do this.*

I can do this.

She can get another tutoring job, or two. Tomorrow (*today, oh God, today*) is the Five Under Thirty party at this loft space in Bushwick that is constructed entirely with reclaimed wood from shipwrecks. Niall Montgomery will be there and so will so many other people she could potentially impress, by telling the story of the time she pretended to go to Devonshire Academy when she didn't, which is a great story but by this point it's barely true.

She can convince everybody that she is the injured one (Hal likes her; Mimi likes her; everybody, everybody likes her); she can be a martyr; she can write a really moving personal essay about the time her boyfriend and her best friend killed themselves, over each other, and about what it feels like to always, always be the one left behind. Gavin Mullaney would probably publish it.

The stars are like nails hammered in the sky.

The sea is just so unrelentingly black.

Once, Louise stood naked, facing it, with the sand in between her toes, screaming *that which we are, we are,* but that is not now, either.

You can do this, Louise keeps thinking. *You can do this.*

She can borrow money from Mimi. She can make five hundred dollars, writing a good *Fiddler* online piece, more for print. She can find a way to get Athena Maidenhead off her back (she has only to *think*). She has the keys to Rex's apartment (she never wants to go to Rex's apartment again). She can fix everything (Louise can always fix everything).

Except, of course, there's Cordelia.

She can make it so Cordelia is crazy. Everybody already knows Lavinia is crazy; maybe it runs in the family. She can make such a big deal about how poor Cordelia, poor *troubled* Cordelia attacked Rex in the apartment—if it ever comes to that—how this sweet well-meaning kid with a narcissist for a sister is growing up just like her, because if the Greeks taught us anything it's that we can't control Fate. She can make it so nobody believes whatever Cordelia says about her sister and the steamer trunk and Rex and Big Sur and the phone calls; people don't do such things; they don't even believe you when you tell them straight-out you've done such things.

She can't make Cordelia believe her.

She doesn't want to.

A ping on Rex's phone, on the sand. Hal. I need to talk to you.
Please.
Please.

Louise has such pity for everyone.

She has such pity for everyone in the whole, wide world.

A ping on Louise's phone. Gavin.
Get ready to ACE tonight!

A ping on Lavinia's phone. Cordelia. Twenty missed calls.

They all sound so fucking loud.

Louise thinks the stars will fall from the sky, shook loose by that sound.

So here, *here,* is what Louise does next:

She dyes her hair.

She leaves Rex's body on the beach. Mimi posts a photo of Rex and Louise at the MacIntyre, kissing, and it must be the moment he told her he loved her because the confetti is streaming down all around them.

She leaves Rex's phone there (*drunk, lonely Hal, won't stop calling him*).

She gets on the subway. (*Gavin is posting a lot of promotional material about Five Under Thirty and reminding everyone on Facebook it's the closest thing to an anointing you can possibly have and if you're important enough to edit for* The Fiddler *you can get away with saying shit like that and nobody will roll their eyes at you in public and he tags all of the five people who are Under Thirty and announces the winners formally on all social media channels but he writes something extra nice about Louise Wilson and calls her "the one to watch."*) She takes the Q from Coney Island. (*Beowulf Marmont is drunkenly ranting about how some people think that they're the shit because they're Five Under Thirty but actually it's just like a giant racket meant to appease a certain kind of emotive, feminine aesthetic and has nothing to do with real literature, anyway.*)

She takes it all the way to Forty-second Street. (*Athena Maidenhead has just gotten engaged to Mike from the opera and she is showing everybody her ring, and she posts the video and it sparkles so gorgeously in the MacIntyre lights.*)

Everybody is drunk. Everybody is loud. There is vomit and confetti everywhere, and glitter and tassels and discarded 2016 glasses and street preachers with signs. (*Now Cordelia is posting a long public Facebook post that begins "When you read this, you will think I have gone insane. I am not insane. My sister is dead. Louise Wilson has killed her."*)

The police horses are being loaded, one by one, into their vans. Australian tourists are singing "Auld Lang Syne."

(*Now Hal is messaging Louise and Lavinia, both, to tell them that Cordelia's had a typical Williams breakdown and probably swallowed a fistful of Mommy Williams's Xanax, too, and maybe everyone in that whole fucking family should deal with their shit, already, okay?*

And if Lavinia says "okay," it will buy Louise more time.)

———

Hey? Mimi hasn't even noticed Louise isn't still dancing. Where did you go?

Are u still here?

Dancing flapper emu.

Louise goes to a 24/7 Duane Reade near Bryant Park.

She gets hair dye, whatever clothes they sell—black leggings, a plain white T-shirt, the sort of anonymous things nobody notices anybody wears.

She doesn't have any money left, so she just shoplifts.

Nobody even notices this, either.

Louise walks right into the public bathrooms at Bryant Park, the nice ones, the ones that there are even flowers in. She locks the door.

She takes off her wet clothes.

She washes off the salt, the blood.

She washes her hair in the sink.

She opens the box. She puts on the gloves.

The water is so red, through her hands.

People are knocking (of course they're knocking; it's New Year's Day, and she's in midtown, and people who have been standing in line all night need to pee) and their knocking is so loud but Louise ignores them; Louise doesn't care; Louise keeps her gaze focused on the mirror, and thirty minutes go by and Louise just stands there, naked, staring at herself, and at the fake ID of some twenty-three-year-old redhead called Elizabeth Glass who probably never existed in the first place.

Louise looks so different with red hair.

She looks paler. Her cheekbones look higher. She is not as beautiful as she was, when she had Lavinia's hair. She is no longer the kind of girl you'd stop, when you saw her. You wouldn't check her out, or turn around, or stare.

You might see her on the street, and not even know her.

Louise should be horrified. Maybe she is horrified, because Lavinia is dead and Rex is dead and Rex's body is bobbing up and down on the water and Lavinia is rotting in a steamer trunk at the bottom of the East River but there is no justice on earth that can make this right, any longer, so the only thing to do now is not be who you are, and that is the best and the worst thing in the world, and also all Louise has ever wanted.

Today, Louise tells herself, *is the first day of the rest of your life.*

"Hey! Fuck you! We all have to pee."
She elbows past them.
Lavinia's phone, smashed, is in the trash.

It is morning. Times Square is still so full of people.
Louise walks faster, now, and then faster still, and Cordelia has posted I am not insane. My sister is dead. and all her Exeter friends keep telling her to calm down, that she can call them if she needs to, and there will be a moment for Cordelia, when Cordelia checks her phone and among all these expressions of placating sympathy she sees that Louise Wilson, too, has Liked this status, but when she goes to click on it she will see that Louise Wilson does not exist.

There is no way in which Louise can fuck up because she has already done all of the worst things, and maybe nobody will ever love her again and maybe that's okay, too, because why else do you set things on fire except to burn them, and maybe they will find her or maybe they will never find her but Louise hopes if somebody finds her it is somebody who deserves to.
Louise hopes Cordelia will.

Now Louise has one dollar and forty-six cents in change. She has a fake ID. She has one set of clean clothes and auburn hair so dark it's almost violet.

She doesn't even have a phone.

Louise keeps walking, into Times Square. She walks so quickly. She walks into the crowd, and then we have to crane our necks to keep her in our field of vision, because there are so many people in this city and so many of them have violet or auburn hair, many, many white women, about five-foot-five, who are reasonably thin, who walk very quickly, or who are wearing black leggings, with white T-shirts, under dark but flimsy coats, and then Louise, or someone who is not Louise, turns a corner, or crosses the street, and then we do not see her.

Acknowledgments

With immense gratitude to everyone who has made this book a reality: to my agents, Emma Parry and Rebecca Carter at Janklow and Nesbit, for their faith, their patience, and their work in shaping the first draft of *Social Creature,* and reminding me to tell a good story, first and foremost, and worry about the rest later.

And to my wonderful editor, Margaux Weisman, whose sharp eye and editorial acumen helped me see the manuscript with a fresh eye, and make it so much better, and to the entire fantastic editorial, marketing, and design teams at Penguin Random House and Doubleday, who have made this book look and feel so beautiful I'm almost afraid to touch it.

Thank you to Simon Worrall, my mentor, who set me on the right path early on!

And a special thank you to Brian McMahon, who has been reading drafts (and drafts and more drafts) of this story since 2009, and who has been putting up with my chaotic tendencies nearly as long, whose faith and guidance alike have made telling this story possible. I owe this book to you—and I'm so glad I do.

Tara Isabella Burton is a writer of fiction and nonfiction. Winner of the Shiva Naipaul Memorial Prize for travel writing, she completed her doctorate in nineteenth-century French literature and in theology at the University of Oxford. Her essays have appeared in *National Geographic, The Wall Street Journal,* and *The Economist*'s *1843,* among other publications. She currently works for *Vox* as their religion correspondent, and divides her time between the Upper East Side of New York and Tbilisi, Georgia.